THE SECRET COLLECTOR

Abigail Johnson wrote *The Secret Collector* while completing the Curtis Brown Creative three-month novel-writing course, where she was tutored by author Laura Barnett. It was longlisted for the 2021 and 2022 Bath Novel Award. Her writing has also been longlisted for the Exeter Novel Award and shortlisted for the 2021 Edinburgh Flash Fiction Award, and she was a Friday Night Live finalist at the Festival of Writing in 2017. She lives in Birmingham.

THE SECRET COLLECTOR

ABIGAIL JOHNSON

PAN BOOKS

First published 2025 by Pan Books
an imprint of Pan Macmillan
The Smithson, 6 Briset Street, London EC1M 5NR
EU representative: Macmillan Publishers Ireland Limited, 1st Floor,
The Liffey Trust Centre, 117–126 Sheriff Street Upper,
Dublin 1, D01 YC43
Associated companies throughout the world
www.panmacmillan.com

ISBN 978-1-0350-5775-7

1 3 5 7 9 8 6 4 2

A CIP catalogue record for this book is available from the British Library.

Illustrations © Shutterstock and Sinead Hayward

Typeset in Freight Text Pro by
Palimpsest Book Production Ltd, Falkirk, Stirlingshire
Printed and bound by CPI Group (UK) Ltd, Croydon, CR0 4YY

For Noah and Joby – follow your dreams

BIRMINGHAM, 1999

1

A change in the weather

Alfred had not let anyone inside his house for almost three years. Not that anyone cared. The overgrown weeds and bushes that swamped the small front garden were usually enough of a deterrent to any potential callers. If the postman arrived, Alfred opened the door the couple of inches that the chain allowed and instructed him to leave whatever he had on the doorstep. It was better to keep yourself to yourself. The trouble with people was that they liked to interfere, and Alfred had had quite enough of having his business poked into.

He lifted a record out of its sleeve and dusted it with a soft nylon brush before placing it on the turntable of his favourite record player – number twelve in his catalogue of collections:

Dansette Imperial 1965
Green and cream, condition good. Output 8 watts, undistorted.

He'd found it in a skip, of all places. Things that other people had thrown out, discarded or considered worthless were often given a place in his heart. He didn't choose them according to their value, but rather their beauty, uniqueness or even an imagined past. In fact, he often wondered if they chose him. If required, he cleaned them and restored them with linseed oil, lacquer paint, silver polish or superglue.

As the needle found its familiar path in the well-worn grooves, the violin notes of *The Lark Ascending* filled the living room. Alfred turned up the volume and closed his eyes, imagining that he was soaring through the sky. He stretched his arms out slowly, feeling the cold breeze against his cheeks, the wind ruffling what was left of his hair, the sun smiling through the clouds and warming him through his buttoned-up coat.

When the music ended, he opened his eyes again and was immediately flattened by the stuffiness of his semi-dark living room. Some time ago he'd decided to cover the windows up with newspaper to keep prying eyes out. It saved all the bother of curtains and also meant he had an encyclopaedic knowledge of the news stories of 22 February 1997. It would be his *Mastermind* specialist subject, if ever he was asked. Dolly the cloned sheep stole the headlines that day, but it was the smaller, blink-and-you'll-miss-them stories that he liked best. The one about the council health-and-safety meeting that ended in an officer breaking his leg on the way out still made him chuckle.

It was almost tea-time. He'd reheat the beef stew he'd made earlier and take a couple of slices of bread out of the freezer to toast. As a war veteran, Alfred knew quite a bit about being prepared. However, it took rather a lot of planning, which was becoming harder as the years passed. Nevertheless, he'd ensured that his larder was packed with two months' worth of tins, in case the millennium bug did its worst. He had three smoke alarms, four torches, a sprinkler system, twenty spare light bulbs, a box of ballpoint pens, three hot-water bottles and an emergency backpack filled with Kendal Mint Cake and a whistle, just in case.

This was the time of day when he was usually restless and the house began to feel too big, despite bursting at the seams with his possessions. He searched for his crossword book, remembering a particularly stubborn seven across beginning with the letter D that he'd been unable to solve the previous day. It was always a good idea to keep busy – that way there was less time to think. He rummaged through several boxes, but was unable to locate it. However, buried beneath a patchwork eiderdown he stumbled upon his barometer, one of his all-time favourite objects.

All at once his thoughts were with Ida, his wife. It had been five years now since she'd died. He knew she wasn't coming back, and yet sometimes he'd think of something that only she would understand, and the fact that he couldn't share it with her splintered his heart. At first, one of the hardest things about losing her had been the empty space beside him. It followed him around like an extra shadow. The bed seemed vast, and the dining-room table mocked him with its two chairs set at either end, knowing that one would remain empty. And so he had filled the space with objects, so many of them that, for the most part, his grief was simply squeezed out.

Ida had given him the barometer for their twenty-fifth wedding anniversary. It had been a while since he'd last seen it, as he'd hidden away most of the things that reminded him of her. It was as beautiful as he remembered; carved from magnificent honey-coloured oak, with a series of interlaced ornate flowers and fleurs-de-lis stretching around the tip.

He cradled it in his arms, comforted by the familiarity of its weight and the way it seemed to join him to Ida with an invisible thread. Oh, how he missed her. Time wasn't a healer; it was simply a measure of how long he'd had a gaping hole in his life. With a simple tap on the glass face, the calibrated dial swung downwards. It left its current station, FAIR, and rested on STORMY.

Alfred made his way to the window to look outside, clambering over the collections that had spilled over from various sideboards onto the floor: Staffordshire pottery dogs, two vintage typewriters, a congregation of tobacco jars, an assortment of lamps and various-sized picture frames. He peeled a corner of yellowing newspaper from the window and peered through the gap, squinting into the late-afternoon sunlight. For the fifth consecutive day there wasn't a cloud in the sky and the fallen leaves scattered along the pavement were scorched and crisp. An Indian summer. For a short moment Alfred was tempted to step outside and kick his feet through them, just to hear them crunch. Like a doomed romance, summer was refusing to accept that it was over. The barometer had never been wrong, though. A change was on its way. Luckily, Alfred was prepared for anything.

2

Stop the clock

Kian was late, as usual, so he had to sprint the last stretch to Cannon Hill Park from the bus stop, ignoring the burning in his chest. He really should give up smoking. The can of Coke in his bag was rattling around and fizzing, a bit like his stomach.

It had been weeks since he'd last seen his little brother, Dan. Their contact order allowed weekly meetings, but if Kian messed up and missed a few, it sometimes meant a whole month went by without them seeing each other. It wasn't deliberate – he hated letting Dan down – but it wasn't his fault if he'd been out the night before and slept in. Kian was seventeen; he was meant to be free from responsibility. He was desperate to see Dan, but simultaneously as nervous as he'd been in yesterday's job interview. Kian knew he wouldn't get the job. It became obvious when the interviewers stopped writing down what he said halfway through. It was a familiar story.

He slowed down to a jog as he reached the boating lake, and then to big strides as he got further up towards the bandstand, trying to catch his breath. It would have been quicker to take a shortcut across the grass, but he stuck to the path, wanting to keep his trainers clean. He smoothed down his shirt and ran his hand through his hair. Although he really wanted a cigarette, he left them in his pocket, instead tipping some mints into his mouth to try to disguise his hangover breath. As far as role models went, Kian knew he set a low bar, but he had to at least try.

As he turned a corner, he spotted his brother in the distance and time stood still. He couldn't take his eyes off him. Dan was kicking a ball underneath the shade of a huge oak tree. He'd got taller since Kian had last seen him, time cruelly measured out in centimetres as well as hours. His brother was growing up without him.

When Dan looked over and noticed Kian, he abandoned his ball and ran straight at him with his arms out, almost knocking him over. Kian held on to him, trying to steady the emotions he usually tried to pretend didn't exist: love, sadness and guilt.

Last time they'd met here had been during a long stretch of hot summer weather, when the sky was a bright strip of cloudless blue that went on for ever. Families were enjoying picnics and bike rides, the air filled with the noise of tennis balls and roller skates and hissing fountains. They took a boat out on the lake and then fed the swans their leftover sandwiches, running from one that had got too greedy. Afterwards Kian had bought Dan a huge ice cream that made his eyes pop. They'd had the best afternoon and it was right then, when Kian got back home with his bare arms still warm and damp grass stains on his knees, that he decided he was going to apply to be Dan's legal guardian. But summers end. Kian looked up at the desolate trees lining the path, struggling to regain that feeling of optimism, despite the autumn sunshine. He didn't have enough money for anything fun this time. He hoped the Coke made up for it.

Kian said hi to Simone, Dan's foster mum, who'd suggested they meet at the park after school, even though he was allowed to pick Dan up and take him out on his own. She said it was to make things easier for Kian, as it was halfway between them and she had to take Dan shoe shopping afterwards. Kian could read between the lines. He hadn't exactly proved his reliability of late. But all that was about to change.

'Here you go, mate,' Kian said, handing Dan the drink. 'Open it later, though. It got shaken around a bit in my bag.'

'I'll leave you both to it,' Simone said. 'I'll be sitting just over there, okay, Danny?' She pointed at a bench near the play area.

Dan nodded.

'So what's new, D?' Kian said, ruffling Dan's hair in the way grown-ups did.

'Mrs Shelton says I should go for my eleven-plus next year. I mean, loads of other kids have tutors and stuff, but she thinks I'll be good enough anyway.'

Kian's heart burst a bit. This kid, this soppy kid, was so damn smart. He was stupidly proud of him, even though he had no right to be.

'Course you're good enough. Right, I'm gonna tell you something. Don't end up like me. You can be, like, a lawyer or a doctor or anything. Then your life will be sorted. You won't need to rely on anyone. Right?'

'Right.' Dan smiled, wrinkling the freckles on his nose. 'And I'll get a big house and you can live with me!'

Kian's fizzing stomach went flat. His little brother was finally realizing that he was a write-off. He should be providing a home for Dan, not the other way around.

'Want a kickabout?' Kian asked, dismissing his thoughts and rolling up his sleeves.

'Yeah, I'll be David Beckham, you be Gareth Southgate,' Dan said. He swiped the ball and ran off with it towards the goalposts.

'No way – you're Southgate and I'm Beckham!' Kian caught up with him and tackled the ball away, before shooting a goal and running a victory lap with his arms in the air. Dan jumped on his back and they tumbled onto the muddy grass. Kian no longer cared about his pristine trainers. Soon they were throwing huge piles of leaves at each other, giggling as they scooped up more ammunition while trying to run.

'Getting outta breath, huh?' Kian said. 'Time for me to get some more goals past you then!'

It didn't seem like more than ten minutes had passed when Simone appeared next to them, looking at her watch. Kian wanted to stop the clock right now, freeze this moment for ever: he and Dan hanging out, laughing and playing footie like normal brothers. Whatever time they got to spend together, it was never enough.

Kian brushed some of the leaves off Dan's coat, although what he wanted to do was grab his hand and run off with him. He had to play the long game, though. In a few months he'd be eighteen, and then they couldn't stop Dan living with him. He'd apply to be his brother's legal guardian, then he could put everything right, make it up to Dan for being useless and give him the family he needed – the one he deserved. He just had to stop drinking, get a job, sort his life out and get a bigger flat. It was an exhausting list, but Dan was worth it. Kian didn't know if he had it in him, though.

Dan wrapped his arm around Kian's waist. 'Can I come home with you?'

It was like a kick in the ribs every time. Sometimes Kian wondered if it would be easier on the kid if he stayed out of his life altogether.

'Mate, you know you can't. Not yet. But I'll see you soon,

yeah? Practise your keepy-ups. I want to see you do a hundred next time.'

Dan released his grip and sloped off in the opposite direction. He kept looking back, and Kian stood there, feeling like he was sending a puppy off to the pound. He gave Dan a thumbs-up and a fake smile before getting out his phone.

'Gav, mate? I need a bender tonight. What time you getting off work?'

3

Checkmate

Alfred had just finished watching the news and he muttered his despair into the empty room. The leading story had been that the Millennium Wheel was being lifted into place on the South Bank in London. It was a feat of engineering; he'd give it that. At 400 feet high, it was taller than Big Ben and St Paul's Cathedral, which was, quite frankly, showing off. Alfred certainly wouldn't be going on it. Not only did it look far too dangerous, but it was also a colossal waste of money.

He settled down to polish his chess pieces. In truth, he didn't really need one chess board, let alone three. After all, he had no one to play with. He'd taught his daughter Maggie to play when she was younger, and she had become a fierce opponent. He set up his chessmen and put the board to one side, annoyed that Maggie had slipped into his thoughts unbidden. It was much easier when he simply forgot she existed. It was a very particular sort of pain, losing your daughter when she was still very much alive. Unlike separation by death, when the door was firmly closed, it had been left ajar to taunt him.

He opened a cupboard, looking for more polish, and noticed his walking boots at the back, neatly laced. The last time he'd worn them was when he'd scaled Scafell Pike decades ago. As quickly as a passing breeze, something brushed over him: the promise of something different – some purpose. Some hope. He closed the cupboard and sat down again. Those days were long gone.

A loud knock on the door made him jump. It was less of a knock and more of a pounding, the sort he sometimes felt the morning after too many glasses of malt whisky. Alfred gripped the arms of his chair and hoped it would stop. Instead the banging got louder, or perhaps it was his heart thumping against his ribcage. The door banged again. What if it was Maggie and there was an emergency of some sort? He would have to take a look.

Alfred shuffled closer to the window and knocked his wine onto the carpet, tutting as it bloomed into a continent the colour of blackberries. He crouched down and lifted the bottom corner of the newspaper. Thick red spray paint covered the glass. Blood-red. The banging continued, angry and purposeful. He stood up again and leaned against the wall. He scrunched his eyes shut and began to count slowly to ten, the way he did whenever things simply got too much.

One, two, three . . . breathe slowly. Air was racing out of him as if his lungs were on fire.

Four, five . . . his shirt collar felt damp.

Six, seven . . . it wasn't working.

In his mind he assembled an inventory of the boxes closest to him, in the hope that there was something sharp or heavy in at least one of them. Ordnance Survey maps of the Lake District – no. No good unless he planned to foil a potential murderer with paper cuts.

Eight . . . what else? His George III copper kettle? It would crumple at the slightest force.

Nine . . .

Alfred didn't reach ten. An explosion forced him to the floor underneath a shower of glass, the noise reverberating through his body. A startling pain shot through the side of his face as something hard collided with his cheekbone. His beef stew revisited him just as the second pane shattered inwards. And then, at last, all was quiet, apart from a low ringing in his ears.

It was hard to know exactly how long he lay there on the floor. His body was right back on the front line, with mortar and shells and the smell of Bonfire Night. Freezing feet, holes in his boots. His heart marching, left, right, left, right. Left . . . right . . .

Don't stop, keep going, man.

At some point the air grew crisp and the light changed from slate to tar. He fumbled around the floor for the phone, trying to remember where he'd last seen it. He stretched his arm underneath the walnut console table and, miraculously, his fingers curled around it tightly as if it was a life-raft. It was difficult to speak, with the crushing pain in his left shoulder, but imminent death gave him a kind of impetus to get on with it.

'Hello? I'd like to report a crime. Yes, Alfred Ainswick, one-three-two Bartholomew Row. I think I need an ambulance.'

His eyes closed and a luminous white light pulled him upwards as if he was being sucked through a straw. He was a boy crying in front of a crackling fire, his ears rang with the roar of gunfire, his tongue tingled with his first taste of watermelon, and cool Windermere water lapped at his shoulders as he swam along the shore at sunset. Even though his life was flashing before him, Alfred spared a moment to imagine the coroner laughing as he wrote down his cause of death: *brick through living-room window*. He had not been expecting that.

4

Someone else's pyjamas

Wearing someone else's pyjamas was more than a little disconcerting. Reassuringly, they smelled of soap powder, so at least Alfred knew they were clean. Still, his were stripy and made of soft flannelette. These ones were stiff and covered in little dots that made his eyes glaze over if he stared at them for too long. This was the least of his worries, though. In the four days he had spent so far in hospital, he had got quite used to the bleeping heart monitor and the blinking lights of the machines that he'd been wired up to. However, it was fair to say that being brought back from the dead really wasn't all it was cracked up to be. He had not experienced an epiphany, had no fresh perspective on life and certainly wasn't invigorated with any sense of enthusiasm or gratitude for being here.

Instead he felt distinctly annoyed, like the time he'd forgotten to cancel his newspapers while on holiday in Hastings years ago. Near-death had sparked a chain of interactions with official agencies that made him as uncomfortable as if he had paraded around in nothing but his underwear. He was exposed, vulnerable and at the mercy of people brandishing clipboards.

It was the police who had informed social services. Apparently they were concerned about the state of his home. Initially they'd assumed the vandal responsible for the smashed windows and graffiti had broken in and trashed the place, but after investigating every room in the house, it soon became clear that this was how Alfred lived. His own choice. It was none of their business, as far as Alfred was concerned, but no one seemed to care what he had to say on the matter. He hadn't told them about Maggie, about the fact that his daughter had more or less disowned him, so now he was stuck with Sandra, the do-gooder social worker.

The hospital ward had a rhythm to it and, despite longing to be back in his own home, he enjoyed the morning rounds, the tea trolley and the nurses fluffing up his pillows. The footsteps behind the curtains would probably be the tea now, right on time at 10.03 a.m. Too early for elevenses, of course, but a suitable gap since breakfast for him to be sufficiently parched.

Oh, it wasn't the tea.

'Morning, Alfred. How are you today? You did remember I was coming?' Sandra said, her voice booming across the length of the ward.

Her frame filled the chair beside him without invitation. Even though the curtain had been pulled around his bed, it was a given that the other patients were all listening in. There wasn't a lot else to do, after all. Once your vitals had been checked and your progress monitored, the only excitement was the promise of lunch, which never quite lived up to expectations.

'Of course I remembered,' Alfred replied. He remembered everything. In any case, he'd been fretting about her arrival all night. As a result, he had yawned most of the way through Dr Mukerjee's assessment after breakfast, which must have appeared quite rude.

Sandra took a notebook out of her bag and commandeered

a flowery pen. It seemed a little unfair, being cross-examined in his pyjamas. He might as well have his hands tied behind his back. She set about her interrogation, easing him in with some seemingly innocuous questions about dressing, washing and shopping.

'All fine in that department, thank you,' Alfred assured her. 'I'm perfectly capable. I don't have any family or friends, you see. I do everything myself.' There, that should nip this in the bud and convince Sandra that he was completely independent. He didn't need to rely on anyone but himself. She could pack away her things and leave him alone.

'No family or friends?' she asked, in a voice so loud that Alfred winced.

When Alfred nodded, she underlined something three times on her paper. She obviously wasn't ready to go yet.

'So tell me a bit about your day-to-day routines. Do you get out much? What do you do in your spare time?'

Answering these questions seemed simple enough, and yet Alfred was convinced there were hidden mines planted in Sandra's words. One wrong move and *kaboom*! If he told her about his collections, she would probably deduce that he was senile. If she knew he rarely left the house, she'd get him signed up to some programme of activities for the elderly – perish the thought. He considered the matter for so long that she repeated the question.

'Ah, yes, my spare time,' Alfred said. 'Well, I don't have much of it, I'm afraid. I volunteer at the local charity shop five days a week, I'm a member of the ramblers' club and, um . . . I also play badminton at the weekend.' That should do it.

Sandra's mouth fell open a little. 'Do you think perhaps you've been overdoing things? I'm sure, when you attend your cardio rehab appointments, they'll discuss with you how to get back to your usual routines. But you will take it easy for a while, won't you?'

If he nodded in all the right places and let her feel she'd done her job, maybe she'd leave and everything could get back to normal. Oh, what he wouldn't give for normal. The idea of it was as comforting as warm woollen socks on a wet Wednesday.

'Well, that's all been really useful, Alfred. Thank you so much for your time this morning. I think I have everything I need.'

Thank goodness – he was off the hook. It hadn't been that awful after all. The badminton had really impressed her, he could tell.

'The pleasure was all mine,' Alfred replied, releasing his fingernails from his palms. He sank into his pillow. Perhaps, if he coughed loudly enough, one of the nurses would come and fluff it up again. Tomorrow he would be back home among all his possessions, and this unpleasant business could be put behind him.

'I've put your next appointment with me on this card,' Sandra said. 'I'll give you a couple of days to settle back in at home, then we can have another chat. Lovely meeting you.'

'My next appointment?' Alfred repeated, but Sandra had already left, leaving a dent in the seat next to him so that he couldn't forget she'd been there.

5

Someone else's shoes

The borrowed suit was too big, dwarfing Kian. It belonged to his mate Gav, who was built like a rugby player – unlike him. Despite Kian's usual swagger, he felt like a little boy pretending to be a grown-up. His barrister, Thea, had reminded him to dress smartly to give the right impression – so along with the suit, he'd sprayed on an extra dash of Lynx before leaving the house. An underage pall-bearer wasn't really the look he was going for. Still, it had to be better than jeans.

This time was worse than all the others. He could tell from the way Thea's eyes had flickered behind her Armani tortoiseshell glasses, when he'd asked her what his chances were of getting banged up.

When he'd been a kid, he could rely on his soppy smile and his big blue eyes to get him off just about anything. Now that he was almost eighteen, charm and cheekiness wouldn't cut it. He ran through the excuses in his head, knowing none of them sounded convincing: there was nothing to do, he grew up in care . . . there was nothing to do. He got a thrill from it all, he couldn't deny that. A kind of crazed high from going into places he wasn't meant to go and doing things he wasn't meant to do. It was like sticking his fingers up at the world, only now it seemed like the world was sticking its fingers up at him.

'So you do understand the seriousness of this, Kian?' Thea asked, while they waited in the freezing corridor. Although she'd represented him before, it hadn't occurred to him until now that she only looked a few years older than him. How was it that she had her life so sorted? Money, probably. It's what everything always came down to. He'd place bets that she grew up in one of those big, posh houses in Edgbaston. When he went past them on the bus, he'd stare through the lit windows, wondering what it would be like to live on the other side of them – to drink posh coffee instead of instant, and to play the piano instead of a games console. He scrolled through his phone messages and shrugged in Thea's direction as if he couldn't care less. But it couldn't be further from the truth.

'We've agreed on your guilty plea,' Thea said, her eyes doing that flickering thing again. 'I'll do everything I can, of course. But I want you to be aware that I can't promise anything.'

'Whatever,' Kian replied.

He tapped his feet, uncomfortably encased in Gav's squeaky black shoes. The waiting was the hardest part. Too much time to think. He replayed the incident that had landed him here. The details were a bit hazy, thanks to the several cans of cider he'd downed after his afternoon at the park with Dan. There was no question that he loved seeing his brother. It was just that it left him with a hollowness that could only be filled with drink. His mood had sunk further after a phone call confirming that he hadn't got the job he'd gone for. Again.

Kian did remember this: it wasn't his fault. Not really. The old geezer had it coming. Who knew what he got up to, in that hellhole with papered-up windows? He'd only meant to shake him up a bit, spray a few obscenities on his house for a laugh. Only, fuelled by the bitterness of Diamond White and rejection, he'd got a bit carried away. The bricks lined up beneath the window were simply asking to be thrown. It felt good to hurl something with all his weight behind it and hear a satisfying smash, to actually have an impact on something. So good that he threw another one. Looking back, it hadn't been the smartest of moves. Still, it wasn't his fault the old dude had a heart attack. Just a massive unlucky coincidence, which was how he felt about his whole life.

'Kian? They're ready for you.' Thea's pencil skirt was no-nonsense-straight and she held her black folder close to her chest, like a secret. She looked the business, like she could get him off after all. She strode ahead, while he hung back and fiddled with his suit jacket. The truth was, he really didn't want to go inside; he'd never admit to anyone that he was scared of prison. However, now that he was looking that possibility right in the face, he was properly bricking it.

A silent promise rang through his head: that if he got off, this was the last time he'd end up here. He couldn't do this any more. His little brother needed him to step up. After a deep breath, Kian straightened his tie and followed Thea in.

Even though he'd been inside a courtroom before, his knees floundered as he entered the dock. He wasn't the only one who looked like they were at a funeral. A row of serious faces in dark suits stared up from rustling papers. He pulled at his shirt collar, sweat forming around his neck.

'All rise,' the stiff-shouldered court clerk announced.

Kian tried to fix his face into a neutral position, so that he didn't look arrogant or bored or, worse, guilty. He settled on looking down at his hands, noticing that his knuckles were nicotine-stained and his nails bitten down. This was it, then. Time to swear he'd tell the whole truth and nothing but the truth. The only thing was that the truth wasn't going to do him any favours right now.

Walking fast to outpace everyone else exiting the courtroom, Kian yanked off his tie, stuffing it into his trouser pocket. He should be grateful that he'd got off lightly. He should also be grateful the old geezer didn't actually die. But instead of gratitude, a ball of fury was building inside him, a small ember burning more fiercely with each passing minute. He was suddenly incensed about every last thing that had happened to him in his life that hadn't been his fault, which was mostly everything. His mobile buzzed and he pulled it next to his ear while reaching for his cigarettes.

'Gav? Cheers for the suit, man. Yeah, it did the job. I got off, only I've gotta do this community-service crap. "Restorative justice" the magistrate called it. I'd have preferred prison, mate.'

That was a lie. He shuddered, feeling the imaginary grip of handcuffs around his wrists as he pictured himself being thrown in the back of a police van and decked out in prison stripes. It had been close, he was sure of it. Thea said as much, warning him that he'd end up right back here if he didn't complete his community service satisfactorily. He'd reached the end of the line.

A pint would take the edge off whatever this feeling was, this buzzy, electric anger racing through him. Even though it was only 4 p.m., the street outside the courts was empty, apart from a woman with carrier bags stacked onto the back of a buggy on the other side of the road, and a guy eating chips at the bus stop. A siren sailed past as Kian dodged the broken glass on the pavement. There was a game he used to play when he was a kid, where he jumped over the cracks so that he wouldn't get bad luck. If only that was all it took now. He lengthened his stride to avoid them, just in case.

He'd walked this way thousands of times and no longer noticed the graffiti sprawled across broken doorways, the chip papers at his feet and the barbed wire above the row of boarded-up shops. He looked towards the Birmingham ring road and his chest tightened, as if the concrete highway that gripped the city was also gripping him and would never let go.

6

Three sugars

It had been so long since someone had been inside his house that Alfred had trembled as he put on a suit. It had taken three attempts for the buttons on his shirt to meet their corresponding slots. In fact, as he combed his hair and dabbed on some Old Spice that he hadn't worn in years, he was reminded of taking Ida out on a date for the very first time. A current of nerves had flowed through him as he'd practised how to say 'Hello' in front of the mirror, as if learning a new language. That was all a very long time ago, of course.

Sandra was at most half his age. Despite this, she seemed to have taken it upon herself to behave as if she was his mother, asking him how he'd slept and if he'd eaten. She'd even wanted to make the tea, but he had insisted. He stirred three sugars into her mug, although he heard perfectly well that she didn't take any.

'So, Alfred, how have you been feeling since coming out of hospital?' Sandra asked before taking a gulp of her tea.

A smile creased the corners of Alfred's mouth while she politely put her tea to one side and tried not to pull a face. Somewhere in the room, a hidden clock was making itself known, painfully scratching away the seconds between Sandra's questions and Alfred's answers.

'Oh, I'm feeling marvellous,' Alfred lied. He had barely slept a wink since he'd returned home from ward ten at the Queen Elizabeth Hospital. Each night he lay down in the hallway, gripping an old cricket bat until the morning came. 'Never better. I mean, the heart attack was a bit of an inconvenience obviously, but, you know, I'm fine now, glad to be home really. With the medication they've given me and a bit of rest, I'm right as rain.' He tapped out a rhythm against his heart with two fingers, as if to demonstrate the effectiveness of his pulmonary artery. 'And they caught the blighter who threw the bricks, so, you know, he'll be suitably punished, I'm sure. All's well that ends well. As you can probably tell, I really don't need a social worker,' he added for good measure.

In response, Sandra pointedly scanned the room and pulled her coat tighter. Alfred understood that if you weren't used to it – if you didn't comprehend the importance of all his objects – it might look a little chaotic. Messy, even. It might help if she knew that all of his items were comprehensively catalogued. Sandra clicked her pen several times, looking from floor to ceiling, and began to write some notes. Then again, it might not help at all.

The good thing about never having company was not having to bother with the trivial matter of tidying up. Before Sandra's arrival, he'd filled several bin liners with magazines, tissues and wrappers. He was so breathless afterwards that he'd worried another heart attack might come his way and had to lie down on the sofa for the rest of the afternoon. Admittedly the place probably needed a bit of a vacuum, some dusting what-have-you, but it was perfectly habitable. He had already demonstrated that he could get in and out of his kitchen with only the smallest amount of manoeuvring and squeezing. Sandra really had nothing to worry about.

'Alfred,' Sandra said, lowering her voice, 'I don't think you're looking after this place, or yourself, very well at the moment. I'd suggest you need a bit of help getting on top of things. Wouldn't you agree?'

He shook his head vigorously to show her that he most definitely did not.

'I know it must be a little overwhelming. Just remember I'm here to help,' Sandra continued. 'We don't need to deal with everything at once. Let's talk about the incident when the young man threw a brick through your window.'

'Two bricks,' Alfred said. The least she could do was get the facts straight.

'I'm sorry?' Sandra looked down at her notes. 'Yes. Sorry, you're quite right: two bricks. Anyway, have you heard of something called "restorative justice"?'

The walls began to inch towards him. For the first time in a long time, Alfred wanted to open the window and let the outside in. The air was heavy, pinning him against his chair. Before Sandra even said the words, he knew what was coming next. They wanted him to meet this criminal, give him the chance to get off scot-free. Well, he wouldn't have it.

'I am not,' Alfred said, his voice turning itself onto its loudest setting, 'meeting the juvenile delinquent who caused me to have a heart attack. Absolutely not. Now clear off and leave me alone!'

'It's just a mediation session at first. We'll meet somewhere neutral and I'll be with you. Alfred, I do hope you'll give this some thought. I really think it will help you to achieve some closure. Restorative justice is fairly new, but it's already been shown to have a really positive impact on both the victim and the perpetrator. It gives you a voice, lets you tell him to his face how you feel. It also gives him a chance to make amends, and you can both move forward with your lives.'

'No, thank you,' Alfred replied, folding his arms across his chest. He didn't want to move forward. He was quite happy staying exactly where he was.

'I'm going to leave you some information to read, in the hope that you'll consider it,' Sandra went on. 'Also, I think we should look at what the next steps should be, in regard to your living situation. We can assess things properly in a couple of months and I can draw up a care plan, once you've had a chance to get back on your feet.'

A care plan? Sandra didn't need to spell it out. She wanted to put him in a care home. She didn't think he could manage by himself. Alfred suddenly felt smaller than a postage stamp and wished he could disappear down the back of his armchair. Even though she was still talking, he tuned her out as if she was a radio station he didn't like. Why was this happening to him? He'd been happily minding his own business. Maybe his house needed a bit of a tidy-up, but that didn't mean he couldn't look after himself.

Sandra had managed to retune herself to a frequency he couldn't ignore.

'So I'll make an appointment for an assessment in the New Year, Alfred. Obviously a cleaner would be a good start, but that's not possible until we've managed to get on top of some of this . . .'

She stumbled over her words and Alfred was sure he heard her utter 'mess' before quickly changing her mind and saying 'these items'. He wanted to respond with something, but his voice was buried somewhere deep inside him and wouldn't come out. She didn't understand, and he didn't know how to make her see. He couldn't go into a care home. He wouldn't! He would have to leave everything behind, and that was unthinkable.

'I know you've probably got a few questions,' Sandra continued, standing up and looking towards the front door. She stepped over his records, her arms wobbling at her sides as if she were a tightrope walker. 'So I'm going to leave you this leaflet over here . . . I tell you what, I'll just hand it to you.'

Alfred took it from her and crushed it beneath his fingers.

'It's got my phone number at the top,' Sandra said. 'So please, you know, ring me if you want me to go over anything again. I'll pop in to see you next week anyway, to find out how you're doing and what your thoughts are. I really do think you'll feel much better for taking part in the restorative-justice programme. I can help you put your victim statement together. There's nothing to worry about. We've got your best interests at heart, okay?'

No, it was most certainly not okay. Alfred slammed his front door behind her, creating a cyclone of dust. After a short sneezing fit, he slumped onto the three-legged divan in the hallway. He lay there among the coats until the sound of early morning rain crashing onto the pavement stirred him from an unsatisfying sleep. Standing up, he groaned with pain. His bones had somehow rearranged themselves into a different order overnight. He tumbled backwards and almost fell into one of his boxes, only a few inches from being speared by a perfectly formed Meccano Spitfire. There was no way in the world he was going to let Sandra do this to him. If she wanted to remove him from his house – his *home* – it would have to be in a body bag.

7

The photograph

It was lashing it down with rain, making the sky dark, and Kian's mind even darker. His trainers were soaked through, just from sprinting across the road for a pint of milk. His toes were numb as he tried to stuff them into a pair of dry socks that were crispy from the radiator. All that was left in his cupboard was a box of Coco Pops. After blasting himself all over with a hairdryer and eating two bowls of cereal, the day lay ahead of him as a series of hours to fill until it wasn't too early to head to the pub with someone. He didn't care who.

He washed up his bowl in the sink, ignoring the mould beginning to bloom underneath the single glazed window. The drunken conversation he'd had with Gav after the court case still lingered in Kian's mind. He'd told Gav it was like he'd been given a second chance and he was going to make the most of every day now, not waste it. Gav had laughed, not realizing that Kian meant it more than he'd ever meant anything in his life.

His focus had to be on staying out of trouble and getting Dan back. But a week had passed and the most he'd managed to achieve was to level up in *Grand Theft Auto*. Making his way through the New York underworld, high on cyber-induced adrenaline, was as good as the day got. The promises he'd made already seemed like a half-remembered dream, something he could disregard, like a New Year resolution that he'd never intended to keep. Who was going to hold him accountable anyway? His social worker? Kian was merely a number, a folder of paperwork to be dealt with as he passed through the system. The only people in his life who claimed to care about him were paid to. That didn't count.

He wasn't even sure he was cut out to look after Dan. One time, when he was younger and they still lived together, he'd tried to cook them both some tea. Dan was moaning in his cot quietly, like he didn't want anyone to hear. Kian was hungry, so he figured his brother must be, too. His mum had been out for hours, and he didn't know when she'd be back.

'It's okay, Dan. I'll make us something,' Kian said, wandering into the kitchen, where the sink was overflowing with dirty plates and the surfaces were covered in empty cider bottles.

He whooped as if he'd scored a goal. Right at the back of the fridge was a handful of Dairylea triangles, and in the freezer box at the top was half a bag of oven chips sitting on top of an empty ice-cube tray. That was an okay tea – better than his mum usually made, if she remembered at all. He turned the knob of the oven round until it made a humming sound, poured the chips onto a tray and popped them in.

He lifted Danny out of his cot, and they played with his toy cars while they waited for the food to cook. 'You got to be careful with this, Dan. It's my best one. Don't put it in your mouth, okay?'

Danny was tiring and he usually didn't listen. Kian loved him, though – more than his Tonka truck – and so he let his brother drool all over it and chew on the wheels. They crashed their cars into each other's knees, and Kian made a mini-garage out of the mugs and ashtrays that were lying around.

When Kian went back into the kitchen, there was smoke coming from the oven. Danny began wheezing and coughing. Kian yanked the door open, his eyes stinging as he pulled out with a tea towel the tray of black matchstick-like French fries. He'd promised Dan some food, but it was all ruined. Tears streamed down Dan's cheeks as he lay down on the floor and howled . . .

Kian had no idea why he kept thinking about the past now. It was his future he had to worry about. He ran his fingers over his stubbled chin. His mediation meeting was tomorrow, so there was no point in having a shave until then. Slimeball Chris, his probation officer, had presented him with the impact statement during their preparation meeting yesterday. Kian had glanced over it with about as much interest as he had in a copy of the *Financial Times*: *Long-lasting consequences . . . blah, blah . . . mental health . . . blah, blah . . . living in fear.* It was so over-the-top, like it was designed to make him feel bad. Chris made Kian produce a statement about how reading it affected him. All it did was wind him up. It was only a broken window – no one had died. If there was anyone who deserved some pity, it was him. No point writing that, though. He knew the drill.

With nothing else to do before lunch, Kian made his way over to his oldest mate Ryan's place. Hanging out there was like pressing pause on real life for a bit. While Kian seemed to be stuck climbing a steep staircase, Ryan was cruising on an escalator. His flat was bigger than Kian's, as he took great pleasure in reminding his friend. It was warmer, too. It had a huge archway between the kitchen and lounge, and he had a fish tank full of brightly coloured tropical fish. Kian loved watching them. The ones with zebra stripes were the best, but they were all pretty cool. Some had neon lights running across their backs, and others were half-orange, half-blue, like they'd been dipped in paint. They were mesmerizing, the way they shimmered in bubbling water and dived in and out of the rocks and bushy plants. He'd like to get his own small aquarium, only Ryan would never shut up about the fact that he'd copied him.

'I'm starving,' Kian said. He'd kicked off his sodden trainers and was sitting on a stool next to the breakfast counter, while Ryan drummed his fingers to the bass line blasting from his new wall-mounted speakers. It was a mystery how Ryan could afford all this nice stuff when he was on the dole too, even if his dad stumped up for his rent. Whenever Kian asked him, Ryan's voice went all weird and he said something about being careful with his money, implying it was something he was better at than Kian. It was a fair point. Kian was always skint. It was as if he had a hole in the pocket of his jacket, despite all the budgeting advice his social worker had given him.

'Wanna go halves on a Domino's?' Kian asked, dropping his wallet on the counter.

'I'll get it, mate,' Ryan said. 'Just cashed in my giro. You order it, though.'

Ryan had the biggest gob ever, and it never failed to amuse Kian that he was scared of talking over the phone. Kian wandered into the lounge, leaned against the radiator and ordered an extra-large Hawaiian with garlic bread, deep-fried potato skins on the side and a bottle of Coke. Well, Ryan was paying. When he came back into the kitchen, Ryan was rifling through Kian's wallet.

'Mate, what you playing at? I offered to go halves. Give it here,' Kian insisted, holding out his hand.

'Come and get it,' Ryan said and chucked his wallet on the floor.

If there hadn't been a pizza on the way, Kian would have grabbed his bank cards, which were now pooled on the lino, and left. When Ryan was in one of these moods, it only ever ended badly.

'Who's the mystery brunette then, eh?' Ryan asked, unfolding the photo that had been tucked inside Kian's wallet. 'Got yourself a secret girlfriend?' He raised his pierced eyebrow.

Kian wanted to swipe the smug look right off his face. Instead he reached across to grab the picture from him. Ryan held it further away and slammed his other palm into Kian's forehead.

'Seriously, hand it over,' Kian said. 'Now! I'm not even joking.' He was about to lose it, big time.

'Ooh, Kian's not joking. This must be one special lady, eh?'

'Just give it back.'

'If she's not special, you don't care if I tear it into tiny little pieces.'

He was bluffing. Ryan was always winding him up. If he ignored him, he'd stop. Except that he didn't. Ryan held the photo right in front of him and began to tear it, ever so slowly, down the middle. A volcanic anger rushed through Kian and he charged at his mate, knocking him to the floor. He didn't even realize he was punching him until Gav walked in and pulled him off, pinning Kian's arms behind him and yelling at him to chill out.

'Psycho,' Ryan said, as Gav helped him up from the floor. His face was puffy and red, and blood drizzled from his nose.

Kian's fists stung as if they'd been cut and dipped in vinegar.

'What the hell, Kian?' Gav said. Still in a shirt and tie from work, he opened the fridge and pulled out a beer, looking hassled, like a dad fed up with sorting out his bickering kids.

Kian looked away, waiting for the urge to launch himself at Ryan again to die down. After a few minutes he turned to face him. 'That's the only picture I've got of my mum, you prick!'

He scooped up the photo pieces, his wallet and cards, put on his wet trainers and slammed the door behind him. It turned out he didn't feel like hanging out with Ryan after all. He really could have done with a slice of that pizza, though.

8

Postcards from the past

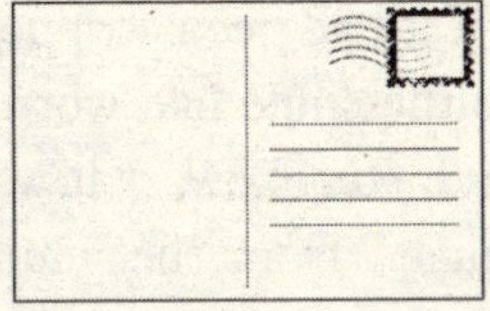

Alfred was attempting to have a bit of a clear-out following Sandra's visit. She had made it clear that she would be coming back. The trouble was, he hadn't made very much progress. Within minutes he'd become distracted by looking through an album of postcards from all the seaside towns in Britain. He had only reached Barmouth, unable to take his eyes off the sweeping bay, the little white sails beyond the harbour, the children splashing in the waves beneath the backdrop of Snowdonia. It was where he and Ida had honeymooned. On the first day it had rained non-stop, so they'd huddled in a pub along the sea front, damp strands of hair plastered to their faces. It was too early for a drink, so they put some money in the jukebox and argued over which song to choose, although there was never any doubt that Ida would win. Soon Bing Crosby crooned in the background while they swayed in each other's arms. Afterwards they sat at the near-empty bar with salted crisps and lemonade, recounting little moments from their wedding day and making plans for their future – an empty book waiting to be filled with their adventures.

Once the rain cleared up, they ate fish and chips on a wall next to the beach, their toes dipping into the shingle beneath them. A couple of dogs ran across the beach with sticks while cyclones of sand swept along the shore and the sea roared. They'd been here once before in the summer, and the beach had been tightly packed with coloured windbreaks and striped deckchairs. There was a raw beauty in the various shades of grey before them, as if it had been stripped back to its natural state. Like love, once the shine had worn away, you were left with the real thing and, somehow, that was even better.

Ida's hair was tangled from the whipping wind and her mascara had smudged around her eyes. She was the most beautiful woman in the world.

'I'll always love you, you know,' Alfred said, finishing the last of his battered cod. He wiped his hands on his trousers and gripped her hand in his, her fingers stiff from the cold.

'And I will always love you, Alfred. You're the one I waited for. No matter what happens in life, we'll face it together.'

She leaned over and kissed him, catching his breath in hers, the world around them melting into nothing. They would always be together. Ida knew him inside-out, better perhaps than he knew himself, and still she wanted him. He was so grateful to have found her. She had got him into collecting, and he always told her that she was his best and most precious discovery. The only one that truly mattered.

Now, despite Ida's promise, Alfred had to face everything alone. Although he was completely fine by himself, he couldn't help thinking about the retirement they'd planned together. With no responsibilities at last, this was going to be their time, when he and Ida could do as they pleased. They were going to complete all the routes in his favourite book, *Best of British Scenic Railway Journeys*. Then they were going to take Spanish classes and travel around Spain. Ida was excited to see the

Gaudí monuments in Barcelona and had borrowed several travel books from the library. After that, they planned to get an allotment. He would grow string-beans and potatoes, and she would have crops of salad. It had never crossed his mind that he'd spend his retirement stuck inside his house, without her.

He looked up from the Barmouth views to the more immediate landscape of his living room: the skyline of boxes, the cluttered carpet, the mess that had multiplied across every available surface. He'd grown so accustomed to it that he hadn't stopped to think whether he had let Ida down. Yes, she'd loved his collections, but surely she'd be horrified if she could see the state of the place? A little kindle of shame forged inside him. It was hopeless, though. Nothing here could be thrown out. Even if Alfred wanted to, he had no idea where to start. Anyway, Ida wasn't here any more.

He put down his book as the phone rang. After staring at it for a moment to see if it would stop, he picked it up.

'Maggie? Oh, hello, I was about to ring you,' Alfred said, knowing full well that she wouldn't believe him. On principle, he hadn't ever rung his daughter since The Incident. She called him occasionally to check up on him, although she'd given up trying to visit long ago, which was just as well, as he had no intention of letting her in. It was her fault that their relationship was fractured, and therefore he wouldn't be the one doing the mending. She obviously only stayed in touch with him out of some sense of duty, so he always did his best to get her off the phone as quickly as possible. Speaking to her was awkward and strained and left him feeling like a plaster had been ripped off, exposing a raw wound.

He wouldn't mention what had happened lately, although a part of him wished he had someone to share the weight of it all with. It had been hard coming out of hospital and realizing that no one had noticed his absence. There were no Get Well Soon cards on the mantelpiece or home-cooked meals left in the fridge. No one to bring him cups of tea or get his medication from the pharmacy, or even check that he took his tablets. No good would come from telling Maggie, though. He didn't need her pity. She had already written him off as unable to cope and that was without having a clue about his heart attack, or the social worker's involvement and the criminal he was expected to befriend.

'Hi, Dad, how are you? It's nice out. Make sure you go for a walk today. Fresh air and exercise will do you good, remember? And are you taking your vitamins?'

Honestly, he was not a child. Goodness knows what she'd be like if she found out he'd been in hospital.

'Already been out, Maggie – fit as a fiddle, you know me. I took a long walk around the pond this morning. Even fed the ducks.' That was probably taking things a bit far. He hadn't fed the ducks since Maggie was small.

'You do know I can come and visit if you need anything, don't you? I honestly don't mind the mess. We could have a proper chat. It would be good to . . . talk.' Maggie sounded like she was sniffing. Perhaps she was the one who needed to monitor her vitamin intake.

'Yes, yes, but we know that won't happen, don't we? Frankly, I don't know why you even bother to call. You've made it quite clear how you feel about me.' Alfred had too much on his mind already, without having to deal with Maggie. He put the phone down so hard that the receiver bounced out of its cradle. At least he wouldn't hear from her again until a few weeks before Christmas, when she would inevitably feel guilty that he'd be spending Christmas Day alone. Same as any other day, if you asked him, but slightly better television and an excuse to eat more cheese. He was already looking forward to the bumper issue of the *Radio Times* and the afternoon that he would spend circling the programmes he wanted to watch.

What made the situation with his daughter difficult to fathom was that they had been so close when she was younger. 'Two peas in a pod,' Ida used to say. Maggie would follow him everywhere. They would make jam tarts together on a Saturday morning while Ida hung out the washing, or he'd push Maggie on the swings at the park. He'd read her stories at bedtime, putting on different voices for Ratty and Mole in *The Wind in the Willows*. Sometimes he'd make a treasure map and hide sixpences in the garden for her to find. She'd dig them up and clean and polish them, so they shone like the hoard of collectible coins that Alfred kept in a little wooden chest.

Of course they went through the usual teenage stage, when Maggie rolled her eyes whenever her father opened his mouth, wouldn't be seen out with him in public unless she walked at least fifteen paces ahead and they argued about the decreasing length of her skirts. However, she emerged from those tumultuous years and things settled back into how they'd always been, although treasure hunts and stories were replaced by discussions about politics or advice about boyfriends. How had it gone so terribly wrong?

When Ida died, he had been so grateful that he still had Maggie – the only other person in the world whom he loved. She was an anchor that he clung to while the land beneath his feet drifted away. Then, a year after Ida's death and after months of nagging and arguing, Maggie took it upon herself to explain to him that hoarding was an illness, and that Alfred might require some help – of the psychological variety.

There was absolutely nothing wrong with his mind. He was as sharp as a tack. Actual bile rose to his throat as he explained, in a not-so-kindly manner, that he wasn't a hoarder; he was a collector. The fact that his own daughter failed to see the difference was both heartbreaking and enraging, in equal measure. Anyway, she had loved his treasure troves when she was a girl. Admittedly there hadn't been quite so much of his stuff back then. At some point after Ida's death, his collections had grown out of control like an untended garden, until it reached the stage where no amount of pruning would improve things. It was simpler just to let it grow wild.

Then, after the arguments, came The Incident. The one he would never forgive her for. She had arranged for him to have a week in St Leonards. He thought it was a peace offering. They both agreed it would do him good. But while he stood on the train platform, surrounded by bustling people with briefcases, suitcases and pushchairs, his ears filled with a whistling sound. The floor began to tilt, and he had to grip the wall behind him to stay upright. He froze as the train came and went, his newspaper tucked under his left arm and his wheeled case by his feet.

He couldn't go through with it, and he returned home to find a house-clearance van outside his house and a man dragging his coat-stand across the pavement as if it were a carcass. Alfred had screamed at him and demanded that everything was taken out of the van and put exactly as it had been found. It had been lucky he'd returned when he had, or there might have been nothing left. He would never go on holiday again. Maggie had pleaded with him, tears in her eyes as she tried to explain.

She'd said she thought it was the only solution, that she just wanted to help. Apparently his home was a fire hazard, and he might trip and hurt himself. Alfred didn't need to listen to her excuses. Her actions had revealed that she could never be trusted again and, worse than that, she didn't accept her father for who he was.

There was a time when his house had been full of love, rather than things. He no longer had a daughter to speak of, or a wife to share his life with. There was no way in the world he was going to lose his home and all his collections. It was all he had left. He took a slug of whisky and picked up the phone.

'Sandra? Hello there, sorry to disturb. I've given it some thought, and I'd like to discuss this restorative-justice scheme. You're right. It would help me to move on.'

The truth was that he had no intention of moving anywhere.

9

Gunmetal pocket watch

The table between them wasn't nearly big enough. Alfred scraped his chair back until it was pressed against the wall, only that made it feel like there wasn't enough air. He felt for his gunmetal pocket watch and rubbed his thumb rhythmically over its decorative casing. It was on page five of his inventory, the details engraved in his mind:

> **Swiss verge fusee pocket watch**
> *Circa 1750. Gilt plates and matching hands. Signed by the maker.*

An unwanted cup of tea grew cold in front of him. Alfred assessed the plate of biscuits. Disappointingly plain, the sort you found lurking in the bottom of the tin and that were only brought out in times of desperation, which he supposed this was. He wasn't hungry anyway, despite the fact that he hadn't managed to eat his porridge earlier.

The meeting was in a small room in the church hall that smelled of coffee mornings and acrylic paint. It was too hot and the sun snuck in through the gaps in the half-closed blinds, creating slanted lines across the paperwork laid out on the table. Alfred undid the buttons on his blazer and looked at the posters advertising yoga and playgroups. He looked at the soothing pattern of the polished parquet floor. He looked everywhere, apart from at the young man sitting in front of him.

Sandra sat beside him, her leg almost touching his as she scoured the pages of her ring-binder. Alfred wanted to climb over her and run out of the building. He wouldn't, of course. Apart from the fact that at his age it would be like scaling Everest, pretending everything was fine was his forte. Still, he couldn't bring himself to look at the lowlife who had put him here in the first place. His eyes stung with the force of avoiding the youth's gaze.

'Okay, well, I'll start things off by acknowledging that this isn't an easy process,' Sandra said.

That was putting it lightly.

'And if you need a break at any point, please ask. Alfred in particular has been incredibly brave in agreeing to take part. So let's do some introductions, shall we?'

Nobody said anything. In the silence, Alfred tried to calculate how many steps lay between him and the exit. Then, after a cough, one of the men sitting on the other side piped up.

'Morning, all. I'm Chris Wilton, Kian's probation officer. He'd like to start proceedings by formally apologizing to Mr Ainswick, here. Isn't that right, Kian?'

Despite himself, Alfred looked up and faced his perpetrator, trying to stare just beyond him rather than directly at him. His vision blurred and his cotton shirt felt cold against his back. Never look the enemy in the eye, especially when held captive. And don't admit defeat. Even when it seems that all is lost. Don't admit defeat.

The perpetrator snapped into focus – a boy, sitting with his legs splayed open, his arms stretched out behind his head as if he owned the place. His mop of hair skirted over his eyes, and he chewed on a piece of gum. He wore a checked shirt, but had left the top button undone, a micro-act of rebellion that niggled Alfred and made him straighten his tie. The boy couldn't have looked less apologetic if he'd tried.

'Yeah. Sorry,' Kian said eventually. Then, as if the probation officer had kicked him beneath the table, which perhaps he had, he took a deep breath and began a monotone speech that sounded as if it had been written for him. 'When I read your victim-impact statement, I realized the effect of my actions. I can see now that what I did was very wrong, and my behaviour has caused you a lot of upset and inconvenience, and so . . . yeah. Sorry.'

'And how do you feel about that?' Sandra asked, ready to write down whatever it was Alfred said.

How did he feel? Humiliated, angry, tired and insignificant. And more than a little scared. But he wasn't about to let anyone know the truth, especially that criminal.

'I appreciate the sentiment,' he said after a few moments, hoping that might be enough to draw this excruciating meeting to a close.

'I don't want to dwell on how this has affected you, Alfred, as I know it's very painful. You did so well by getting everything down on your statement, and I think we can all see that Kian understands the consequences of his actions. So if it's okay with everybody here, I'd like to look forward now and agree on how Kian can make amends.'

For the rest of the meeting Alfred tried to nod in the right places. He'd actually stopped listening, transporting himself to where he would rather be – at home in front of his inventory. Each new discovery was like an ointment to smooth over the cracks in his life. Right at the top of page 278, he had recorded the details of his recent find, unearthed at a car-boot sale in Smethwick. Finding it among the generic-looking vases, ramshackle radios and clocks, he'd had to squash his enthusiasm down, so that the seller wouldn't know how special it was. One of the benefits of having a near-photographic memory was that he could feel close to his objects wherever he was.

Chinese cloisonné egg
Circa 1950. Blue foliage arabesques, no hallmarks, condition good. Seven inches tall, carved mahogany base.

'And I think that's a brilliant solution, don't you, Alfred?' Sandra had stopped writing and clasped her palms on her lap. Alfred stared at her, as though he could rewind the conversation with the power of thought. Unaware of what the proposed solution was, he supposed he ought to agree to its brilliance. Just to keep her onside.

'Yes,' he said, forcing a grin her way for good measure. 'Marvellous.'

'Perfect. That's agreed then. Kian, you'll come and help clear out Alfred's house once a week for ten weeks. That satisfies the courts, yes, Chris? And I know it will be a huge help to Alfred, won't it? It'll be supervised, obviously. Then we can see what steps we need to take after that. Thank you so much, everyone. I'm really pleased with how well it's gone today – so, you know, well done all.'

The scaffolding holding up Alfred's smile collapsed. Kian stood up, muttering something Alfred didn't quite catch as he walked out, letting the door bang shut behind him. Meanwhile Sandra and the probation officer moved into the corner of the room and huddled deep in conspiratorial conversation. Alfred was glued to his chair. He should have said no, obviously. That young hooligan wasn't going anywhere near him again, let alone inside his house. No one came inside his house – that was the rule. Sandra had been an exception, due to circumstances beyond his control.

'I'm so pleased you've agreed to this,' Sandra said, beaming as she strode towards him. 'I can't wait to see what a difference Kian makes to the place. This will be so good for both of you. You take care now, Alfred. I'll call you in a couple of days and we can discuss the arrangements and make sure you're happy with how this will work.'

Happy? He wanted to throw himself to the floor and grab her by the ankles to make her stop. It didn't take a genius to work out what the next steps that she'd cryptically referred to would be. Ever efficient, Sandra had probably already filled in the paperwork securing his place in a care home, just in case he refused to go along with the whole thing. It was very clear that he had no choice.

10

The orange lighter

Kian kicked a stone across the car park and it pinged against a metallic-blue, rundown Volvo that he hoped belonged to Chris Wilton. The mediation meeting had been a complete waste of time. No surprises there. It had taken everything he'd got to stay awake while everyone else droned on. Chris had loved every minute of it, obviously, lording it over him and making him apologize.

His punishment could have been loads worse than a bit of tidying, Kian knew that. What got to him was the thought of having to go round to that freak's house every week. There could be bodies buried under the floorboards, for all he knew. And what were they supposed to talk about? The old guy couldn't even look him in the eye, like Kian was a mass murderer, not just some kid who got a bit carried away with some spray paint and a couple of bricks. Was he going to sit there and watch Kian, inspect what he'd done at the end of the day and find fault? Sod that. He'd try to get it all done in a day, so he didn't have to go back. How messy could it be? Even when his flat was a total tip, it never took more than a couple of hours to get it sorted.

He arrived home, took off his trainers and flung them across the room. They bounced off the wall, leaving a tired grey smudge behind. He stepped over a leaflet on his doormat for the local kebab house and noticed a handwritten letter hiding beneath it. The only letters he usually received were official ones that meant some kind of trouble. He recognized the slanted writing straight away. It was from Lucy, his last foster placement and the best he'd ever had. The two years he'd spent with her were probably the only good ones of his life. The only time when he hadn't felt like a piece of unclaimed lost property. Lucy used to cook his favourite food, bacon-and-tomato pasta, and actually tried to play the computer games he'd liked back then. She'd cheer him on in the rain when he played football, and would sit next to him on the sofa to watch *Match of the Day*. Most of all, she cared. Unlike his real mum.

It wasn't him who stole the money, and Kian wished more than anything that Lucy had believed him. When she'd said it was out of her hands, he'd been crushed. His social worker agreed there had been an irreparable breach of trust and it was best for everyone if he moved out to supported accommodation, as he was already sixteen. He should have refused. He should have proved he was innocent. Instead he let his social worker and personal adviser write up a Pathway Plan that was meant to map out his life for the next two years. A road to nowhere. He opened the letter:

Dear Kian,

How are you? It's been a while since you've been in touch. I was so pleased to hear things are going well for you – a traineeship at a global tech firm sounds very promising! I knew you were destined for great things and I'm so proud of you. I bet you've got some exciting plans for New Year's Eve. The millennium! It's going to be a big one, eh? I know you're really busy, but if you have time I'd love to hear your latest news.

Love, Lucy x

A weight sank to the pit of his stomach like a dodgy kebab. He'd forgotten that he'd lied about getting the global tech job. It was supposed to keep Lucy happy, stop her from thinking she needed to check up on him or feel bad about the way his life had turned out. If she knew what a mess it really was, she wouldn't be using the word 'proud'. She'd stop writing, that was for sure. How was it he'd ended up with no family, no job, useless friends, no money and a couple of months of hard labour facing him?

As he opened the window by his bed and lit up his last cigarette, a heaviness worked its way between his ribs. The darkness was coming again. It had started a few months earlier, in August. There was this total solar eclipse that everyone was making a big deal about – a once-in-a-lifetime thing apparently. Kian got some free cardboard glasses from the newspaper and headed into the beer garden of The Hare and Hounds with his mates, expecting it to be a laugh. Loads of people stood there, beers in hand, wearing these stupid-looking glasses, but nothing was happening. Kian was about to sack it off, go back inside and try his luck on the slot machine when everything changed. He hadn't even noticed the birds were singing until they stopped, and then goose bumps worked their way up his arms. It got cold and he had to put his jacket back on. Minutes later the whole sky went dark, even though it was the middle of the day, and while Gavin and Ryan whooped and laughed, Kian struggled to breathe. All he could think about was that this was it: the world was ending. He never told anyone; it was too weird. Since then, the same sensation hit him every now and again, out of nowhere. He'd be back in that beer garden, an invisible cloud twisting around him until he choked.

He put out his cigarette now and took some deep breaths.

Normally when he got like this in the middle of the day, he'd ring Ryan. Gav worked during the week, but Ryan could always be relied upon to meet him down the pub. An afternoon of drinking would obliterate enough brain cells to stop the feeling of doom. True, he'd usually end up doing something stupid, like stealing a bike or getting into a fight, but it was worth it to feel he was in control again. There was no way he was going to call Ryan now, though. He'd never see that waste of space ever again. He'd taken things too far this time.

Kian pulled out the torn photo from his jacket pocket, tipped the pieces onto the table and tried to put them together, like a jigsaw. His mum's left cheek was missing, and he scrambled through the old bus tickets and chewing-gum wrappers in his pocket until he found it. Even with the missing piece back in place, her left eye had a white gash running through it and her smile was crooked now. Closing his eyes, he tried to conjure up an image of her in his head, one that wasn't scarred with Ryan-induced rips. He could picture her red shirt with buttons that shone like tiny shells, and her long curls tied back in a ponytail. He could even remember the weight of her arms when he tried to drag her out of bed in the morning to find him something for breakfast.

The last time he'd seen her he'd been eight. She'd smelled of cigarettes and sweets. Danny was asleep in his pushchair. She was sitting at the table flicking through a magazine and told him to stop swinging his legs, because it was getting right on her nerves. Then she took a Wham bar out of her handbag and handed it to him for lunch. He could still remember the dark-blue wrapper and the pieces of popping candy zapping on his tongue like little electric shocks. His hands were sticky and, when he wiped his mouth, it was stained with a bright-pink smear like his mum's lipstick. Before he was even halfway through it, she asked him to be a love and fetch her lighter from the bedroom. He didn't mind, his jaw was beginning to ache from chewing. The lighter was refillable and made from orange plastic. He used to like flicking it, to make the liquid inside slosh about.

Resting his Wham bar on the bedside table, he tipped everything up, trying to find it. He wanted to get it right, to please his mum, but he was useless and couldn't find it anywhere. He must have been looking for ages, because by the time he came back empty-handed she'd vanished. Then, instead of the lighter, he began searching for her – behind doors, inside drawers and cupboards, hoping she'd jump out and say, 'Got you!' He looked under his bed and in Dan's cot. She wasn't anywhere. He climbed on a chair and ran his fingers along the top of the fridge, his hands fastening around something hard and plastic. Her lighter. He screeched with delight, as if he'd won a prize. She could come out now. Only she didn't. Dan woke up, and Kian gave him the rest of his Wham bar to stop him from crying.

The house got quieter and darker, so he switched on the lights in every room and turned on the clock radio and the TV, trying to drown out the thought spinning around his head: she wasn't coming back. Usually when she went out, she at least said goodbye. He sat by the window all night, freezing in his T-shirt and shorts, and waited. One of the neighbours must have spotted him, because the next thing he knew, the police were at the door, coaxing him to let them in – the start of an unhappy relationship between him and the local constabulary. The start of his and Dan's life in care.

If he'd found her lighter sooner, maybe she would never have gone.

11

One man's trash

Kian had been standing on Alfred's doorstep for a good five minutes, so Chris couldn't say he hadn't turned up. But Chris was nowhere to be seen anyway. He'd give it another two, then he'd be off. It wasn't his fault if the old guy didn't let him in. What had been the point of getting up before lunchtime for this? It was cold, and his breath turned into vapour as he shuffled his feet. He folded his arms and looked up and down the street of terraced houses. In comparison to the one he was standing outside, they were all completely normal-looking. The paint on their doors wasn't blistering like a bad case of sunburn, and they had net curtains fixed in the windows instead of newspaper. Their gutters hung straight, and their hedges were neatly trimmed – unlike this one, which was so tangled and overgrown it was practically a forest. With a bit of luck, Alfred wouldn't answer the door.

A seagull was swooping near some bins and, further along, a kid was kicking a football against a wall. The repetitive skid-thwack was doing Kian's head in. Still no sign of Alfred. Waste of time. As he turned to jump off the step onto the pavement, the door finally opened. Without saying anything, Alfred handed him a note. He looked like he'd just got out of bed. His grey hair stuck up at crazy angles and he had wild eyebrows, like some mad professor. A toothpaste-stained shirt hung loosely over his trousers, drowning his thin frame. He'd made a decent stab at looking like a normal human being at their mediation meeting. Now it was clear he was a nut-job, exactly as Kian had suspected. Great.

'Sign this,' Alfred said.

'All right, Al? How about a "hello"?' Kian replied, scanning the crinkly handwriting on a tatty bit of paper, which appeared to be a list of rules:

CONTRACT FOR KIAN MATTHEWS

All rules must be strictly adhered to. Failure to do so will result in this contract being terminated and the agreement severed. I, Kian Matthews, agree to abide by the following rules:

1) No swearing.

'You've gotta be—' Kian began, before Alfred held up his hand.

'I mean it,' Alfred said. 'No swearing or I'll terminate the agreement and inform your probation officer.'

Kian gave the drainpipe a sharp kick and it collapsed onto the floor.

'You can fix that before you leave,' Alfred went on. 'Go on then, read the rest of it.'

Kian sighed and dragged his eyes down the list.

2) Nothing to be thrown out without my approval.

Okay, fair enough.

3) No smoking or drinking.

As expected. Kian chucked the end of his cigarette into the empty skip below the bay window and noticed how huge it was. Surely he wasn't expected to fill the whole thing? He carried on to the final point on the list.

4) No questions!

'Seriously? I'm not allowed to ask you anything?' Kian shoved his hands in his pockets, wondering if he'd ever be let in, out of the cold, or if Alfred was going to pull out more pages of rules.

'I'm afraid you're already contravening point four of our contract,' Alfred said. 'Shall I phone – now what's his name? – Chris, that's right. Shall I call Chris and tell him you would be more suited to some other form of punishment? Behind bars perhaps?'

Fair play to the man: he knew how to get his own way. Kian took the pen Alfred held out to him and quickly scrawled his initials on the paper. Anything to be let indoors and into the warm. Only, once he was inside he realized the house was colder than his flat when the electric had run out. How was the old guy not dead? The place stank, too, like a school canteen – floor polish and over-boiled cabbage. Even though he'd left school more than a year ago, a familiar fear rippled through him – the dread of being put on the spot to work out unsolvable algebra equations or make sense of sonnets.

'Bloody hell!' Kian muttered, as he stepped into the hallway.

'Point number one!' Alfred waved the contract at him.

It was unlike anything Kian had ever seen. Instead of being an entrance that led to the stairs, with a coat-rack or one of those little tables with a lamp on it and a phone, the hall was a labyrinth of bulging cardboard boxes. They towered on either side of him, making him feel far smaller than his six feet. Everywhere was dirty, not just a bit, but layers of proper filth and cobwebs. Then there were the random objects that lined the entire staircase. Kian flicked his eyes upwards and took in a bronze statue of some naked dude, an ugly gold clock with pointy bits coming out of the sides, a model aeroplane, a globe resting on a shiny stand and, on the bottom step, a set of wooden soldiers, lined up and ready for an imaginary battle. It was like a retirement home for all the useless rubbish nobody else wanted. He'd been expecting a bit of a mess, not an indoor scrapyard. There was no way this place would be sorted in ten weeks. It would take more like ten years. He'd been properly stitched up. Chris must have known, the tosser.

Kian picked up one of the little soldiers and moved its arms while making machine-gun sounds. Alfred snatched it from him.

'Don't touch that,' he said quietly.

Alfred's doorstep bravado had disappeared, along with any glimmer of daylight, as the front door shut behind them. He seemed to shrink as he rushed into the kitchen to make some tea. Kian had an uncomfortable feeling, which he thought, for a moment, might be guilt. The guy looked like he might actually be scared of him.

'Make a start in the front room,' Alfred called out from the kitchen. 'I'll tell you what you can throw away. I'm pinning your contract on the wall right here, so you can remind yourself of the rules each time you come. And where's your supervisor anyway? You're not meant to be here alone.'

'I dunno, do I? Ring your social worker. Ask her.'

Alfred appeared in the doorway and shuffled from foot to foot. 'Maybe there's been a mishap with the paperwork. I suppose we don't need someone else sticking their nose in, do we? It's easier this way. As long as you stick to your contract.'

'Whatever,' Kian replied. It wasn't like he was ever going to look at it again. He could do without someone else snooping over his shoulder, too. Any hope that the living room might be an improvement on the hallway vanished instantly. The room was dimly lit, like the colour of weak tea. When was the last time Alfred had opened a window in here? Kian coughed as he forged a path through the collection of cabinets, bookcases, sideboards and armchairs, all buried under mounds of dust. He had to stop himself from stretching his arms out and pushing it all over. It made him feel claustrophobic.

The table closest to him was draped with a red tasselled tablecloth. He examined the jumble sitting on top of it – a box stuffed with silver teaspoons, a huge bowl filled with hundreds of brightly coloured marbles, some glass bottles with crystal stoppers, a twisted wooden candlestick and some little china bells. None of it seemed to have any purpose or any connection to anything else. He picked up one of the marbles that looked like a cat's eye and rolled it between his fingers. The guy had well and truly lost the plot. Even the yellowing walls were completely covered with paintings, mirrors, lamps, stag antlers and clocks. There wasn't an inch of space that wasn't filled. He should have done the geezer a favour and torched the place, instead of lobbing some bricks through the window.

A bound A4 notebook was resting on the edge of the sofa.

Its pages were worn, and little corners of paper poked out from it. Kian picked it up and had a nose through it. Each page was split into columns with a date of entry, name of item and description. There were pages and pages. It looked like all this random stuff actually meant something to the guy.

Alfred arrived with tea, which Kian drank quickly, avoiding looking at the mug too closely in case it wasn't clean. He made a mental note to wear his oldest clothes next time. There was no way he was ruining his decent jeans or making an extra trip to the launderette.

'What's this then?' Kian asked, holding out the notebook. 'For the skip?'

'Certainly not. It's my inventory, if you must know. It's a record of all my collections. I know all that information off by heart. Go on, pick one out and test me on it.'

Kian laughed, before realizing Alfred was serious. He handed it over and watched Alfred squirrel it away in a drawer. Then he picked up one of the boxes next to the sofa to make a start.

'No! Not that one,' Alfred said, grabbing it out of his hands.

For a scrawny old guy, he was actually pretty strong.

'Do I need to go through the contract again?' Alfred asked. 'I decide what you can throw away.'

'Okay, okay. What do you want me to shift then?' Kian looked around at the boxes squashed between endless pieces of furniture. They were spoilt for choice, and he could guarantee that nothing was worth keeping. It would be quicker to take a box at a time and dump it straight into the skip, although even that tactic would take for ever. So much for getting it all done in one go.

Alfred made his way over to the far side of the room and hesitated. After a few minutes of appearing to stare into space, he lifted up a brown lampshade, ran his fingers along the rim and grunted.

'Here, take this.'

'Seriously? That's it?'

'No questions, remember? Well, go on then, pop it in the skip. Gently, mind.' Alfred handed it over and stepped back quickly. They'd be here all day at this rate.

Kian's fingers left imprints in the dust. The lampshade wasn't brown at all. Underneath the dirt, it was originally a pale-orange colour with a garish pattern of flowers. From the doorstep, he hurled the hideous seventies-looking shade into the skip. When he came back into the living room, Alfred was slumped on the sofa with his head in his hands. His whole body was shaking. As if the day couldn't get any worse, the old geezer was now having some sort of breakdown. This wasn't a punishment. It was a curse.

'Er . . . you okay?' Kian asked. 'You seem like, I dunno. I mean, you're not upset about that gross lampshade? It's well ugly.'

'You know nothing about me, young man,' Alfred replied, a vein on his forehead bulging as he spat out his words. 'I don't want you here in my house, snooping through my belongings and throwing them away. Do you understand? You're only here because Sandra will throw me in a care home if I don't go along with this whole thing.'

'I don't wanna be here myself, mate!' Kian shouted. 'I'll be sent down, if this tip isn't cleared to Chris Wilton's liking!' The thought of Chris made him curb his fury. He flexed his fingers and took a long, slow breath. He couldn't risk Alfred reporting that he'd lost his temper. Even so, Kian half wanted them to have a proper blazing row. He was ready for it, his rage ignited and ready to fire, but Alfred got up from his seat and quietly left the room, eyes down to the floor.

Kian's anger burned itself out as he looked around at the mess surrounding him and it changed to dread. On the one hand, he had agreed not to throw anything away without Alfred's say-so. On the other, he was very aware of the ticking clock that lay between him and a prison cell. There were only ten weeks to empty out this place, before his probation officer decided if his sentence had been served adequately; and Chris had it in for him, as it was. He'd just have to get on with it. The guy clearly wasn't in charge of his own marbles. And he had a lot of them.

With Alfred nowhere to be seen for the rest of the afternoon, Kian emptied a total of eleven boxes into the skip and only had three cigarette breaks. He felt quite pleased, until he realized exactly how much was left. It was like climbing a mountain when you couldn't see the top. He tried not to root around in the contents, in case he uncovered something totally gross, like a jar full of belly-button fluff or a box of toenail clippings. He wouldn't put it past the old guy.

Despite the cold, he was now dripping with sweat and had to tie his jacket around his waist. There was no way he was putting it down – he'd never find it again. The last box he shifted might well have been lined with lead and had finished him off. His back was killing him and he collapsed onto the divan in the hallway, only to jump in alarm at finding Alfred beneath a pile of coats.

'What the hell are you doing under there?' Kian yelled. The man was certifiable.

Alfred looked like he'd woken from a nightmare. His skin was the colour of ash and shiny with sweat. It would be just

Kian's luck, if Al went and carked it. Kian would be up for a murder charge on top of everything else. He pushed his way through the gap between the boxes and the kitchen and filled a glass to the top with tap water.

'Here,' Kian said, handing him the glass.

'I . . . I was just having a little nap,' Alfred replied, after knocking back the water, the way Kian drank lager on a Friday night. 'Anyway, it's getting dark. I think it's time you went home.'

'Best thing I've heard all day,' Kian said, racing out of the front door before Alfred could change his mind. He was getting straight into the shower to wash this place off him. There was no doubt about it: if he made it through the next couple of months, they were going to be the longest of his life.

12

Hornsea coffee pot

British Summer Time was almost officially over. Since the attack, Alfred had found himself hesitant to be out after dark – which was silly really, as he had been indoors when it had happened. Nevertheless, the evening had crept up on him and now he was stuck inside, despite having been desperate to empty the skip as soon as Kian had left.

Instead he made some tea and sat in front of the television to watch an episode of *Inspector Morse*. It was a repeat he'd already seen, yet he was unable to follow the plot. His mind was too busy creating crime stories of its own. Each time he heard footsteps on the street, he turned the volume down and waited to hear if there were any sounds of rummaging in the skip outside. Thank goodness he'd hidden away his most valuable possessions before Kian had arrived. The boy was devoid of any principles and showed absolutely no sign of remorse for his crime. In fact, the young lad seemed to think he was doing Alfred a favour – as if he should be grateful that there was an intruder in his home.

As soon as the sun came up, he was outside in his dressing gown and slippers, bringing everything back inside. All the bending and hauling left him breathless, though. It would be impossible to keep this up. At this rate he'd end up in a funeral home, never mind a care home.

Kian would be back in a few days, so Alfred had to get on with hiding as much as he could. He surveyed his collections again and then stared at his plan. Step one was simple enough: get as much of his collections upstairs as possible. Out of sight, out of mind. Surely Sandra wouldn't be nosing around the entire house when she came back? He would leave a few bits and pieces downstairs for the boy to sort out and get rid of, to give him something to do. Only he hadn't managed to decide what could be thrown away. Every time he picked something up, he could think of a hundred reasons why he should keep it and began to feel dizzy. He pored over his inventories, hovering over them with a pen, ready to cross out any unnecessary items. So far, in the twelve hours since he began this process, his pen had not yet made contact with the paper. Everything here had earned its place. It belonged.

People didn't understand that collecting connected him to the world. Whenever he found something to add to his inventory, it was like he became a part of its history. Every item had meant something to someone at one time, and now they meant something to him. Ida had understood. And she'd also known when to rein him in. Not that he'd really needed it back then. Before she died, it had been a hobby, a bit of fun, not a frame around which his entire life was constructed.

Alfred set to work again and struggled upstairs, saddled with overflowing bin bags that were almost heavier than he was. Each step required him to heave a deep breath, while his ribs rattled. His arms ached and his back was on fire. It had occurred to him more than once that perhaps this wasn't such a good idea. Unfortunately, it was the only one he had.

Very quickly it became apparent that there was a bigger problem than the physical challenge of dragging his possessions from one room to another. There wasn't very much space upstairs, after all. In recent years his bedroom had become an overcrowded museum. It was almost impossible to push open the door now, let alone find room to put anything else in it. The spare room resembled a warehouse storage facility. The racks of shelving were fit to burst, and the carpet was completely hidden beneath a patchwork of bags and boxes. The only free space left in the bathroom was the bath. Although Alfred was tempted to fill it, as the shower was occupied by a huge grandfather clock, there would be nowhere for him to wash. Pungent body odour would only give Sandra something else to be concerned about.

The loft was the only space left. He pulled down the ladder from the hatch in the ceiling and carefully climbed the rungs. When he switched on the overhead light, the roof cavity shone with antiquities like Aladdin's cave. This was where he stored the possessions that he had to be really careful with, the ones that needed to be kept in pristine condition. Although he rarely went up there these days, knowing that his best items were tucked safely in his roof helped him drift off to sleep at night.

He'd obviously been much fitter when he'd dragged most of these treasures up here. Now he sat at the top of the ladder and panted for several minutes to recover from the effort of reaching it. The good news was that there was definitely space underneath the rafters, towards the back.

He had collected all manner of curiosities, relics and heirlooms over the years. A quick glance around revealed a Renaissance painting, a Toby jug, a stuffed elephant with sagging ears, a sewing machine, a bronze bust (heaven knows how it got up there, it weighed a ton) and an Art Deco lamp. His pulse danced gently at the sight of them. It was like he'd been thirsty for weeks and was now presented with gallons of water.

Even then, it wasn't enough. A shopping trip was in order.

Leaving the house was fraught with potential danger. Alfred tried to save his expeditions for days when he really needed a lift – when the desire to find something new overtook him, a burning pain that crept over his skin and could only be relieved by the balm of a new discovery. After everything he'd been through recently, he deserved it. He wouldn't get carried away, though. Just one item; maybe two, if he spotted something really special.

He slipped through the streets stealthily, as if on a classified mission. With his coat collar up and his hat pulled down to meet his eyebrows, he focused on his footsteps to avoid meeting anyone's gaze and to ensure he safely navigated any trip hazards. The last thing he needed was another hospital visit and more busybodies.

The local charity shops were his favourite place to hunt down items for his collection. There was the thrill of the chase, not knowing what he would uncover. Then the joy of bartering, even if it only cost a few pence in the first place. And he could chat to people who seemed happy to see him and would listen if he told them the history of a particular type of glass bowl, or the origins of a sideboard.

In the Animal Rescue shop he delved into a box of bric-a-brac, feeling his way around the objects without looking, like it was a lucky dip. More than once he'd found a couple of priceless collectibles in this way. It had practically been theft, the price he'd paid for them. Still, it wasn't his fault if they didn't bother to find out the true value of things.

'Hello,' the woman behind the counter said. Her hair was tied up in a bun and a colourful shawl was draped over her shoulders. She was putting some books out on a shelf and stopped to look at him. 'Nice day out there, for the time of year.'

Alfred hadn't noticed. He realized he had been staring at the Hornsea coffee pot in his hand for several minutes, without saying anything. He wanted to explain that he'd already got several of the teapots and most of the rest of the tea set. This was a most welcome addition, but he couldn't let her know that. He'd have to put on his most extensive charm to get the price down from the £5 tag.

'Well, good afternoon, how lovely to see you.' Alfred smiled and handed over his spare hand for shaking. 'Keeping well? I have to say, you certainly look it.' That's right, reel her in.

'Oh, thank you,' the woman said, darting her eyes downwards as she shook his hand. 'I've been doing a bit more walking lately. Not far, you know, just around the lake really.'

'You're right, it is a rather beautiful day out there, isn't it? Perfect for a walk. Perhaps I could join you, if you wouldn't mind? What time do you finish?' He willed her to say no.

'Oh, what a lovely offer. I can't, though, I'm afraid. I have to go straight home today. I need to get some shopping done for my neighbour. Housebound.'

Thank goodness for that. 'Well, aren't you a kind soul? Volunteering for charity, assisting the needy. Another time perhaps. Anyway, what do you say to knocking a few pounds off this old crock for me?'

With the pot safely tucked into his bag in a blanket of bubble wrap, Alfred left the shop only £2 lighter than he'd gone in. He was not losing his touch. There was no point stopping here, not when he was doing so well. Who knew what he might find in the next shop?

13

Friends like these

The last person Kian expected to see standing outside his flat, waiting for him when he got home, was Ryan, but there he was, headphones plugged into his ears and a skateboard under his arm. Kian was about to tell him to sling his hook when he caught sight of the bruise on Ryan's right cheek and thought better of it. He let his mate in and they stood in silence while the kettle boiled for the longest two minutes ever. Kian took his last two Pot Noodles out of the cupboard and pushed one towards Ryan on the counter, as if they were about to have a Western-style brawl.

'All right?' Ryan asked, as he peeled off the lid.

'All right,' Kian replied. 'Soz about your face.'

'Don't sweat it. My fault. I didn't know it was your mum, mate. Sorry.' Ryan reached into his coat pocket and handed him a can of lager. It wasn't a supermarket own-brand one. A peace offering.

There was no point in staying angry. They'd been mates for ever. Without Ryan and Gav, Kian would be completely alone. Yes, he had friends he saw down the pub every now and again – kids he knew from school, or from knocking around the neighbourhood – but no one else had ever really stuck by him like Gav and Ryan had. Maybe he was difficult to like, or maybe it was the fact that he just found most people annoying. Maybe some quack with a white coat and an expensive degree would tell him he had trust issues. He'd never really figured it out, but what Kian did know was that friends, even ones who did your head in from time to time, were worth hanging on to, especially when you had no family. Anyway, he'd managed to tape up the photo and it didn't look too bad. He wouldn't tell Ryan that, though. No harm in him thinking he owed Kian one.

'You ever tried to track her down?' Ryan asked.

'My mum? No point, she made it clear she wants nothing to do with me.' Kian sat down on the sofa and passed a game controller to Ryan. He always dealt with personal questions by shutting them down. Considering he'd known his mates for such a long time, Ryan and Gav only knew the scantest details about his family life. Then again, so did he.

'That sucks, man,' Ryan said. 'Don't you ever wonder, like, what she's doing right now?'

Of course he did. Constantly. The game had only just started, and Kian was wasted by a grenade. He kicked his controller across the floor and opened his lager. How was he supposed to concentrate on prowling the streets of San Andreas, working for Uncle Fu's gang, when Ryan had filled his head with thoughts of looking for his mum? There'd been loads of times when he'd thought about trying to track her down. But he wasn't sure he could take it if she wanted nothing to do with him. Anyway, shouldn't she be the one trying to find him? Apologizing for never being there and for letting Kian and Dan go into care?

'What about your dad then?' Ryan asked. 'Why didn't he hang around?'

'Dunno, you'd have to ask him.' His dad had never been in the picture, so somehow it hurt less. It wasn't personal. It was probably his mum's fault that he scarpered. All Kian remembered her saying about him was that he was a waste of space and was in and out of prison. Kian couldn't shake the feeling that he was a chip off the old block, even though they'd never met. There had been times when he was younger when he'd dreamed his dad would come back for him – a hero who would whisk him off to a better life. He soon learned that dreaming got you nowhere and that heroes didn't really exist.

'So what we doing for New Year's then?' Ryan asked, putting his controller down and stuffing steaming noodles into his mouth.

Kian shrugged in reply. The way things were looking at Al's place, he'd probably be banged up by the New Year.

'C'mon, man, we need to decide. It's the biggest New Year ever. It's, like, the millennium!' Ryan went on, as if Kian didn't know.

It was all Ryan had talked about since last New Year's Eve, when he'd spent the entire night throwing up in the toilets at Zanzibar's, convinced he'd missed out on pulling some chick wearing a feather boa. This year *had* to be the party of their lives apparently.

'When you're like an old geezer, people will ask you what you did for the millennium. We gotta do something amazing,' Ryan said.

'I dunno, man. You sort some tickets for something – I don't care what we do.' With only a handful of weeks of 1999 left, Kian was fairly confident that the next century wouldn't be any better than the one he was currently stuck in, and that really wasn't worth celebrating.

Sunday nights were the worst. The weekend was over, and reality hit again. Kian should be getting ready for the week ahead, or at least looking forward to something. He rang Dan and got through to Simone, who knew him well enough to realize that he didn't want to waste time with small talk.

'When can I come and live with you?' Dan asked, breathless from rushing to the phone.

Kian flinched. 'Hold up, you didn't even say "hi"!'

'Hi.'

'And I'm working on it, you know that. What've you been up to? How's school?'

'Good. We're doing about the Second World War. We've got to do a project for homework.' It sounded completely boring, but Dan seemed happy with it.

'Like any girls?'

'Don't be stupid,' Dan said. 'I'm ten. Can I watch the England game with you?'

The Euro 2000 qualifier match was coming up. Kian had already arranged to watch it with Ryan, so he'd have to cancel. He'd understand. Dan was more important.

'Yeah, I'd love that. We need to square it with Simone, though, yeah?'

'She already said yes!'

Kian smiled, thinking of the fuss he'd make when Dan came over to watch the match. He'd get him an England flag, buy Dan's favourite crisps and a bottle of Coke, because he knew his brother wasn't allowed to drink it usually. Sometimes life threw out some good moments, just to remind him that it was worth living after all.

14

A house of cards

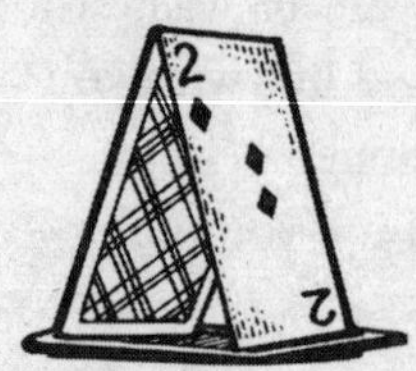

It was a pretty good feeling, getting one over on people. Without anyone's assistance, Alfred had transferred almost half of the contents of his living room to the loft. It hadn't been at all easy, which made it even more rewarding, like building a tower from a pack of playing cards. It had taken perseverance and a great deal of determination. He'd proved something to everyone, even though no one knew what he'd done. All he had to do was complete the job, wait a few weeks, cart the whole lot downstairs again and life would return to exactly the way he liked it. No interfering, no hoodlums in his house and no threat of going into an old people's home. He would, of course, have to do his best to tolerate the infernal youth in the meantime. Keep your enemies close.

Somehow, in all the business of his self-congratulation, Alfred had lost track of time. The doorbell was already alerting him to Kian's arrival. He turned down the volume of his *Die Fledermaus* record, tucked in his shirt and opened the door.

'Oh, it's you,' Alfred said, as if there was a possibility of someone else coming to visit.

Once again, Kian was unaccompanied, but Alfred wasn't about to chase up his errant supervisor. Whatever admin error had occurred, it had resulted in a tiny bit of fortune being on his side in what was undeniably a most unfortunate situation. At least this way, Alfred was in charge and didn't have to answer to anyone.

Kian's tracksuit bottoms were hanging so low, they looked as though they would fall down if he so much as sneezed. 'Need to borrow a belt, young man?'

Kian grunted something incomprehensible and yanked up his trousers. Judging from the smoke drifting around his ankles, he had hastily stubbed out a cigarette on the doorstep before ringing the bell. Alfred held the door just wide enough for him to walk through, and let Kian go into the living room first.

'You should give up, you know,' Alfred called after him. 'Dreadful habit and such a waste of money.'

Kian charged back into the hallway. 'There's more stuff in there than last time! We're meant to be emptying the place, not filling it with even more junk!'

It was possible that his recent shopping spree had undone some of the youth's hard work, but surely the room was better than before? Alfred eyed up the new boxes. There really weren't that many. Kian should take a look in the loft, if he wanted to see what a packed room really looked like.

'You're overreacting,' Alfred said. 'It's a few bits and pieces. If you work like last time, you'll have it done by lunchtime. Tell you what, do a good job and I'll even make you lunch.'

'Nah, you're all right.' Kian wandered off, expletives escaping under his breath.

It was tempting to remind him of the no-swearing clause in their contract, only Alfred was in such a good mood that he decided to let it drop. This visit from the dreadful lad was so different from last time. He was in control. Now that he knew he would simply have to empty the skip himself the next day, he had no need to worry about what Kian threw away. Buoyed up by his recent shopping trip, and thoroughly pleased with his plan to hoodwink both Kian and Sandra by storing most of his collections in the loft, he reclined in his armchair with the latest copy of the *Collectors Gazette* and an early glass of claret. A joyous paean floated out from his record player and the afternoon sun filtered through the newspaper-covered windows, dappling the room in a Golden Delicious glow. It was turning into quite a splendid day.

Kian had only been working for about half an hour when he sighed in an exaggerated manner and sat down on one of the boxes on the floor. Alfred could feel him staring right at him through the pages of his *Gazette*.

'Can I help you?' Alfred asked.

'Well, yeah, actually. How about helping me shift some of this bloo . . . this lot?'

'I'm sorry? Was it me who threw two bricks through an elderly war veteran's window and terrified him almost to death? No, it was not. You did the crime, and now you serve the time. Don't expect any help from me.' Alfred took a large sip of wine and began humming along to the music.

Kian grumbled some more before lifting another couple of boxes and dropping them in the skip. Alfred imagined their contents being crushed and took an extra-large gulp of wine. He had lost his place in the article he was reading and decided they could both do with some tea. The wine was making his head fuzzy. He brought in a teapot on a tray, with half a packet of Bourbons. The other half remained in the tin. The last thing he wanted was Kian eating him out of house and home.

'Sit yourself down in that chair,' Alfred said, realizing at once that he hadn't thought this through. Now they were sitting opposite each other with nothing to do, they would have to talk. Putting up with Kian and wanting to be in his company were two entirely different things. He tried to remember how conversations usually went when there was no ulterior motive involved, or if he wasn't talking about his collections. Of course he could quite happily sit in silence. It didn't bother him one bit. He lived by himself, after all. No, he couldn't care less. There was nothing he liked more than peace and quiet. By the time his cup was half empty and two Bourbons had been consumed, without so much as a word from Kian, Alfred cracked.

'So what sort of name is Kian anyway?'

'Dunno. What sort of name is Alfred?'

Alfred huffed. An obstinate young man, just as he'd thought. 'What do your parents have to say about your recent behaviour then?'

That was clearly the wrong question. Kian's eyebrows knitted together as he stuffed a fourth biscuit into his mouth. It had been wise to bring out only half of the packet.

'Grew up in care,' Kian said after a while. Now that he'd finished eating, he was pulling strips of cardboard off the side of one of the boxes and letting them fall to the floor. It was making a terrible mess.

Never in a million years would Alfred have thought they would have anything in common. If he hadn't signed up to fight in the war at the age Kian was now, he might have ended up on the wrong path himself. Growing up in care had convinced Alfred that he wasn't good enough. It wasn't an easy thing to recover from. He had been lucky – he had found Ida. Perhaps this boy had no one to show him the worth that was hiding inside him. There was a very small possibility that he might have judged Kian a little harshly. Then again, the lad had almost killed him.

'In that case, you can't blame your parents for how you've turned out,' Alfred said, picking up his magazine again. 'I grew up in care myself. It doesn't excuse you from taking responsibility for your actions.'

Kian leapt up from his chair and kicked over a nearby stool before storming outside. It was a wonder the stool didn't splinter in two with the force. Alfred tutted as cigarette smoke snuck its way into the hallway from underneath the front door. Attempting conversation with the lad was a mistake. Alfred wasn't good around people as it was, and Kian was the most trying individual he'd ever had the misfortune of coming across. He might as well get on with the tidying himself.

15

No questions

Feeling like he could explode was becoming a regular thing lately. It was like the dial on Kian's mood was jammed on the insanely angry setting. The old geezer had clearly been and bought a whole new load of crap to replace all the stuff Kian had got rid of last week. Not only that, but Alfred also seemed to enjoy goading him, like he wanted Kian to lose his rag and fail. Well, he'd done his job. Although Kian's thoughts were racing, he was sure of one thing: he couldn't do this any longer.

He took out his phone to ring Chris. He had to tell him this wasn't working. That he'd take any other punishment than this. The man was a loony and needed locking up. He opened his contacts, scrolled through to the letter C, then hesitated. Dan's number was right below Chris's. Completing this programme with Alfred was impossible, and yet if he went to prison instead, there was no way of Dan ever coming to live with him.

He paced the length of Alfred's street and stopped when he reached the corner – a crossroads. A few more footsteps would determine his future. Just then a little boy crossed over the road, holding his mum's hand. A football was tucked under his arm, and in that moment something tugged at Kian's heart. He was back at the park with Dan, running and laughing, being the brother he always wanted to be. He could feel Dan's arms wrapped around him, asking his usual question about when he could come and live with him. Kian blinked back tears. He watched the boy and his mum walk down the street until they became nothing more than specks in the distance. He kicked the kerb, swivelled on his feet and headed back towards Alfred's. He had to see this through, for Dan's sake.

Kian chain-smoked several cigarettes before forcing himself back through the front door. He headed straight for the bathroom, swearing as he stumbled over the gold pointy clock on the stairs. One of the spikes stabbed him in the ankle and he hobbled up to the landing. The bathroom was packed full of useless stuff, exactly like downstairs. There was barely space to take a slash. As he washed his hands, a strange creaking came from the floorboards above him, like an ancient coffin opening in a horror film. He zipped his flies fast. This house gave him the creeps, big time. Kian scrambled back down the stairs, trying not to trip over the collections that snaked their way beneath the banister as he went.

When he returned to the living room, Alfred stood up all of a sudden and dropped his magazine.

'You look like you've been caught stealing,' Kian said.

'Not at all, I just thought I should probably give you a hand after all. I mean, you do seem to be struggling a little,' Alfred replied.

Kian's hands briefly formed into fists, before he released them and lifted the flap of the next cardboard box. A rustling came from inside it.

'A bloody mouse!' he shrieked, hurling the box back onto the floor, glad that Ryan and Gav weren't around to hear him squeal.

'Don't worry about him,' Alfred said. 'That's Monty. I haven't seen him for a few days actually, thought I'd have to get the Red Leicester out. Monty? Monty?'

Someone was messing with him. This whole thing was a set-up, one big joke, only Kian wasn't laughing.

'I've gotta ask, Al,' he said, climbing onto the armchair to escape the free-running rodent.

'It's Alfred, if you don't mind,' the old geezer said, his cheeks mottled pink.

'Whatever. How did this' – Kian extended his arms towards the mess around them – 'happen? I mean, did you wake up one day and think: I know, I'll see how much crap I can cram inside my house?'

Alfred was silent for so long that Kian considered prodding him to check he was still breathing.

'This is why your contract clearly states you are to ask no questions,' Alfred replied at last. 'But since you're evidently not one to pay attention to the rules, I'll ask you one. What on earth has it got to do with you? Shall I interrogate you about your life decisions? It doesn't look like you've made a very good job of things so far, does it? You're headed for prison.'

'Yeah, well, I've had a tough life. How else was I going to turn out?' Kian was sick of people expecting the impossible from him, like it was his fault he'd had no opportunities and a screwed-up childhood.

'Oh, really? Well, let me fetch my violin,' Alfred said. 'My life was far from easy. But I didn't go around behaving like a hooligan and thinking the world owed me a living.'

Seriously, the guy was asking for it. Kian had had enough. 'Yeah, well, look how you turned out! You're no better than me. You've still ended up with a bloody social worker breathing down your neck. If I was well off, like you, and had my own house, I'd keep it nice and wouldn't waste all my money on this total trash!'

Alfred's face was now the colour of beetroot. He shouted at the top of his voice. 'How I choose to spend my money is absolutely none of your business. I've had a respectable job. A wife. A family! I am not a criminal. I made something of myself, fought for my country, while you – you're a nihilistic layabout and haven't done a single good thing in your life!'

Kian stepped right up to Alfred, so close that he could smell wine on his breath and see hairs escaping from his nostrils. His hands trembled with the force of keeping them by his sides. A wave of heat was rising through his body, like a pan about to boil over. If he didn't get out now, he was going to swing for him, then he really would be screwed. Alfred was right: Kian was going to end up in prison anyway, so why was he wasting his time here? He should be making the most of his freedom while he had the chance, not hanging out in this hellhole with a crazy person who was beyond help.

'I'm out,' Kian retorted, stepping back and flexing his fingers.

'Well, see you next time, I suppose,' Alfred said, scooping up the remaining Bourbons.

'As if,' Kian replied. 'It's over, you nutter. I wouldn't come back here if you paid me.'

He yanked Alfred's contract from the wall as he passed through the hallway and then, before leaving, snuck one of the wooden soldiers into his coat pocket, just to annoy the hell out of the old guy. He tried to block out the image of Dan's face, when he came to visit him in prison.

16

Unlucky numbers

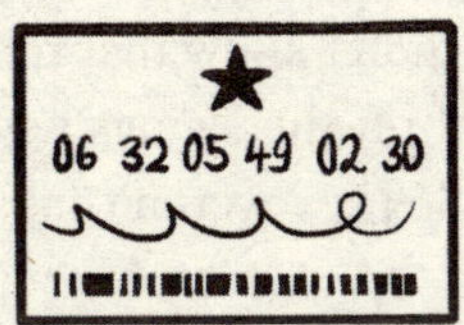

'Dan? Danny, you okay?'

'Kian, they're moving me away. I want to live with you. You said!'

That voice. It ripped up his insides whenever he heard it on the end of the phone. Danny was two when they were sent to different foster carers, and ever since then Kian had wanted nothing more than for them to be back together. With Dan being so young, they thought he had a better chance of being adopted on his own. It was clear they didn't think anyone would want Kian.

'Dan, what d'you mean? Where are they moving you to? Why? You like it with Simone, right?'

'I do like it, but they've found me a match. Sam and Lou. They're going to be my new mum and dad. I'm going to be adopted.' Danny's voice cracked, and he began to cry.

Kian punched the wall next to his bed and watched the thin plasterboard crumble. He shook his hand. The possibility of adoption for Dan had always hung over him, just like the distant threat of a life behind bars had. The longer it went on, the less likely it seemed it would ever happen. Kian only had a few months left until he was eighteen, and he was sure everyone would see that it made sense for the brothers to live together, rather than put Dan with strangers. Sam and Lou? Who the hell were they and how could they look after Dan better than he could? They didn't know that he liked Marmite on toast in the morning, or that he twisted his hair with his fingers when he was nervous. They didn't know that the scar on his left knee was from when he fell off the swings when he was five. They didn't know him at all. They weren't his flesh and blood, like he was.

'Shit!' Kian snapped out of it. 'Dan, listen, it'll be okay, yeah? Adoptions take for ever – I'll have you with me before they've even drawn up a plan. Promise. I'll get us a nice place, look after you.'

'You can't cook! Remember, you burned those chips,' Dan said through hiccupping sobs.

Kian laughed. 'Cheeky sod. I can use a microwave! Don't cry, right? We've got this. I'll sort everything.'

Kian shouldn't have told him that. He was the last person in the world Danny could rely on, and he didn't even know if legally he had a chance in hell. He wasn't sure if Dan really remembered that he burned the chips or if it was simply a story Kian had told him that he'd held onto, in the absence of many other memories of their short time together. The other stories Kian had weren't really worth sharing. Like the times he wrapped up some of his free school dinner in a paper napkin and brought it home, so that he'd know Dan had eaten something that day. Or how he'd climb into Dan's cot to keep him warm when the electric had run out. Or making towers out of the empty beer cans and letting Dan knock them over noisily while their mum slept on the sofa, still in her clothes. He wished he could wipe his mind clean and forget it all.

After Dan's phone call, the day only got worse. Kian stopped off at the newsagent's and bought his weekly Lottery ticket. It was stupid, really. He had the worst luck out of anyone he knew. It was just that the one week he didn't bother would be the week he'd become a millionaire and see all his problems disappear. Of course when he checked later, his numbers hadn't come up.

Now he was in fear for his life, because Ryan was driving like a maniac on the way to some house-party he'd persuaded Kian to come along to.

'Seriously, mate, slow down!' Kian said, his foot plunging hard on an imaginary brake. 'Want me to drive?'

'As if,' Ryan replied. 'You don't have a licence, remember?'

'I've been driving since I was thirteen, mate. I'm better than you. How many times did it take you to pass your test? Er, four, wasn't it?' Ryan hated being reminded of that, and Kian grinned.

Ryan replied by flooring the accelerator. It wasn't even his car. He'd borrowed it from his older brother, Lee, who'd taken a loan out on the basis that in the TV advert for the car Claudia Schiffer took all her clothes off. Like there was even a remote possibility of Lee scoring with someone like that.

Kian didn't want to go to the party, not really. He just didn't want to be by himself in his bedsit worrying about Dan; and Gav was out with his girlfriend watching the new James Bond film at the pictures. And so he'd said, 'Nice one' when Ryan had asked him to come with him. He'd put on a clean T-shirt and splashed on his best aftershave, trying to convince himself he was up for a night of mayhem, when he knew the reality was that Ryan would be loud-mouthed and idiotic and would still end up snogging the face off some girl, while Kian hung around in a corner somewhere, slowly getting wasted until Ryan was ready to leave.

'This estate's massive. It's this left, I reckon,' Ryan said, swerving the car into a maze of maisonettes and high-rises. 'Yep, this is the right place.'

Kian sighed and opened the car door as soon as Ryan parked up. Already, from across the street, it was obvious which house the party was in. The group of lads with no tops on, dancing manically in the front garden, and the woman spewing into a hedge gave it away. Not to mention the music pulsing out onto the street and making the house vibrate. There was a guy out cold on the doorstep, covered in shaving foam, with piles of empty beer cans everywhere and one of the front windows was smashed in. Not Kian's problem. In fact, now that he was here, he welcomed the chaos.

Ryan handed him a bottle of bright-yellow liqueur. 'To get you started. Don't leave without me, yeah?'

Kian took a swig and coughed on the astringent citrus fumes.

'Twenty per cent alcohol, that. Go easy on it,' Ryan said, taking it back and screwing up his face after a big mouthful. He wiped his mouth on the back of his hand and strutted into the house, high-fiving a guy wearing neon face-paint.

Kian followed him in, but had already lost Ryan. It was absolutely rammed inside. Sockets and light fittings had been pulled from walls, holes had been burned in the hallway carpet, and couples with tangled limbs were sprawled over sofas and tables. There was a guy with a set of decks in the living room, pumping out tunes while people went crazy, waving their arms in the air. Among the crowd, he recognized a few people from school and headed towards Vishak, who used to be in his form.

'All right, Vishak, mate. What you doing here?'

'Kian, no way! I love you, mate! Haven't seen you since we left. How's it going?'

Vishak was clearly tanked. He leaned so close that Kian thought he might fall on top of him. He was shouting right in his ear.

'Yeah, good, mate,' Kian replied, taking a step backwards and patting him on the back in a way that implied the conversation was over. Vishak had other ideas.

'Ah, it's so good to see you! What college you at? You're doing A-levels, yeah? Which subjects?' Vishak slurred, his beer slopping over the edge of his can and creating dark patches on his jeans.

Because of course, with only a couple of GCSEs to his name, Kian would be doing A-levels right now.

'Got a job, mate,' Kian said. 'Accountancy firm. Making a fortune.' He rubbed the fingers of his right hand together to suggest bundles of bank notes.

Vishak's eyes bulged, and Kian was about to enjoy getting stuck into a more elaborate lie when he saw her: Millie Hatton, the woman of his dreams.

'Catch you later, Vish. I've seen someone I need to talk to.'

Millie with the caramel hair, who didn't know Kian existed, was wearing a denim skirt with black leggings underneath and a sleeveless white T-shirt. Simple, but effective. She looked incredible. Even at school she was like some sort of untouchable goddess. Kian slugged back half of Ryan's liqueur and tried not to heave. Twenty minutes later, with the bottle almost empty, he was pretty sure he was the coolest guy in the room. Cool enough to talk to Millie Hatton.

'So did you just come out of the oven?' Kian asked, after sidling alongside her and interrupting the conversation Millie was having with one of her mates.

She turned to look at him, rolling her eyes like he was her kid brother. 'What?'

She had perfect teeth. Her friend smirked at him. Kian realized then that he was like an ice cream van turning up in the dead of winter. Optimistic and completely unwanted. He wanted to slink away, but he'd have to see it through now. 'Er, I said, "Did you just come out of the oven?" Cos, you know, you're really hot.' He half closed his eyes, as if it would help him to disappear.

'Seriously?' Millie said. She cracked up laughing, flicked her hair and went back to her conversation.

Kian needed something else to drink. He grabbed a can of lager from the kitchen and went out into the back garden to find Ryan. Exactly as he'd expected, he was there with his arms wrapped around some girl. How did he do it? Kian was going to head back into the house when he spotted Ryan's hoodie hanging off the back of a plastic garden chair. With the aptitude of a seasoned pickpocket, he silently lifted the car keys out of the pocket and left.

17

A jar of Spanish summer

The day had got off to a bad start. Alfred had been repairing the huge scratch that now ran along the walnut bookcase that Kian had thrown in the skip. His own special remedy to breathe new life into wood surfaces involved 150 grams of beeswax, a few drops of lavender essential oil and a healthy dose of grapeseed oil. He stirred the mixture in a clean bowl and applied it liberally to the bookcase with a soft cloth, soothing it better and reviving himself in the process. There was nothing like a fresh coat of polish to make him feel like a new man. However, he hadn't realized he'd spilled some of the mixture on the floor and had slipped, catching his eyebrow on one of the cupboard handles as he fell. He'd had to hold a clean handkerchief to the resulting gash for several minutes to stop the bleeding.

To cheer himself up, he made a breakfast of toast spread thickly with the Seville orange marmalade that Ida had declared 'a jar of Spanish summer'. As he sat down to eat it, Kian's probation officer rang.

'Morning, Alfred, Chris Wilton here. Just touching base.'

Alfred had no idea what that meant, so he said nothing.

'I'm meeting Kian next week, so I wanted to reach out and

see how things are going over at yours? Is he behaving? Pulling his weight?'

Caught off-guard, Alfred didn't have time to concoct a lie. The truth, however, simply wouldn't do. He chewed on a mouthful of toast and considered the matter. The house was quiet without Kian stumbling around his boxes and complaining. If he thought about it, he had actually got what he wanted. The boy had given up. Alfred was free from the hideous arrangement that he'd wanted no part of in the first place. In which case, why could he no longer settle at anything? After Kian left, he'd started and abandoned a jigsaw of a lighthouse, unsuccessfully tried to read the newspaper and put Puccini on the record player, only to lift the needle after two tracks.

'Good, good, yes.' Alfred said. 'Out of interest, what happens if this arrangement doesn't work out?'

'I knew it. Kian causing trouble over there?'

'No, no. Not at all. We're getting on like a house on fire.' Admittedly it was more like an inferno. 'It's just . . . I'm trying to weigh up my options, that's all. See if there's some alternative form of punishment for the lad. I mean, it must be rather boring for him having to come round to my house every week and I really don't need—'

'This is his last chance. Kian needs to be bringing his A-game, and he knows it. Listen, you've got my number, so if he's not giving it one hundred and ten per cent, or he's messing you around, give me a buzz. I'll be round there in a flash to rattle his cage, whip him into shape. He'll soon remember what's what.' The sound of rustling paper travelled down the phone line. 'In fact, it's probably time I paid a visit anyway. I seem to be missing the supervision notes.'

Listening to Chris was like being bashed over the head by a

sound-effects machine. All that flashing and buzzing was enough to bring on a headache. Alfred wanted to get off the phone, fast, and he definitely did not want Chris turning up on his doorstep.

'Thank you, Chris. Yes, I'll certainly call you if necessary, although Kian is doing a sterling job. And there's no need to pay us a visit. A man in your position must be incredibly busy.' Alfred gritted his teeth.

'That's true. No rest for the wicked. I've got case files coming out of my ears. Well, if you're sure?'

'Absolutely!' Alfred replied, with more conviction than was strictly necessary.

'All right then. Sounds like Kian's meeting his obligations for now. Be sure to let me know if there are any problems.'

'There won't be. Things really couldn't be any better.'

Alfred's toast had gone cold and dreams of a Spanish summer had evaporated. He went back into the kitchen, wishing that all thoughts of Kian could be shaken away along with the crumbs from his plate. Would the lad end up in prison if he didn't complete the programme? Chris had said it was his last chance, but it really wasn't Alfred's problem. It wasn't his fault they were in this mess.

A rut of leaflets flopped onto his doormat and, as he picked them up, he saw that one of them was advertising a new luxury care home that had opened up around the corner. If he'd managed to eat his toast, he'd be throwing it back up again, right over the glossy photo of two elderly people laughing over a perfectly ordinary-looking cup of tea. Sandra was not going to get off his case, and it appeared that Chris wouldn't be leaving Kian alone, either. As painful as it was to accept, Alfred needed the boy, and the boy needed him. He knew what he had to do. He just hoped that Kian saw sense and came back.

18

The limit

There was nothing that could beat the open road. With the windows down, the wind rushing through his hair and the stereo blasting out some old school tunes, Kian was untouchable. He belted out the songs playing on the radio as if he was headlining in front of an adoring crowd at Wembley stadium. He was driving double the speed limit and it felt absolutely perfect. The alcohol swirling around his bloodstream gave him an edge, a superhuman ability to navigate the twists and turns of the dark lanes that wrapped around the Lickey Hills. He didn't care about anything any more: not Dan, not Chris Wilton, not Alfred, not even Millie Hatton. It was him against the universe, like it always had been.

There was no real plan. It just felt good to be alive and free. Kian reached the top of the hill, turned sharply into the car park and skidded across the gravel with smoking wheels. He got out and staggered in the direction of the toposcope, which he hadn't visited in years. It was built into a little fort and suddenly he wanted to climb right up it, to feel on top of the world. The sky was a starless deep purple, and the canopy of trees created an impenetrable black wall around him. He fell over more than once and was surprised to feel blood dripping from his left eyebrow.

Once he'd scrambled up the steps of the fort, he lay back on the toposcope. The sky was vast and heading towards him. For a minute or two it was like he was flying – the arctic wind flapping his jacket and howling in his ears. He stretched out his arms. The metal plate he lay on was so cold that his back turned numb. He could freeze to death out here and no one would really be bothered. Millie Hatton would probably laugh her head off. Sure, Gav and Ryan might raise a toast in recognition of his short life. Dan would be upset, but he'd soon realize he was better off without him. He'd have his new family.

Kian got down from the monument and wandered right up to the edge of the hill, ignoring the fact that the ground was swaying. The city lights twinkled beneath him – a reminder of all those families tucked up in their safe little houses. He'd never felt so alone.

His life was one big mess and he'd had it, reached the limit, couldn't do this any more. Going from one crisis to another was no longer fun. It was killing him. Despite the amount of booze he'd drunk, it was clear that he had two choices: sort his life out now or ruin his entire future. He had to show Dan that he was reliable, a proper big brother and not some locked-up scumbag. What the hell was he even doing up here on his own in a stolen car? Ryan was going to go nuts.

He made it back to the car, turned the volume down on the stereo and began to descend the winding roads. This time he wasn't channelling Michael Schumacher. Instead he was acutely aware of the blurring of the catseyes as he veered across the road and he slowed right down, gripping the steering wheel until his knuckles went white. Caught in his headlights, something rushed across the road in front of him – something that shouldn't be there. A deer?

'What the hell?' Kian shouted, thumping the horn and trying not to close his eyes. He braked as hard as he could, but the car was on a tight bend. He lost control and skidded off the road, flashes of trees and sky spinning around him as he bumped and jolted over stones and bracken. Finally the car rolled into a ditch, its front end wedged into a hedge while smoke whistled from the exhaust. His first thought – I'm still alive – was quickly replaced by his second: Ryan's going to kill me. His neck throbbed and his ribs burned where the seatbelt had restrained him. Frozen with shock, he tried to process what had happened. Then, in the wing mirror, he caught sight of a trail of blue lights in the distance and his survival instinct kicked in. Leaving the keys in the ignition, he undid his seatbelt and ran, not even daring to check the state of the car. If the police caught up with him, there was no doubt about it: he was going down.

19

All that glitters

'Good morning, young man. Just making sure you remembered we're meeting tomorrow, yes?' The unmistakably curt voice of Chris Wilton on the other end of the phone.

'Yeah, as if I'd forget,' Kian said. 'Highlight of my week.'

'Glad to hear it. You can give me a full progress update on Mr Ainswick's house, so I can write up my report. And it had better be good, Kian. Remember, you're on very thin ice.'

He'd already fallen through and drowned. The cut on his head throbbed, just in case he needed a reminder that on Saturday night, not only had he stolen Lee's car and driven it without a licence, but he'd also crashed it and left it in a ditch. He turned his phone over, as if hiding the screen would make the six missed calls from Ryan disappear. He'd come round here looking for Kian soon enough. Ryan wouldn't dob him into the police, they were mates, but he was pretty sure he'd demand that Kian pay for the damage to the car. Money Kian didn't have. But right now he had more important concerns, like his meeting with Chris. He had no choice but to get things sorted with Al before then. The old geezer was going to take some persuading, that was for sure. Kian would tell him that he'd made a mistake. That he really was going to work hard and obey everything in the contract. He'd apologize. He'd even stop smoking, if it helped.

The first thing he needed to do was get there on time, or Alfred would be in a mood before he even arrived. He opened the door to leave and stopped still. Dan was standing on the other side.

'What's wrong? Why aren't you at school? You're not meant to turn up like this,' Kian said. 'It has to be organized. Your social worker's gonna blame me. You want to get me in more trouble?'

Sometimes his mouth worked before his brain fired up. He shouldn't have said all that. Dan's bottom lip quivered and he looked to the floor. That's when Kian noticed the sports bag next to his feet.

'What's that?'

'I . . . I've come to live with you,' Dan replied, picking up his bag as if it was a done deal. 'You said I can, and you're nearly eighteen and I can stay at the same school and see you all the time. I won't have to move away. Be adopted.'

Kian rubbed the back of his neck and sighed. What he wanted to do was let Dan in, unpack his belongings and tell him he could stay. Nothing would make him happier. But he had to be a grown-up, prove to the authorities that he was doing this the right way.

'You know I want you to live with me, right?' Kian said, crouching down to Dan's eye-level. 'More than anything. But we can't do it like this. I need to get a job first, get us somewhere nice to live. They'll take one look at this place and say I can't look after you. It's a state. And there's only one bed, mate.'

'I'll sleep on the sofa,' Dan said. 'I hardly take up any room. And I'll be quiet.'

'I don't want you to be quiet, Dan. I want you to make all the noise you want. I want you to have a proper bedroom, with Villa wallpaper. I want to be earning a decent wage, to be able to cook for you properly – and not burnt chips!' He poked Dan in the ribs, trying for a laugh that didn't come.

'You don't want me?' Tears were brimming in the corner of his brother's eyes.

'I do want you, but it's got to be done properly! People are gonna be looking for you – the police, for a start, and I could do without them paying me a visit. How did you even get here? It's miles from Simone's.'

'I got the bus. I know the way. Simone thinks I'm at my friend Adam's house. It's half-term, remember?'

'You shouldn't have got the bus by yourself and you shouldn't have lied to Simone,' Kian said, well aware that his own moral compass wasn't exactly a shining example. 'I'm gonna call a taxi and drop you back home.'

'I don't have a home. Not a real one.' Dan was tearing a tissue with his fingers.

'I know. I'm sorry. I'm gonna sort it, okay?'

Kian opened his wallet. He didn't have any money for a taxi. If he rang Dan's social worker, he'd arrange for Dan to be collected, but Kian didn't have time for all that; and if he called Simone, she'd be worried and would ask him a hundred questions. He was meant to be at Al's by now. Dan would just have to come with him, and he'd take his brother home on the bus afterwards.

'Kian, you came back!' Alfred said, lifting his arms up as if he was about to hug him, before thankfully drawing them back down to his sides.

He seemed so pleased that Kian felt glad he hadn't gone straight in with the offer to give up smoking. Alfred placed his hand over a cut near his eye. It almost matched the one on Kian's face, and he shuddered at the thought that they were alike in some way.

'Come on in. I'll make us both some lunch,' Alfred said.

'Actually there's three of us. This is my little brother, Danny.'

Dan peeped out from behind Kian's back and waved his Luke Skywalker figure at him.

'Oh,' Alfred said. 'This is most . . . unorthodox. I suppose you'd better bring him in, too.' He disappeared into the kitchen.

Dan looked around with eyes the size of gobstoppers. He picked up a set of brass cymbals and, as he went to crash them together, Kian took them out of his hands.

'Just sit there and be quiet, yeah?'

Dan nodded and flicked a switch on the lamp next to him that looked very similar to one Kian had thrown out the other day. If he didn't need to stay ahead of Chris Wilton's sadistic streak, he'd walk out right now and get Dan home. Instead he had to see this through.

Alfred came in, carrying three plates.

'Bloody hell, Al, I thought you were making a sandwich?' In front of Kian was home-made shepherd's pie with gravy, peas – the lot. He looked at it suspiciously before hunger got the better of him and he dived in, the hot, buttery mash melting in his mouth.

'It's Alfred. And no swearing. It's only leftovers, I made it last night.'

'I don't care when you made it,' Kian said, now stuffing forkfuls of it into his mouth. 'It's bloody delicious!' He couldn't remember the last time he'd eaten anything that hadn't come out of a packet or takeaway carton. Alfred could actually cook!

'Swearing,' Alfred said. 'But thank you. Glad you like it. I can look after myself, you see. I've always been a good cook. And it's important to make time to eat properly.'

Just when Kian thought he'd got Alfred sussed, the old man whipped up a culinary meal to rival that Jamie Oliver bloke off the telly. Dan was wolfing his down, too, and Kian wondered how early he'd sneaked out that morning.

Alfred dusted off a pile of old comics and passed them to Dan, who smiled politely and put them aside. Then he coughed and said, 'Were you in the war?'

'Dan, that's rude!' Kian chided him.

'No, no, it's fine. I was, yes. The Second World War,' Alfred said. 'Warwickshire Regiment, Second Battalion,' he added. 'I don't really like to talk about it.'

'Oh,' Dan replied. 'I'm doing it at school. My teacher said we should interview our grandparents and see if they have any memories – but I don't have any.'

'I see,' Alfred said. 'Well then, would you like me to show you a photograph?'

Dan nodded and Alfred handed him an old black-and-white picture of eight soldiers in uniform. They were huddled together – some with their arms around each other, others with hands stuffed in their pockets.

'Where'd ya find this?' Kian asked.

'I didn't find it,' Alfred said, shaking his head, 'I'm in it. That's me, third from the left.'

Kian brought the photo closer, examined it and then looked back at Alfred again. No way was that the same guy. There was a resemblance, he couldn't deny that: the same angular chin and rounded nose. The guy in the photo looked smart, though. He smiled straight into the camera like he wasn't afraid of anything. He didn't look like someone who lived in a tip of their own making, who forgot to brush their hair and was running scared from a social worker called Sandra.

'All of us boys in the photograph, we were in the D-Day landings. The sixth of June 1944.'

'What?' Kian said. Alfred had just mentioned that he didn't want to talk about it.

Alfred frowned. 'Didn't they teach you anything at school?'

Kian was about to tell him that the only subject he'd liked at school was history when Dan piped up, asking him to tell them more. He got a little notebook out of his pocket and started writing in it with his best joined-up handwriting.

'Yes, well, I was about your age, Kian. I lied when I signed up, you see – said I was eighteen. So many of us did. We had no idea. Jim, he's in that photo, right next to me; his left arm was blown off as we stepped onto the beach. Blood everywhere.'

'Seriously?' Dan said, his mouth gaping open.

'You still in touch with any of them? Those guys in the picture,' Kian asked.

'No,' Alfred replied, blinking his eyes several times. 'No, not all of them made it; and those that did, well, we lost touch a long time ago. You know, if you're interested, I could show you my medals.'

'Yes, please!' Dan said, scooting to the edge of his chair.

Alfred lifted the lid of his bureau, took out a black box and handed it to Kian first. They were impressive: shiny silver and bronze stars resting on a sky of dark-blue satin, hanging from colourful ribbons. There were also two medallion-like coins, one embossed with a picture of a king, and the other with a lion holding the head of some weird creature. They were the sort of items that belonged in a museum.

'Take one out, if you like.' Alfred nodded.

Kian unpinned one of the medallions and let it rest in the palm of his hand. It was surprisingly heavy, like it carried the weight of war. The only medal Kian had ever won was on sports day, for the high jump. That was probably only because he was one of the tallest in his class. Even so, he'd been so pleased that he'd run home after school and hung it above his chest of drawers. He had no idea where it was now and, holding one of Alfred's medals, he realized it had been worthless anyway.

'Pretty cool,' Kian said, handing the medallion to Dan, who inspected it from every angle and asked Alfred lots of questions.

'Looking at these brings about so many mixed emotions,' Alfred confessed as he put the medal back in its box. 'Churchill said that a medal glitters, but it also casts a shadow, and he was right. These are my proudest moments and my darkest hours, rolled into one.'

Kian nodded. Memories could be complicated – a web of pain and pleasure that was sometimes hard to unpick. 'Yeah, I get it. Did you . . . in the war, did you kill people?' Kian asked, straight away realizing he'd stepped over an invisible line.

Alfred's eyes darkened. 'Sadly, yes. I don't think you ever recover from being surrounded by so much death and destruction. The other boys became my family, I suppose. With none of my own, it helped that I didn't really have anything to lose. I just feel so lucky that I made it, or I would never have met Ida. Before her, I had nothing.' Alfred's words dried up and a tear rolled down his cheek.

Kian wasn't sure where to look, so he stood up. 'We've gotta get going. Dan, we've got to get you home.'

'Oh, already?' Alfred said, wiping his eyes. 'I could make us some crumble?'

'It's Remembrance Day soon,' Dan said. 'Can we go with you to church?'

Alfred twisted his hands. 'I don't go to the service any more. My daughter Maggie used to take me, but we don't see eye-to-eye these days.'

'I can tell my teacher I'm going and get extra marks for my project. You can come too, Kian!'

Kian and Alfred stared at each other. This was a definite boundary that Kian didn't want to cross, and yet he never could say no to Dan, especially now, when he didn't know how long it would be until he moved miles away.

'Okay, if you like,' Kian agreed, wishing he could stuff his fist into his mouth.

'You will?' Alfred said. 'I don't know what to say.'

No, Kian hoped.

'That's so kind. Really. Thank you.' Alfred stood up and cleared the plates away. 'I am so glad you came back.'

Kian had never been called kind in his life. He looked around the room, noting the complete lack of progress that had been made.

'Do you like school, Danny?' Alfred asked as Dan zipped up his parka.

'Yeah. I might do the eleven-plus next September. Everyone else has got a tutor, though.'

'You're gonna pass,' Kian said. 'No doubt about it.'

'I commend you for your ambition, young man,' Alfred said. 'It's always good to have a goal. I used to be a maths teacher and I know things have changed a great deal since I retired, but I'm happy to help you out, if you like. A couple of coaching sessions? You'd have to bring your own books, of course.'

'Okay,' Dan replied, looking at Kian to check if it was.

'Dan might not be . . . he might be living somewhere else, so thanks for the offer, but it probably won't work out. Anyway, Al, you realize that after today I've only got seven weeks here to sort this mess out? Before you end up in a care home, and I end up in prison.'

'It's not enough, is it?' Alfred said.

'No, Al, it's not. How about I come round again tomorrow? Make up some of the time we've lost?'

He really was going soft.

20

Unsent letters

Alfred turned the photo upside-down as soon as Kian and Dan left. He had caught a glimpse of Jim's smiling face and his stomach flipped as if he was standing on the edge of a diving board. He and Jim had joined up together. They had shared water flasks, socks and secrets. Jim looked so young, so alive, that it was still hard to believe he didn't exist beyond the photo. He wasn't a man; just a boy with high cheekbones and a dash of floppy black hair. He was quite a bit taller than Alfred and had broader shoulders, too. Of the two of them, Jim was the one who looked like he'd make it out alive.

The secret that he had told no one engulfed him at this time of year. The guilt had never left Alfred. It was a part of him. He had lived, Jim had not. Alfred had a raft of medals for bravery, even though he was the biggest coward going. Jim knew it, and so did he. He took out the large envelope that sat in the locked drawer of his mahogany dresser. Inside were twenty-seven letters. All of them were addressed to Jim's widow. None of them had been sent.

Underneath the letters were a few remaining sheets of cream writing paper and matching envelopes. He picked up his pen and began to write:

Dear Emmeline,

Many years have passed since the war, but I've never forgotten. Jim talked about you all the time, how glad he was that he'd married you and what a wonderful, kind person you are. I came across his photo today. He was the best friend I ever had, and I miss him terribly still. I can only imagine your loss. I do hope you can find it in your heart to forgive me. The truth is—

The phone rang, interrupting Alfred's train of thought. He folded the sheet of paper over with a sharp crease and answered the phone.

'Hello there, Alfred, how are you? It's Sandra. I just wanted to check how everything is going with Kian? I thought it might be a good time to make another appointment for a visit.'

Alfred's toes curled inside his slippers as he considered his options. If he said, 'Wrong number' and put the phone down, she'd only ring back. His eyes darted across to the boxes in his living room. Sandra would have him inside that new care home on Cartland Street in a flash, if she came here again before it was sorted. He couldn't let that happen. He needed to get rid of her.

'How kind of you to call. I have to say that Kian is doing a marvellous job. The place is looking so much better already.' He closed his eyes. 'You really don't need to visit – it's all under control.'

'That's brilliant. I know there are a few weeks to go yet, so I'm pleased things have got off to such a good start. Now when's a good time for me to call round?'

Sandra breathed loudly down the phone as she waited for Alfred to say something. He was backed into a corner. It was beginning to look like he wouldn't get away with it, that he actually would have to part with most of his collections.

'Sandra, I think I'm a bit busy over the coming weeks. The badminton has taken off again, you see, with the tournament season and all. But as I said, it's going exceedingly well here.'

'It's great you're doing so well and I'm looking forward to seeing it for myself, so I'll come and visit you on Friday the nineteenth of November . . . let's see, around one?'

A strange mewl escaped from Alfred's mouth, which Sandra mistook for agreement.

'Lovely. See you then,' she said.

Alfred held the receiver in his hand long after the call had ended, the dialling pips ringing out like an emergency siren. After pacing the room for several minutes, he returned to his letter to Emmeline, wrote the address and put it inside the envelope with all the others. How was it possible to be so haunted by the past and the present at the same time?

21

Roller skates

Kian had concocted an elaborate lie about needing to collect an electric heater he'd bought from an ad in the *Bargain Pages* so that Gav would lend him his van. He needn't have bothered. Gav simply threw the keys at him, no questions asked, and even said Kian could keep it for as long as he wanted. He had a works van now, so his only clogged up the driveway. There was no way Kian could explain why he was going back to do more donkey-work at Al's when it wasn't even his designated day. His mates wouldn't understand. He wasn't even sure he did.

'Morning. Come on in,' Alfred said, springing the door open before Kian had even rung the bell. 'No Danny today? He's a lovely young man, I must say.'

'Unlike me?' Kian queried, unable to resist poking the fire.

Alfred didn't reply.

A quick look around confirmed that more items hadn't arrived in the twenty-four hours since he'd last been there. That was something.

'Instead of waiting until the skip's full, it'll be easier if we load up my mate's van and take it all down the tip ourselves,' Kian said. He didn't add that this way, he'd be certain that whatever he got rid of wouldn't find its way back into the house.

'The tip? Do you have a driving licence?' Alfred asked, picking up a red vase and cradling it.

'Yeah, yeah, course.' It just wasn't his licence. Gav's was inside the glove box next to an *A–Z* and half a packet of chewing gum.

Alfred put the vase to one side, clutched his stomach and sat down in his armchair. 'I don't think it's a good idea. What if I change my mind?' He was backing out. When it came to throwing things out, he didn't see straight.

'I totally get this is hard,' Kian replied, even though he didn't understand it at all. 'But focus on keeping Sandra out of your hair, yeah? You want to stay here, in your home? Then you've gotta get rid of this stuff, or she'll think you're a headcase that can't be trusted to live by yourself. We'll look through it together. Sort one pile for keeps and one for throwing away. Deal?'

Alfred was quiet for a very long time. He buttoned up his cardigan. He stood up, wandered over to the window and appeared to read one of the newspaper articles covering the glass, letting out a little laugh. Then he paced back across the room, straightened a picture leaning on the floor and sat down again. 'I don't know,' he said, sighing heavily.

'I'll go then, yeah?' Kian retorted. 'Let Chris and Sandra know it's all over?' He tried to blot out the image of him sharing a cell with a tattooed skinhead convicted of GBH. It was too real a possibility. If his life was bad now, it would be a total non-starter with a few years of prison behind him.

'I know you're right,' Alfred said. 'It's just I don't think you know how hard this is. These aren't only things, you see. They're important. They mean something, in here,' he went on, placing his hand over his chest. 'But . . . I suppose I have to.'

'Finally,' Kian said.

They might actually get somewhere now. Kian picked up a shoebox, the lid held on with an elastic band. Inside was a collection of musty pages, torn from books. 'You do know you can buy whole books? You don't need to collect individual pages.'

'Look at them,' Alfred suggested. 'Each one has an inscription from someone. A message of love. How could I not save them?'

Kian read the first one: *To my dearest Eliza, the poetry on these pages is nearly as beautiful as you.* The next one: *Happy 10th birthday, Arthur! We hope you enjoy reading this and can't wait to see you again soon. How is the rabbit? Love from Aunty Joyce xxx* Seriously, why was Al keeping this crap?

The guy was hard to figure out, that was for sure. Kian put the shoebox down and kicked it underneath the sofa, having an inkling that Al wouldn't want to let go of this one. At least it didn't take up much room. Next he lifted out a pair of roller skates with bright-yellow laces. Junk. He shoved it in the throw pile, before Al could form an argument about wanting to take up senior skating. A moth-eaten tapestry that practically vibrated with dust – this was getting easier, for him at least. Alfred remained seated, rolling and unrolling a newspaper. Kian carried on, undeterred. A door handle, some sort of lamp with a wick running through a green glass tube, a theatre programme from 1966 and a load of ancient copies of *Radio Times*. No one needed to know what used to be on TV. All in the chucking-out box.

'I think that's enough now,' Alfred said, standing up suddenly.

It was hardly worth going to the tip with this lot. 'There's tons of stuff still here,' Kian replied. 'Sandra's coming to check up on you soon, remember?'

'I know!' Alfred snapped. 'Sorry. I just don't see why I have to do this. What's wrong with the way I live? I'm not hurting anybody.'

'Sit back down, Al, take a breather. This house, it's not healthy. If you want people to mind their own business and leave you alone, you've got to persuade them you're – you know – normal.'

'I am normal! That doesn't mean I have to be exactly like everyone else,' Alfred said.

He didn't seem to get that this was about faking it. Kian had spent years trying to fit in, pretending to everyone that he was all right on his own, didn't care about being tossed aside by his mum, wasn't bothered about failing his exams and being skint. It was merely a way to get through life. Alfred had a lot to learn.

'You know what it's like to grow up in care, be discarded and left to fend for yourself,' Alfred continued. 'Ida was the only person that ever cared for me, and now she's gone. Maggie doesn't want to have anything to do with me. There's nothing left. Only my things. Why can't people leave me be?'

Kian did know how it felt to have no one on your side, to have a family that cut you out, but he really didn't understand why Al wanted to hold on to all these possessions. In fact, he didn't really know very much about Alfred at all.

'What was it like? When you were in care?'

Alfred didn't answer. He was looking into the distance as if Kian wasn't there. The only way Kian was going to get him to cooperate was if he did more pretending. He needed Al to think he was on his side.

'I just don't want to see you go into a home. Help me get the room cleared up. Come on, you can do this. You were in the D-Day thing, remember? When we get back, you can tell me some more about the war. Have some hot chocolate?'

'Yes, yes, I suppose you're right. The trick to a good hot chocolate is making it on the stove, not in the microwave. You need to whisk the milk, you see.'

'Whatever you say. What are these?'

Kian tipped a brown envelope onto the table and a bunch of smaller sealed and addressed envelopes fell out.

'Oh,' Alfred said, looking at them fleetingly. 'Only some letters. Nothing important.'

People didn't write letters that weren't important. They were all addressed to someone called Emmeline McGuire.

'Who is she?'

'Ah, well, it's complicated. Perhaps you should sit down and I'll tell you.'

Kian looked at the nearest clock, then back at Alfred, who was fiddling with his shirt buttons. There really wasn't time. However, Alfred clearly needed to get something off his chest and they wouldn't get any further until he had. When Alfred didn't speak straight away, Kian tapped a finger on his wrist.

'Okay,' Alfred said, taking a deep breath. 'Where to begin. Remember the photograph – the one with my best friend Jim in it? Emmeline, well, she was his wife. I suppose you need to have a bit of background.'

Kian slouched down in his seat and yawned. Alfred didn't take the hint.

'So,' Alfred continued. 'We signed up to fight together, Jim and I. He made a joke as we stood next to each other in the queue, and we bonded straight away. It turned out he only lived a few streets away and we'd never met! Can you believe it? Anyway, we were part of the D-Day landings.'

'Yeah, you said,' Kian replied, wondering exactly how long this story was going to take.

'What I didn't tell you was that I was absolutely terrified as we crossed the Channel to northern France. I'd never been on a ship before, and the sea was unbelievably rough. I spent the journey throwing up, as did so many of the others that we had to use our helmets to bail out the vomit from the bottom of the ship. Some hero, eh? Jim was fine, though, excited even, convinced we were heading off on a big adventure. He was always much braver than me. It was one of the things I liked about him. His confidence made me feel less scared than I was. But we knew what was at stake, so we made a promise to each other. No matter what, we wouldn't leave each other's side.'

Kian was more interested now, unable to imagine heading off to war and what it would be like to have a best friend who promised to stick by you, no matter what. Ryan would leave him like a shot.

'We'd been waiting for a clear spell in the weather,' Alfred went on. 'When it finally came, we were buzzing with adrenaline. We were ready. Or we thought we were. Only when we arrived on Sword Beach, the noise, well, it was deafening, you see. You couldn't think straight. Machine guns, snipers, explosions, screaming, commands being shouted left, right and centre. It was so disorientating.'

'Shit,' Kian said, pulling himself upright. Alfred was in so deep that he didn't even comment on his swearing.

'Anyway, I'm not even sure why I'm telling you this. I've . . . well, I've got a secret. No one in the world knows it, apart from me. Not even Ida.'

Kian gulped, unsure whether he wanted to hear what Alfred was about to reveal. 'I can keep shtum.' It was true. He never grassed anyone up. He had values.

'I told you that Jim's arm blew off as soon as we landed. The truth, well . . . the truth is that it did happen, only it was as soon as we entered the water. The waves were pulling him under. He screamed and screamed. The water turned into a crimson pool around him. He called out to me, pleaded with me to save him as he stretched out his remaining arm towards me. I froze when I saw the blood, the tangle of flesh and cartilage. I panicked. I was sinking. I couldn't breathe. Jim's eyes, they looked right through me. The pain in them still torments me to this day. I swallowed huge mouthfuls of freezing, salty water and, to stop myself from drowning, I swam. I swam for my life towards the shore and left Jim behind. I . . . left him behind.'

Kian held his breath. He was right there with Alfred, experiencing his fear and pain and guilt.

Alfred lowered his voice. 'I keep writing to Emmeline to say sorry – not that it would ever make up for what I did. I wanted her to know that the medals I won for bravery are undeserved. I keep them in honour of Jim, to remind me of what he sacrificed and how grateful I should be. He was the brave one. I broke my promise and I'm so ashamed.'

'I don't know what to say,' Kian said. This was way beyond the usual stuff he talked about with his mates, like girls and football. Nothing in his life compared to what Alfred had just told him, but for a minute he tried to put himself in Alfred's place. 'You didn't do anything wrong. Anyone would have done the same; it was, like, a survival instinct. Post these letters to his wife. You need to let all this go.'

'I don't know,' Alfred replied. 'I'm not sure if it's a good idea to dig up the past. I don't deserve Emmeline's forgiveness anyhow.'

By the time Kian had convinced Alfred to bundle up his letters and post them, it was late afternoon. They boxed up the remaining items in silence and loaded them into the van. Alfred wasn't the only one consumed by regret. His melancholy had spread to Kian, who was dwelling on his own mistakes and the fact that he had made so many, he'd lost count.

The queue for the tip was huge. Kian crunched on the boiled sweets Al had brought with him and turned the heater up, as lime-flavoured shards zinged on his tongue.

'Should've got here earlier,' Kian said. He hated waiting.

Alfred had hunched himself inside his coat, collar up. He was staring out of the window and drumming his fingers loudly on the dashboard. Kian might have had a new-found sympathy for Alfred, but it was now stretched to its limit. Finally a bay became available, and he reversed the van into the space. He whistled at the sight of all the objects in front of him as he opened the doors. It somehow looked worse all squashed together than it had spread out in Alfred's living room.

He worked as quickly as he could, knowing that at any moment, Alfred could change his mind. One of the boxes near the back was especially heavy, and he had to drag it across the floor and up to the platform next to the giant skip. He was working out how to lift it over the edge when he heard shouting. A man in a fluorescent jacket was running towards him, and Kian instinctively looked towards the van. Alfred was no longer inside it.

'Oi, get him out!' The man had reached the bottom of the steps and was red in the face. 'You can't get inside the skip!'

'What you on about?' Kian asked, while the man hurled abuse at him. He looked down and saw that somehow Alfred had climbed right inside. Under one arm he carried a tatty rug; roller skates were hanging by their laces around his neck; and his other arm was dragging a wooden giraffe. His pockets were bulging and, if Kian wasn't mistaken, his trousers were stuffed with something other than nature had intended.

'Al, what the hell are you doing? Put that lot back!'

'No! I won't! It's all mine. I don't want to throw them away. You can't make me.'

There was nothing else for it. Kian jumped off the platform and landed in the rubble beneath, while the fluorescent-jacket man's face contorted like he'd swallowed a whole plate of Vindaloo in one go.

'Al, remember what we said? Sandra, remember? You can do this. Put the stuff down. It's time to go now. Just put it down. You don't need any of it.'

Alfred crumpled a little. Then he closed his eyes, slowly dropped the rug, untangled himself from the roller skates and eventually let the giraffe sink back into the bottom of the skip. Kian took his hand, papery and cold, and guided him back towards the van.

'You can't keep doing this,' Kian said, his patience shattered. 'I can't keep doing this. It's seriously nuts. You're screwing with my life here! I get that you probably couldn't care less, but you're practically reserving me a prison cell.'

Alfred looked across at him and nodded. 'Sorry.'

Kian had churned that word out his whole life: sorry for nicking stuff, for breaking things, for being late for appointments, for being rude to teachers – so he knew better than anyone that it meant nothing.

22

They shall not grow old

Despite the biting cold, Alfred left his coat open, making sure his uniform was on display. It gave him some protection, like a coat of armour, even though his shirt was so thin he worried his heart might burst through it. He pulled his beret further over his ears and felt for the wooden cross in his pocket, where he'd written the name *Jim McGuire* with a black marker. Kian was still behind him, dressed in a black suit that drowned him. Dan was wearing a black coat. His paper poppy was drooping, but his hair was neatly combed. It was touching that they'd made an effort. Alfred couldn't remember the last time people had willingly spent time with him and it made his heart beat even faster.

He looked straight ahead at the wreaths resting on the steps at the front of the cathedral and paused. St Philip's Cathedral was in the middle of a square right in the centre of town. It had been bombed in the Second World War and the west half of the roof had to be reconstructed. It had survived, though, like he had – the devastation so carefully hidden that a passer-by would never know what damage had been caused. He craned his neck to look up at the clock tower. It was almost time. All around him, people carried on with their everyday activities. A group of students sat on a bench eating sandwiches, pigeons flocking at their feet. Shoppers hurried between the leaning gravestones, running for buses or clutching takeaway coffees. They had no idea that for him, in less than twenty minutes, the whole world would stop.

As he stepped into the nave, Alfred was held hostage under the light of a huge stained-glass window depicting Judgement Day. A kaleidoscope of reds turned his white shirt into the colour of wine. Feeling Kian at his side, he walked slowly down the aisle, taking a seat in an icy pew to his left. He shivered as he picked up the order of service and read the opening page: *They shall not grow old.*

It had been years since he'd done this and he expected everyone to look around, to tut at his presence. The previous time, he'd had to leave the service as the trumpet began its sombre rendition of 'The Last Post'. He'd dashed towards the exit struggling for breath, feeling a hundred pairs of eyes watching what felt like his final moments.

Last night, as he was laying out his suit on the back of the chair in his bedroom, he'd had second thoughts. And third and fourth thoughts. No one would notice if he wasn't there. He could pay his respects quietly at home like he usually did, then spend the day finding ways to distract himself. Kian was only going because Dan wanted to.

Then he'd thought about Jim. He owed it to him to remember him properly. It was the least he could do.

'You okay?' Kian asked. 'Want a mint?'

The incense drifting from the altar was plunging Alfred into a hypnotic daze. He had to focus on something before he was dragged down, pulled into a memory he did not want to revisit. His eyes were shutters that could only process the smallest of details: the black gloves, the glinting medals and the spots of ruby poppies that coloured the pews like drops of blood. He coughed, to ground himself in the present. Across from him, he swore for a moment he saw Jim, running his remaining hand through soaking wet hair and smiling at him. Alfred's throat was closing. He took the packet Kian offered him and, as menthol filled his mouth, he was plunged into ice-cold water. He was up to his waist in the dark sea, sinking into shushing shingle as bodies floated around him, flailing his arms. His uniform was heavy and itchy, the salt made his dry lips sting. Alfred put his head to his knees as the congregation stood for the opening psalm. A hand touched his arm and he looked round, blinking.

'You're okay, Al. Just breathe. I've got you.'

Kian held him steady, repeating the same phrase over and over. 'You're okay, Al. You're okay.'

He gripped the edges of his sleeves, hardly able to believe they were completely dry, and by the time they reached the two-minute silence Alfred was pretty sure he could make it through the remainder of the service without breaking down. He avoided eye-contact with anyone else as he exited the church and, once outside, laid his cross with the wreaths. No one had called him out. No one had asked him what right he had to be there. He was simply another person remembering those who had been lost. The other veterans carried their own painful memories, exactly as he did.

'You all right?' Kian asked, gesturing to him to stand away from the crowds.

'I'm sorry about in there. It's just, I don't know, a lot of different feelings. Thank you, for getting me through it,' Alfred said. There was so much he wanted to say, but couldn't.

'You did brilliantly,' Kian said, somewhat generously, considering.

'Yeah,' agreed Dan. 'I'm with a real war hero. My teacher's going to be amazed.'

The cathedral in front of them seemed less threatening now, a place of quiet reflection rather than a mortuary of memories. The poppy Alfred wore each November had become a symbol of guilt, a paper weight that reminded him of all his flaws, weaknesses and mistakes. However, as he rearranged the fragile petals, he realized that something else had joined it. A hint of acceptance. Being with Kian reminded him of being with Jim, made Alfred remember that they were only boys, making split-second decisions in fear of their lives in the most awful of circumstances. They had been too young to be in a uniform and to witness the unspeakable horrors of war.

He'd never forget, and he was sure he could never forgive himself. He was the lucky one, though. He was still very much alive, and he had to make the most of it.

'I tell you what,' Alfred said. 'Why don't we all go back to mine for some lunch?' He really didn't feel like being alone for the rest of the afternoon.

23

Cooking up a storm

Alfred had set up a chessboard, but after discovering Kian had no interest in it whatsoever, he was teaching Dan how to play. He'd obviously forgotten about lunch. It was almost three and Kian was starving, so he offered to fetch them something from the kitchen. He stared at the contents of Alfred's kitchen cupboards. He had got enough food to see him through the next year. Not only that, but the tins were all categorized according to the contents, with all the labels facing the front like a regiment. How was it that someone who lived in such a mess had such an orderly kitchen?

He couldn't find any bread, so he grabbed a tin of beans and found some eggs in the fridge. His experience of cooking was limited and at first he thought he was going to be beaten by the tin opener, which seemed to require arms of steel to operate it. How did an old guy like Alfred manage it? Then he emptied the beans into the pan, cracked the eggs onto them and whacked up the heat. The resulting gloopy mess didn't look promising.

Kian switched the kettle on and tried to find the teabags. In one of the cupboards there were about thirty jars with silver lids, containing different herbs and spices. He hadn't heard of half of them and had no idea what to use them for. He took out the one labelled 'ground coriander' and sniffed it. It reminded him of his favourite chicken Balti.

'What's that smell?' Alfred called.

Kian was about to comment on Alfred's super-sensitive nostrils when he realized that smoke was spiralling from the direction of the cooker. He turned off the gas and tried to empty the charred, congealed mess onto a plate with a spoon, but the blackened remains were cemented to the bottom of the pan. Seconds later a loud screeching noise filled his ears as the smoke alarm did its job.

Alfred burst into the kitchen, opened the back door to let the smoke out and put the pan straight in the sink. It made a loud hissing noise as he filled it with water.

'Don't you know how to cook?' he asked.

'Nope,' Kian admitted. 'Just stuff out the freezer that you chuck in the oven. Mostly I get a takeaway or eat cereal or toast. Less hassle.'

'That's the trouble with your generation,' Alfred muttered. 'Always taking the easy option. You need to be able to cook. It's a basic skill. It's healthier and will save you a great deal of money. Pass me that box of eggs.'

Kian expected Alfred to take over. Instead he positioned Kian in front of a glass jug and instructed him what to do, his voice softer now.

'Crack the shells like this, see? That's it. Straight into the jug. Perfect.'

Kian scooped out some fragments of shell before getting a fork to beat the mixture. Next he melted some butter in a fresh pan and poured in the eggs, which spread out like a splodge of yellow paint. Alfred told him to tip the pan from side to side until it reached the edges.

'Nicely done,' Alfred said, while Kian prodded it with a spatula, like he was some fancy chef.

He added some grated cheese and reluctantly, at Alfred's suggestion, a sprinkling of parsley. He was usually wary of anything green, but had to admit it smelled kind of nice. He ate it right in front of the stove and it was hot and fluffy and oozing with melted cheese. It was the tastiest thing Kian had eaten since Alfred had made him and Dan shepherd's pie.

'Thanks,' he said, scraping the last flecks of omelette from his plate.

'Well, young man, you made it. You can make the next one for Dan without my help.'

Alfred obviously didn't know him well enough. It wasn't a good idea. Kian took the eggs anyway and tried to remember the steps Alfred had shown him.

'You know,' Alfred went on, watching him swirl the eggs into the pan, 'I think you're a natural. Have you thought about catering college?'

The thought of him strutting around in one of those big chef hats made Kian laugh out loud. His mates would think he'd lost it, although he'd helped Lucy make a lemon cake once and she'd said he had a flair or something. At the time he'd thought she was just being nice, like always, but what if she'd actually meant it? He pictured himself in the kitchen of a little restaurant, creating masterpieces that people queued round the block for. It would be pretty cool to actually have a profession, to be able to say 'chef' when people asked him what he did, instead of mumbling something about being between jobs. He almost told Alfred that it was a brilliant idea, before getting a grip. The chances of it happening were about as likely as him winning the Lottery, and that hadn't worked out for him so far.

'If you like,' Alfred said, 'I can show you how to cook another dish next time you come round?'

'Maybe.' Kian knew Alfred would do anything to avoid clearing out his house. He didn't goad him, though. The geezer wasn't some joke any more. He'd seen another side to Alfred, dressed in his uniform, with his medals proudly on display. The way he struggled to breathe in the church was exactly how Kian got sometimes. He was a person, with real feelings.

Instead of rushing off afterwards as he'd planned, Kian hung around while Alfred told them how he used to sneak through the turnstiles at Villa Park when he was a boy to watch the matches, then afterwards collected all the empty beer bottles to sell to the local pub. Kian teased him about having a criminal past, and Dan asked if Alfred wanted to go to a match with him, before telling him all about his favourite players and reeling off league stats. Kian mouthed 'sorry' as Dan chatted on and on, but Alfred shook his head and laughed, as if he was enjoying every minute of it. This might be what it would be like if they had a grandad. Sunday afternoons filled with jokes and stories and warmth.

'Oh, Kian, I almost forgot; I have something for you.' Alfred presented him with a small box. 'I noticed you don't have a watch and I have . . . well, too many to count.'

Kian stared at the stunning silver watch nestled in green satin.

'It's an Audemars Piguet,' Alfred said. 'You don't see these very often. Beautiful craftsmanship and it still has all its original parts. It's to say thank you for coming today and for helping me with all this. And I'd love to help Dan with some coaching, so do bring him around again, won't you?'

Kian was without words. He couldn't remember the last time

anyone had given him anything, apart from a pint. Even though he could tell the watch was probably worth a fair bit, he knew instantly he'd never part with it. It meant something. He didn't care about its value and finally understood a little bit more of the puzzle that was Alfred.

'You know,' said Alfred, 'I think you'll get into college and go on to become a chef. Pop the watch on, that's it. Every time you look at it, I want you to remember that the past is behind you and the future is yours for the taking.'

Kian rubbed at his eyes, worried the tears forming there might fall. 'Thanks,' was all he managed to say.

It was late when they left and, as Kian turned back to say goodbye, Alfred was sorting through some old football programmes to give Dan next time he visited. Kian watched him for a few moments and, as he did so, a light that had been extinguished within him a long time ago flickered again, faintly. Perhaps there really was more to Alfred than met the eye.

24

A bad hand

Kian hadn't exactly been in any rush to see Ryan since the incident with the car. When they'd finally spoken on the phone, Ryan had gone ballistic. Apparently his brother went for him, even though miraculously there were only scratches on the bodywork, a cracked bumper, a small dent in the passenger door and a smashed headlight, which his insurance would cover. Lee had told the police that the car had been stolen, so it wasn't even as if he was in any trouble. Even so, Ryan made it very clear that Kian owed him, big time.

However, the real reason he hadn't seen Ryan or Gav lately was that he'd been busy. Over the past couple of weeks he had spent a few extra days helping at Alfred's. He'd also sneaked Dan in for a couple of coaching sessions without Simone's knowledge. There was no way she'd have agreed to it without a whole heap of questions and official checks, and Kian could do without that sort of headache, so he'd picked Dan up as usual and told her they were going bowling. It took some effort to convince Dan that lying with a good reason didn't really count, but at least now he was getting the extra help he needed and the chance he deserved. Who could argue with that?

It was strange, but the more time Kian spent with Alfred, the more distant he felt from his old life and his friends. When he wasn't with Alfred, he had meetings with Chris or appointments at the Job Centre. His days sort of filled up and by the evening he felt too knackered to do anything but sit and worry about the situation with Dan.

His mates had moaned at him a few times for being AWOL and had now taken action. They'd turned up uninvited at Kian's flat, with sculpted hair, humming with aftershave and wearing slick, ironed shirts. Gav was carrying a four-pack of beer and Ryan had brought a giant bag of crisps. Kian really didn't feel like company.

'You avoiding us?' Gav asked, as he walked in and stuck the beers in the fridge.

'Course not, just been busy.'

'Yeah, looks like it,' Ryan said, pointing at the console, jumping over the back of the sofa and landing on the cushions. 'You're coming out with us tonight, no excuses. It's gonna be a blinder.'

'Yeah,' Gav agreed. 'You can't bail on us tonight – Ryan needs his wingman back.'

'Shut up,' Ryan said. 'Kian's the one who needs a wingman. When was the last time you pulled? Also, you owe me money. My brother had to fork out eighty pounds excess on the car insurance and he's hounding me for it.'

Things only ever got worse. Where was he supposed to get that from? 'Yeah,' Kian replied. 'Sure. I'll sort it.'

He joined Ryan on the sofa while Gav pulled up a chair and dealt out a pack of cards. Ryan's legs were sprawled out, so that Kian was squashed into the corner. Kian helped himself to a handful of crisps and explained that he'd have a few beers with them, but he couldn't go out tonight, as he had to be up early in the morning to help Alfred.

'You what?' Gav spluttered, nearly choking on his crisps.

'Alfred's freaking out, cos his social worker's coming round,' Kian said. 'He needs me to straighten the place out a bit more before then.' He should have found some other excuse, one that was a lie. Too late now.

'You're losing it, man,' Ryan laughed. 'Hanging out with an old guy has turned you into one. So if he's like a war vet, has he got medals then?'

'Yeah, a few. He showed me them one time.' Kian left out how impressed by them he'd been, and there was no way he was telling them about going to church for the Remembrance service.

'Worth a bit, I bet,' Ryan said. 'Anyway, me and Gav have come up with the best idea. We're gonna spend next summer in Ibiza and you're coming with us!'

Kian let himself get swept up for a moment in the idea of hanging out with his mates for a summer of Balearic beats, booze and birds. Only a few months ago, it would have been living the dream: T-shirts and shorts, nursing hangovers by a pool and swimming in the sea, maybe hiring one of those mopeds. Kian had never been abroad and the idea of it – the thought of actually jumping on a plane and leaving everything behind – had always been intoxicating. Only now it didn't hold the same appeal. His priority had to be Dan. If he played his cards right, they'd be living together by next summer. Maybe the two of them could go on holiday, somewhere by the sea. Kian could hire a caravan and they could try surfing. He'd buy Dan as many ice creams as he wanted. They'd be a proper family.

'Nah, I don't fancy it,' Kian replied, keeping his cards close to his chest. 'It's gonna cost loads, right?'

'That's the good part,' Gav said. 'My sister's working at a travel agent in town. She can book out this awesome villa for us for dirt-cheap, with her staff discount. We just need to get her one hundred quid each by the end of December, and then we pay the rest next year.'

'No can do. I'm skint. Sorry, lads.'

'You're joking, right?' Gav said.

When Kian said nothing, Ryan slanted his eyes in his direction. 'You're seriously not going to come with us? To Ibiza?'

'Like I said, I can't afford it. I don't finish at Al's place 'til just before Christmas, and if by some miracle it gets signed off, I need to get my head down, find a job.'

'Some mate you are,' Ryan said. 'Stick this CD on. Your music's crap.'

Kian took the CD from him and shoved it into the stereo, letting a wave of drum and bass wash over him. There was no point arguing with him.

'Speaking of jobs,' Ryan said. 'I'm starting a new one in January. My dad's mate's got this plumbing business and said he'd take me on. Five years from now, I reckon I could take over as manager.'

'Nice one, mate,' Kian replied, forcing a smile. He tried to imagine his life five years from now. Would Dan be living with him, or would he still be stuck in this bedsit, waiting for Ryan and Gav to finish work, so he had someone to hang out with? Kian looked at his cards and laid them on the table. He'd been dealt a bad hand again.

25

A slippery slope

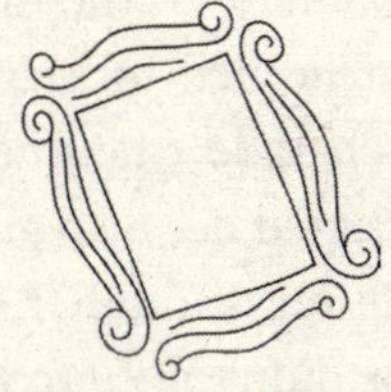

The trouble with telling lies was that at some point you started to believe them yourself. The first ones came swiftly after Ida's death. Their friends – well, her friends really – rallied round and brought home-cooked dinners and peace lilies to accompany their sympathy. Alfred was not okay. Far from it, and yet he found himself telling them that he was doing fine. He had done such a convincing job that Doris, who had sung in a choir with Ida, actually sat in Ida's favourite armchair and sobbed for fifteen minutes, right in front of him. He had to fetch her a tissue and comfort her as if she was the one who had lost her spouse.

Talking to people who thought they had a share in his grief was exhausting. His heartache was all-encompassing, bitter and hard, but it belonged to him. No one had noticed that Ida's death had changed him structurally somehow. He may have looked the same, but he was a different person now; one with rattling bones and a hollow chest, and an untamed rawness that left no room for anyone else.

Sympathy was of no use to him. He wanted Ida here, alive and well, to hear her telling him what the weather was going to do that day, to listen to the clacking of her knitting needles, to visit the Birmingham Museum and Art Gallery and discuss the merits of the Pre-Raphaelites. Instead he had to make do with the remnants of her existence: a ball of wool and some knitting needles on the bedside table – a jumper that would never have sleeves; a magazine with curled pages; her paintings on the wall; and her jewellery on the dressing table.

It followed then that he lied to Maggie, too, although she could see through his charade when he told her that he was perfectly fine. Maggie carried her own grief, and he didn't want to add to it with his. He reassured her that his collecting was keeping him busy, so she didn't need to worry. She did, though. She said he was pale, so she brought round vitamins and fruit and insisted that her father go for a walk every day, saying the fresh air would do him good.

Alfred tried, but each time he did, he was paralysed by a sensation that he was going to sink right beneath the paving stones. His knees stiffened and his breathing got so shallow that he thought his lungs might give up completely. The walks became shorter, until he barely made it to the end of his garden path without having to return home and double-bolt the front door. He stopped answering the door to anyone, preferring not to bother with appearances or small talk just to make other people feel better. He reassured himself that he was fine, that this was the way he lived now. The greatest lie of all was to himself. Deep down, he knew that everyone was right: he wasn't doing well at all.

And those lies kept on coming. He'd told himself so many times that his collecting was under control – it was everyone else who had a problem. It was best all round to shut out the ignorant world, but now he wondered if they'd had a point. His run-in with the truth wasn't limited to facing up to his guilt over Jim's death. He'd also realized it wasn't true that he didn't need people. The time he'd spent recently with Kian and Dan proved otherwise. Despite the emotions of Remembrance Day, he'd gone to bed feeling thirty years younger. Coaching Dan and seeing him grow in confidence had brought him real pleasure. Alfred wished he could hold on to that happy feeling, instead of being weighed down with the dread that accompanied Sandra's visits.

Changing into a suit had been a bad idea. Sandra would arrive in a little under three hours and Alfred could already feel huge moons of sweat under his armpits. To say he was still unprepared for her visit was putting it mildly. The impending deadline had failed to accelerate his progress. If anything, the pressure had had the opposite effect and he'd sat drowning his sorrows, watching the hours tick past at twice their usual speed.

He'd made a fresh batch of ginger biscuits first thing, which had been exceedingly difficult, on account of the two tables and model railway that he'd hidden in the kitchen, out of Sandra's view. Even with them out of the way, he could see that the living room might be considered akin to an earthquake zone. He managed to get his sideboard halfway across the floor, but couldn't push it any further and now it was an island in the middle of the room. In the past few days he'd developed a hacking cough and was getting breathless more easily. He had to battle on. Don't admit defeat.

It didn't seem possible that he had achieved so little by the time someone knocked on the door. Typical of Sandra to arrive early, in the hope of catching him out. Alfred plodded towards the hallway and opened the door on its latch.

'Kian? I thought you were Sandra.'

'Want me to go?' Kian swung round to face the street.

'No. Don't go. I'm glad you're here. I could do with your help.'

Alfred gave him a list of instructions, pointing to the new

temporary home for each item that needed relocating. The living room looked marginally clearer once half of the furniture was in the garden, creating an obstacle course that the squirrels were already making good use of. He had checked his barometer several times that morning and it was insistent that a storm would arrive, even though the sun was heating up the pale winter sky like an electric blanket.

'Now,' Alfred said. 'You will bring everything back inside the moment Sandra leaves, won't you?'

'I should have brought Gav's van again and taken it all to the bloody tip. I can get it now? We've still got a bit of time.'

'Swearing!' Alfred said, wiping his brow.

He did not want to visit the tip for a very long time, if ever again. Although he'd managed to keep hold of some of the smaller items, which he'd stuffed in his pockets, the giraffe that he'd left behind played on his mind. Was it upset that it had been abandoned, as if Alfred didn't care about it? It had looked so at home in his living room next to the umbrella stand, and it would have no idea what it had done to deserve being thrown away like that. Alfred knew it was merely an object – he wasn't insane. He also knew how it felt to be dumped and to believe you were to blame. It wasn't his mother's fault she could no longer take care of him, once his father upped and left, and so Alfred had concluded that it must be his. Closing his eyes, he pictured the giraffe drowning in rubbish and then, worse, being crushed into sawdust. He couldn't let that happen to anything else.

'Very kind of you to offer,' Alfred said. 'Only, I think it really does need a proper sort-out first. I'll make it my absolute priority over the next few days. Don't want to throw away any family heirlooms by mistake.' He then ate one of the ginger biscuits, just to make sure they were acceptable.

Kian looked at his new watch and then gestured towards the armchair. 'You look a bit peaky. Sit down for a bit, yeah? But make sure Sandra thinks it's all under control. She's reporting back to Chris, so, you know, don't screw this up.'

Alfred had no idea what Kian could possibly mean. As long as Sandra didn't look in the kitchen, didn't open the hallway cupboard, didn't ask to use the bathroom and didn't look out of the window to the back garden, everything would be fine.

The central heating groaned from its first use in months. Alfred was boiling, but he didn't want Sandra thinking he couldn't afford the heating bills. She wouldn't understand that he'd rather wear extra layers and spend money on his collections, instead of lining the pockets of a swindling fat-cat energy firm. Not to mention that he hadn't let anyone in to service the boiler in years, so it was best to switch it on only when absolutely necessary. He opened the back door and let the cold air steady him. Already it didn't look like home any more. He couldn't see his velvet footstool and his Russian dolls, the hurricane lamp and the mustard pot. He actually missed the wind-up penguin that was prone to starting up all by itself and scaring the life out of him. The pictures and mirrors that usually hung on the walls were stuffed behind the sofa, and now there were brass hooks and an assortment of slightly faded squares and rectangles where they used to be. The marbles he liked to run his fingers through each day were dispersed into three different vases, and his favourite books had been posted beneath the bureau. The record player was balanced perilously on top of the fridge, and he had to remember to shut the door with the gentlest of nudges so as not to send it tumbling to the floor. He scratched at a scar on his thumb and ate another biscuit to distract himself from the fact that he was on the verge of throwing Kian out, locking the front door and putting everything back where it belonged.

He didn't have time to give it any further thought. The doorbell rang.

'Sandra,' Alfred whispered, jumping up from his chair. 'Just follow my lead.' He looked down at the Willow-patterned plate of biscuits. Only two remained. How had that happened? He couldn't present a plate with only two biscuits. He shoved them behind a cushion and rushed to the door, flattening down his hair and realizing too late that his hand was covered in biscuit crumbs.

'Sandra, how lovely to see you,' he said.

'Good morning. Well, I can see there's some improvement in here already,' she replied, taking off her coat this time.

Only *some*? Was Sandra being serious? It looked like a completely different house.

'Kian, nice to see you again. How have you two been getting along? It's cold out there today, isn't it?'

Sandra laid her coat out on the chair before sitting on it. She had a habit of disguising her questions in between fragments of small talk, but Alfred had her all worked out.

'He's been marvellous,' Alfred said. 'As you can see.'

'Yeah,' Kian agreed. 'We've made some progress and, you know, we're getting on well, too.'

Even if Kian was saying it to keep Sandra happy, it made Alfred smile.

'It certainly looks that way,' Sandra said. 'I knew this would be good for both of you.'

Alfred added 'know-it-all' to his imaginary list of Sandra's extensive flaws. 'Would you like a cup of tea?' he enquired, before coughing loudly in the direction of the hallway. He was still standing up, not quite willing to join the summit that was taking place in his own living room.

Sandra started to nod, then changed her mind. 'No. No, thank you. Let's just get through some paperwork and then I can be out of your hair.'

That suited Alfred fine. He would happily complete an entire forest of paperwork if it meant Sandra would leave him alone.

'That cough sounds nasty, Alfred. How long have you had it?'

He knew her game. 'Oh, do you know, I had a little smoke earlier. First time in years and it clearly doesn't agree with me. Shan't be doing that again. I'm fine, I can assure you.' His voice was raspy from the effort of suppressing another cough.

'I see,' Sandra replied, writing words that Alfred couldn't see in her pad. 'So how have the first few weeks gone? I mean, you've both said you're getting on well, but what have you learned from the experience, now that you're over halfway. Alfred? Be honest.'

Alfred looked across at Kian. 'I've learned that I did need a little help after all.' If Kian hadn't turned up this morning, there was no way he could have got through this ordeal.

Sandra smiled as if she'd swallowed a sunbeam. She wasn't satisfied for long, though. She asked Kian if he would make some tea and, while he was ensconced in the kitchen, followed up with more questions about how Alfred was coping, again coming back to washing and dressing and cooking. It was verging on impertinence. He was obviously dressed, in a suit no less. He was clean, bar the biscuit crumbs and sweat patches. He thought about getting the remaining ginger biscuits out from behind the cushion to show her that he could cook, but realized in time that the sort of person who concealed food behind soft furnishings might be considered unhinged.

'Okay, let me check what else is on my list. Ah yes, I think we should look at whether you're meeting your financial commitments, Alfred. We can give you some budgeting advice – see what you might be entitled to. That sort of thing.'

The absolute gall of the woman. His meticulous records ensured he never overspent. He was frugal in every aspect of his life and prided himself on never getting into debt. The very idea of benefits was not only absurd, but insulting.

'I've got my records right next to me. I keep tabs on everything, so I really don't need any help. Have a look for yourself.'

Alfred took out his record book to show her. Only now that he looked more closely at the recent pages, something didn't quite add up. It appeared he had become a little lackadaisical in his record-keeping. There were objects he definitely remembered buying that weren't written down. He glanced into his folder and saw a pile of bank statements that had remained unopened, and some red reminder bills he'd forgotten about. There was no doubt about it: he was in a bit of a mess. He would get it sorted, though. He didn't need Sandra's advice, that was for sure.

Thankfully Kian arrived with the tea, just in time. 'He's a wicked cook. Makes an awesome shepherd's pie.'

'Wonderful,' Sandra said, scribbling away.

One point to Alfred. 'I'm teaching Kian to cook as well, aren't I, Kian?'

'Oh, that is so lovely!' Sandra gushed.

Kian squirmed in his seat. Another ten minutes of questioning ensued, until finally Sandra closed her folder. Thankfully she appeared to have forgotten about his finances. Alfred let his head fall back against the headrest of his armchair. He'd won. A smile slowly spread across his face, and he stretched out his legs so far that one of his slippers dropped off his foot and landed on the carpet. It couldn't have gone any better. He was almost tempted to ask Sandra if she'd like to ask him anything else, before remembering his barometer's prediction of a storm. It had never been wrong, so he wanted his things back inside, where they belonged, as soon as possible.

'So,' Alfred said, dusting down his trousers, 'I suppose we won't be seeing you again then.' He was already picturing his living room back exactly as he liked it. Maybe he could find a replacement giraffe. No, a whole herd of them.

'This was an interim visit,' Sandra said. 'To check everything is going okay so far. I did mention that to you in my phone call. I'll be coming back to carry out a needs assessment in January. And of course we'll have the review meeting at around the same time, with Kian and his probation officer. I'll write to you to let you know exactly when it will be. Nothing to worry about, though. I can see you're right on-track and I'm sure a few more weeks will make all the difference. Do let us know when you're ready for the skip to be taken away. It looks like it's filling up! Lovely to see you both. I'll see myself out.'

Kian put everything back where it belonged, as he had promised he would, though it had been a battle to stop him chucking it all straight in the skip. Luckily, it had been getting steadily filled by other people dumping their rubbish in it.

'I meant it,' Alfred said as Kian put his jacket on, ready to leave. 'When you come back next week I'll give you a cooking lesson.'

'Al, we've got more important stuff to do. Like getting rid of all this stuff. You do realize that, right?'

'Yes, yes, there's plenty of time yet. We'll do a bit of cooking first and then we'll have a good clear-out. No arguments.'

26
Diving watch

Kian arrived at the probation service to meet up with Chris with no idea whether he was going to tell him the truth about what was going on at Alfred's house. He'd barely made a dent in the mess and was convinced the old geezer was still buying more stuff. It was like an addiction. Kian was nowhere near qualified to help him, only it looked like he was all Alfred had. One lost cause helping another.

Chris Wilton was the sort of person who'd enjoy telling someone they only had weeks to live. He was born to be an offender manager. Kian would bet money on him having ironed socks and a wardrobe divided by the colour of his clothes. Chris loved reciting all the rules, trying to trip Kian up and prove that he was hopeless.

'You're two minutes late,' Chris said, tapping his watch as Kian sat down opposite him. 'Like this, do you? Diving watch, top-of-the-range. I can go to depths of three hundred metres with this.'

Kian stopped himself from asking what the point was, when you'd be dead at that depth. He also suspected that the only diving Chris had ever done, if any, was at the local swimming pool. He twisted the watch Alfred had given him. It was probably worth loads more than Chris's dodgy counterfeit.

'You're not the only person on my caseload,' Chris said. 'You keep me waiting, you keep everyone waiting. You know this is part of my role, don't you, Kian? To challenge you to stick to rules and keep time, and to transform you into a young man that society can be proud of?'

In any other circumstances, Kian would tell Chris to do one. In this instance, he simply had to suck it up. They both knew the man literally had Kian's life in his hands.

'So before we go over this week's goals, let's have a review of how things are going so far at Mr Ainswick's house. His social worker tells me you've made good progress. Is that right?'

Kian couldn't do it. He couldn't tell Chris about the collections that were completely out of hand, and about Alfred's total unwillingness to throw anything away. He didn't want to see the old guy go into a home, and he didn't want to give Chris the satisfaction of thinking he'd failed. And, more than any of that, he didn't want to go to prison. He had yet to come up with a plan to fix all this. For now, he'd just have to fob him off.

'Yeah, it's going good. I've got rid of loads of stuff. Al's even teaching me how to cook.' Chris didn't need to know that all he'd done was crack some eggs, and that most of the stuff he'd got rid of seemed to find its way back into the house.

Chris cracked his knuckles. 'Well, that's a turn-up for the books, isn't it? Shows this restorative-justice thing works. So you're on-track to have completed your service effectively before Christmas?'

'No problem,' Kian said, wishing he could take the words back as soon as they'd left his mouth. There was no way that was possible. It would take a miracle.

The rest of the session was even more depressing than usual.

Kian had to circle his strengths and weaknesses from a long list and then write down what he wanted to achieve between now and his next meeting. In his head, starting with the most achievable, he thought: beat Ryan at *Grand Theft Auto*; get Alfred's house cleared out; win the Lottery; save Dan from being adopted. On his paper he wrote: *manage my temper more effectively, using the techniques Chris has discussed with me; eat healthily; look at possible apprenticeship schemes.*

Chris grinned as he read the list, truly believing his work here was done. Smug git!

Kian swung the doors to enter the outside world and zipped up his coat, fending off the downpour that greeted him. Water was flooding from the gutters and pooling into huge puddles on the pavement. There was no choice but to walk, as he couldn't afford the bus fare. Cars sped past, spraying him with bucketloads of icy water that soaked through his jeans. The street lights blurred as he tried to blink away the rain from his eyes. No one in the world felt as miserable as he did right now.

Just when he thought it couldn't get any worse, the storm upped its game, adding a vicious wind to the mix and doubling the weight of the rain. Kian ducked into the lit doorway of the nearest building. Behind him, an automatic door opened and he spun round. It was the library. Kian was transfixed by the warm glow of lights, rows of books and circles of armchairs. It looked like the sort of place he could sit by himself for a bit to keep warm, without needing to spend any money. Only until the rain stopped. Had he even been inside a library before? He didn't remember anyone ever taking him. He shook the rain from his coat and stepped inside.

If he seemed to know what he was doing, it was less likely he'd be asked to leave, so Kian walked purposefully to the corner of the large room and avoided eye-contact with anyone he passed. A little sign hanging from the ceiling told him he'd arrived in the reference section. He sat down in a jaded brown chair and noticed that the shelves were labelled alphabetically. He was sitting right next to the one marked with the letter A. Despite the fact that he was dripping water onto the carpet, he had an idea that might keep him in there longer than he'd first thought.

The antiques guide he took from the shelf was a heavy bound book with a gold spine. He turned the pages, examining the photos and descriptions and mentally cross-referencing them with the objects he'd seen at Al's place. The trip to the tip had been a disaster. Maybe if Al could see that he could get some money in return, he'd have some motivation for getting rid of some of his possessions.

'Want some help?' A girl a little older than Kian with wavy red hair had crossed the floor from the counter, without him noticing. His time was up; he'd be booted out. She was wearing a black shirt, and a purple beaded necklace poked out from underneath. He looked at the badge on her jumper and read her name: Chloe.

Kian looked over her shoulders, half expecting a security guard to be standing right behind her, but there wasn't anyone else. His words took some time coming out and, when they did, he wished he could swallow them back down.

'What, me? Er, no. I mean, yeah. This book. Can I borrow it? What do I do?'

'No library ticket?' Chloe asked. 'Fill in a form at the counter over there. If you've got some ID, you can take them home with you today.'

'For free?'

'Yes,' Chloe laughed. 'For free. So you like antiques then?'

'Not really. I'm just helping someone who does.' He sounded like a total freak.

'That's nice of you. My nan loves *Antiques Roadshow*. She wells up when someone brings along some ugly painting from their loft and it ends up being worth thousands.'

'Yeah,' Kian replied, wishing he'd at least seen one episode so that he had something to say. He followed her to the counter and completed the form, taking extra care over his usually illegible handwriting.

'Anything else?' Chloe asked, when Kian hadn't moved.

'Er, what? No. No, thanks.' How hard was it to ask someone out? He practised the words in his head until they sounded more and more ridiculous, and then he pictured Millie Hatton laughing at him as she flicked her hair. He couldn't do it. Instead something else entirely came out of his mouth. 'Do you have, like, records of people? I mean, if I wanted to find someone, could I do it here, at the library?' Where had this train of thought come from? True, he thought about his mum more at this time of year, but he'd never before come close to looking for her.

'Depends,' Chloe said. 'You'd need a few details to get started, like their full name, which town they live in.'

'Yeah, I know some of that stuff. I mean, she's somewhere in the West Midlands, as far as I know. Her last name's Fernsby, unless she got married. I got my dad's surname.' He had no idea why he told her that. He wished he knew when to shut up. 'First name's Cathy. My mum, I mean – not mine.' This was going from bad to worse. If he could kick himself, he would.

'Okay, come over to the computer. See if we can find what you're looking for.'

It seemed pretty obvious, now that Chloe had spelt it out for him. He'd thought he would have to trawl through official registers or something. Get copies of birth certificates. All these years Kian had hundreds of questions for his mum, and now he could simply look up her number on a computer. But what if they didn't find her? He pulled at the cuffs of his sleeves as Chloe sat down in front of the monitor. Kian had the feeling he used to get at the start of a football match. Boots tightly laced, waiting for the whistle to blow, all he'd be able to think about was trying not to be sick all over the pitch.

'I've changed my mind. I'll just go and see if there's anything else I need.'

Chloe shrugged.

Kian hid behind a bookshelf and closed his eyes. He waited for a few minutes, trying to work out what his next move was. The door was near enough to make a run for it, and he was about to when he realized that the book he'd borrowed was still on the counter. He'd have to face Chloe again. He strode over as if he wasn't dying inside and pointed at the book, not trusting his mouth to say anything else. She handed it over and gave him a smile that made her eyes sparkle and made Kian trip over the rug as he headed to the exit.

He tucked the book under his arm as he walked right into a swirling snowstorm that had replaced the rain. The dirty pavements looked as though they'd been sprinkled with icing sugar – a clean slate, something ugly becoming beautiful. If it continued to fall like this, very soon his footsteps would be covered, as if he had never walked this way at all.

27

Cared for

Alfred woke up, panting and drenched with sweat. The dreams had started a few days ago – for the first time in months. He put off sleep for as long as he could, terrified of being back with Jim. Eventually his eyes would close and he'd be dragged into the warfare, unable to change the pattern of dreams that repeated over and over again.

He boiled the kettle, needing coffee. The lack of sleep had left him brittle. In the week since Sandra's visit, most mornings he'd gone shopping. He couldn't help it. The objects he bought made him feel better, held him together like a tourniquet. And somehow one day of shopping had turned into five. Each day he'd place his new items out on the floor, repair them as necessary and add them to his inventory. It was all so predictable and calming. When he'd finished, he was sure that was enough – he had satisfied the urge. But by the next day the pain from his dreams blended with the harsh reality of his current situation, which was enough to practically push him out of the front door and he'd find himself at the shops or the market again. He'd even bought things from the classified section of the newspaper: a rocking horse, a fire guard, a box of mixed cassette tapes even though he no longer had a tape player and a panel of stained glass. As his house filled with more items, his mood lifted, like he was a balloon being filled with helium. Only the effect was always temporary.

He'd hidden as much as he could in the loft and had no idea where he was going to put anything else before Kian became suspicious. Alfred's genius idea to teach him how to cook would hopefully keep the lad occupied for now and buy him some time.

When Kian arrived, he handed Alfred a roll of bin liners, as if he would forget their agreement about the cooking lesson. Alfred took them from him, pulled a book from the shelf above the microwave and dusted off the cover. It was the cooking encyclopaedia he'd learned to cook from himself. The pages were tatty, and the most well-loved recipes were splattered with the sauces and batters of family meals that were now all a distant memory. 'This will teach you everything you need to know,' he said, passing the book to Kian.

Kian turned the pages slowly, shaking his head. 'It's like a foreign language. Who's Julienne? What's a rux?'

'A roux,' Alfred said. 'It's a mixture of flour and fat. It thickens sauces.'

'Forget it.' Kian slammed the book closed. 'It's like being back at school.'

Alfred had started in the wrong place. Kian was overwhelmed by the terminology before they'd even begun. He'd have to rely on intuition instead of facts. Go back to basics. He put the book away and handed Kian a notebook and pen.

'Let's start again. Okay, write down the name of a meal you remember really enjoying. Got one?'

Kian nodded.

'Good. Now underneath that, I want you to write down how it made you feel when you ate it.'

'Full?' Kian said.

Alfred tutted. He turned his back to make another coffee and clanged his teaspoon loudly against the side of his mug, wondering if it was best just to give up. He'd been a teacher; passing on his skills and knowledge should be easy. His patience had clearly diminished since retiring. He would have to try harder.

He drank his scorching coffee and took a deep breath, before taking the notepad from Kian. He'd written: *bacon-and-tomato pasta*. Underneath were the words: *cared for*. Alfred smiled. That was the power of food. It could be a way to communicate, when words let you down. There was no argument with Ida that couldn't be put right with a batch of fruity scones straight from the oven and a pot of home-made strawberry jam. Food and love were intertwined.

'So,' Alfred said, turning on his teacher's voice that he hadn't used in years, 'we're going to try to recreate this. The meal, and the way it made you feel. It won't be exactly the same, because this time it's going to have a bit of you in it.'

Kian rolled his eyes, yet to be convinced. Alfred made him wash his hands and told him to help himself to what he needed. Kian paused in front of the open cupboards before grabbing a bag of penne. He held it out towards Alfred to check whether he'd chosen correctly.

'You don't really need me,' Alfred said, lifting up both of his hands. 'If it feels right, it is.'

Kian stared into the cupboard for a full five minutes. Alfred leaned against the counter and resisted the urge to do it for him. Kian opened some spice jars and smelled them, sneezing after inhaling too much ginger. This was how you learned. He eventually chose a pot of smoked paprika and two tins of tomatoes, trusting his intuition, as Alfred had hoped. He took a packet of thick-rind smoked bacon out of the fridge, paused, closed the door and then opened it again.

'I reckon onion and garlic? I mean, I think so. And then . . . yeah, Lucy would put loads of grated cheese on top, so we need that, too. Oil. Black pepper?'

'Perfect,' Alfred said. 'And you can taste it as you go along, see what you think.'

He showed Kian the correct way to chop the onion, lengthwise, with the root end furthest from the knife. Kian hunched over the chopping board and clenched his fingers around the knife as if it would fly off. His arms were rigid at the elbows.

'Let's put some music on,' Alfred suggested. 'You have to relax into it or this tension will make the food taste bad. When you cook, you need to let go of everything.'

He turned the radio dial away from Radio 4, through varying degrees of hiss, until he landed on some music. It wasn't to his taste – a dissonance of psychedelic sounds against a tinny drumbeat – and the only thing stopping him turning it off was the obvious effect on Kian's mood.

'Love this one,' Kian said, loosening his surgeon's grip on the knife. 'Chemical Brothers. You know it?'

'No,' Alfred admitted. 'It's catchy, though.' He hadn't really meant it and yet, by the chorus, he was bobbing his head along to the beat.

Kian glided from one task to another, sometimes singing along into a wooden spoon as if it were a microphone. He became animated as he chopped and stirred. He tasted and asked questions. As the bacon crisped up in the pan and the tomato sauce bubbled, it was as if all his apprehension had been replaced with joy, something Alfred had never seen even a spark of in Kian previously. Alfred tapped his feet as he drained the pasta, unsure if it was the music or Kian's happiness that was infectious.

When the food was ready, they sat down opposite each other at the table. Alfred waited for Kian to take the first mouthful.

'Is it nice? How does it make you feel?' Alfred asked, expecting Kian to open up. Instead he just nodded. 'Okay,' Alfred went on. 'Close your eyes as you eat each mouthful and really think about it.'

'I feel . . .' Kian opened his eyes again, 'like an idiot. This is stupid. It's only food.'

'Well, I'll start then,' Alfred said. 'For starters, this tastes delicious. I'll certainly be making it again for myself! Beyond that, I feel . . . friendship.' He opened his eyes to check that Kian wasn't laughing at him. It was a relief to see that he wasn't, so he continued. 'The smokiness of the bacon, the sweetness of the paprika – they balance each other out. Work well together. I can feel the effort and care you took to cook this, and that makes me feel, I don't know, appreciated.'

'You got all that from a plate of pasta?'

Alfred put his fork down and undid the top two buttons of his shirt. It was uncomfortably hot all of a sudden.

'Okay, okay,' Kian continued. He took another mouthful, then closed his eyes. 'I'll try. I feel . . . satisfaction? I didn't think something I made would taste this nice. It reminds me of feeling safe with Lucy, my foster carer for a few years. She'd cook this for me; well, a version of this. It sort of makes me think about being young, when I didn't have so much crap to worry about. It's like – comfort?'

'All that from a plate of pasta?' Alfred raised his eyebrows.

Kian grinned. 'Yeah, okay, you were right. I've never given

this sort of stuff much thought before. Have you got memories of food from when you were in care?'

Alfred pushed his plate away, even though he hadn't finished eating. The memories of that time were locked away in a box and he'd never opened the lid.

'I don't really remember the food, no.'

'What was it like?' Kian asked. 'The children's home? I still remember the wallpaper of every foster home I ever stayed in.'

There was something about spending time with Kian – who never tried to hide his flaws or present himself as perfect – that made Alfred more willing to share a part of himself.

'Well, it was all so long ago. I do remember the first night I arrived, though, vividly.' Alfred shivered. 'I was seven and felt completely alone; abandoned, I suppose. I clutched my only possessions as if my life depended on them: a small teddy bear and a die-cast model car, a Morris Eight Series E saloon, if you're interested. Red. While the house-mother was busy upstairs, a group of older boys snatched them from me. They threw them in the fire in the kitchen. I couldn't cry because then I'd be a target, you see, so I pretended I didn't care, when what I really wanted to do was jump in the fire after them. Everything I'd ever had was taken away from me at such a young age. A lesson in life, I suppose.'

Alfred didn't share that that night he had stayed under the tangerine-coloured beam of a torch, beneath his scratchy blanket, for as long as he could keep his eyes open. He committed every detail and stroke of paint of the car to memory. He imagined its wheels against the palm of his hand, and pictured the marks on the bonnet where the red paint had been scratched – a souvenir of its daring races. If he held onto it in his mind, it was as if he hadn't really lost it.

'Maybe it's why you collect?' Kian said. 'A way of getting your own back on those kids who took your stuff. Now you can have whatever you want?'

Alfred resented being put under a microscope. He didn't need a reason to collect. He was a collector; it was who he was, and that was that.

'Well, you did a great job today. Your cooking skills are coming along nicely. Now you can work on perfecting your washing up,' Alfred replied, handing Kian a tea towel. There was a reason why lids shouldn't be opened.

'The washing-up can wait,' Kian said, discarding the towel and picking up his bag. 'I brought this book round for you. This page here – it's like yours, isn't it? The clock on the stairs. I thought it was gold, only it says here it's "gilded bronze". *A stunning French mystery clock, circa 1900, with a Louis XVI-style setting*. Al, it's worth a couple of grand!'

'As I've said to you before, young man, it's the beauty of the objects that fascinate me. I don't care about their monetary value.'

'Yeah, but if we sell them, then we clear the house and you make a nice little profit out of it. You can even buy some more stuff, once we're all done and Sandra's left you in peace.'

Alfred was aware of his heart beating inside his ears. He could no more part with his belongings than he could willingly lose a limb. And it was true: he didn't care about their value. It was just a piece of arbitrary information, no more important than their date of production or a hallmark. At the same time he couldn't deny the faint but very real tremor of relief that he felt at the chance to put all this behind him. A life free of Sandra, where he was left to do as he pleased, was too good a chance to pass up, even if it meant selling his beloved mystery clock.

'Exactly how many things do you think I'd need to sell?' Alfred asked, already mentally ticking off the objects in his collection that he absolutely, most definitely wouldn't part with . . . There were too many to count.

'The way I see it,' Kian said, 'is we pick the big-ticket items. It's two birds with one stone, yeah? You make some space in here, so it looks more . . . normal, so it's all sorted in time for Sandra's inspection.'

There was no way in the world that Alfred could go through with this. He couldn't let go of his belongings. Even his own daughter had given up trying to persuade him. Although he hadn't been living with the threat of losing his home until now. He looked at Kian's expectant face and then across at the calendar, which would shortly be turned over to December. He really had reached a dead end. However, his life wasn't the only one in a mess. Kian needed some guidance, too. A little bit of care.

'Okay. I'll do it,' Alfred replied uncertainly. 'But on one condition: you apply for catering college.'

'Are you, like, blackmailing me?' Kian asked, scratching his head.

'Of course not. I'm just ensuring that you stay on the straight and narrow and have something to aim for. If I've got to make changes, then so have you. And I have every confidence that you would make a marvellous chef.'

'Yeah, right. You've only seen me whisk up a few eggs and make some pasta. You might have noticed, Al, I'm not big on achieving.'

'Call it intuition. I can spot talent a mile off.' Alfred wanted Kian to have a focus, so that he kept out of trouble. 'Forget about the past. All the mistakes you've made, the bad things that have happened, they're behind you. Everyone's capable of change.'

Kian looked at the floor, reminding Alfred that behind the facade he was simply a boy who was lost and vulnerable. Alfred had to do this for both of them. He helped Kian wash up and drew up a list of all the possible items to sell, cross-referencing them with the antiques guide. As each item was added, Alfred felt like he was losing a layer of skin. They began packing his possessions in sheets of newspaper, while he counted slowly to ten and kept telling himself there was no other way, even though he was hot and nauseous and just one silver teaspoon away from screaming the house down.

'These worth anything?' Kian handed him a box of glass teardrop baubles.

'Only to me.' Alfred removed the crinkled tissue paper tucked around the gold-and-purple decorations and lifted one out. He held it up to the light. Although it had a tiny crack in it, it still gleamed beautifully as it spun from its nylon thread.

'If you're gonna keep them, put them on a tree this year,' Kian said. 'No point them being in a box.'

'I haven't bothered with Christmas decorations since Ida died. It's a shame, really; these are so pretty.' Their Christmas tree used to take pride of place in the front window, covered in lights and baubles and home-made decorations that Maggie brought home from school. He hadn't realized how much he missed it.

'You can still make the place look nice – for you,' Kian suggested.

Alfred looked again at the baubles. He couldn't bring himself to bury them back beneath the tissue paper, where no one could see them shine. They still had some life left in them. It wasn't worth going to any effort when it was only him at home, though. 'I don't suppose . . . No, it's silly.'

'What?' Kian looked up from the pages of the antiques book.

'It's just that I'll be roasting a turkey on Christmas Day. I always do, you see, and there'll be too much for one, and so . . . I wondered if you might like to join me? If you're not busy, of course.'

Kian hesitated before replying. 'Hmm, I dunno. I was kinda looking forward to my microwave dinner in front of the telly.'

'Oh.' Alfred put the box of baubles down and pressed the lid on firmly. Obviously Kian didn't want to come over on Christmas Day. He probably couldn't wait to see the back of him, once all this was over. Alfred had got caught up in some misguided notion that they were friends, forgetting that Kian was being forced to spend time with him to avoid prison. He turned away and shook out a sheet of newspaper.

'Er, I was joking,' Kian said. 'I'm not gonna turn down a proper roast dinner, am I? I'll only be sat at home, waiting for the pub to open, anyway. There's gotta be pigs in blankets though, yeah? They're the best bit.'

Alfred nodded, although now he wanted to retract the invitation entirely. He didn't want Kian to say yes because he felt sorry for him. However, his embarrassment was slightly outweighed by the anticipation of having someone to cook Christmas dinner for. It had been a long time since anyone had marvelled at his home-made stuffing with fresh cranberries and sage. Also there was a box of Christmas crackers in the kitchen cupboard, which were useless because no one was there to pull them with him. It was settled then.

An hour into the packing, Alfred began to feel a little better and the nausea faded. The trick, he discovered, was to pretend that he had merely been the custodian of his objects for a limited period. He was simply sending them off into the world to be fully appreciated, as if the love and care he'd shown them had helped them to realize their potential and meet their true destiny. Although he would miss them, he would be able to look through his inventory and recall them. It reminded him of the pride and sadness he'd felt when Maggie went off to university.

He closed his eyes and tried to picture a new life – one where his house was tidy and organized, and where Maggie came round for tea. The image was rather blurred, but it was there, like a photograph that had not fully developed. It was a possibility.

28

The perfect apple pie

'So,' Alfred said, flattening the page of the maths book, 'last question, Dan, and then we're done. You've come on leaps and bounds. George baked one hundred and eighty apple pies. If one tray holds twelve pies, how many trays does he need to hold all the pies?'

'Why did he bake that many pies?' Dan said. 'He'd be sick.'

'Yeah, bit greedy,' Kian agreed, puffing out his cheeks to make Dan laugh.

'I love apple pie – I could eat two hundred! Anyway, I know how to do this one.' Dan scribbled down the answer and held it up for Alfred to see.

'That's right! Perfect. You're going to fly in this exam, young man. I'm very impressed.'

Dan stood up, beaming, and flung his arms around Alfred, who momentarily recoiled in surprise. He couldn't remember the last time anyone had hugged him.

'Thanks for helping me,' Dan said. 'You're the best ever.'

Alfred was sure he'd grown two feet taller as he squeezed Dan back. 'You're the best ever, too.'

Kian rolled up his sleeves. 'Yeah, cheers, Al. You've been

brilliant helping Dan like this. Time for lunch, I reckon. What we making today then?'

'I thought we could make a risotto and, for afters, how about apple pie?'

'Just the one, though, yeah?' Kian said, holding a finger up towards Dan and laughing.

He rolled out the pastry, while the apples Alfred had chopped simmered in a pan with a pinch of cinnamon and a dash of sugar. The smell of Sunday mornings with his family prickled at Alfred's memories.

'My Ida used to make one of these pies every week. Risotto needs a stir,' he said, nodding towards the pan.

'Do you miss her?' Kian asked, adding some more stock to the pan of rice.

The obvious answer was yes, only that didn't go nearly far enough. How could he explain the magnitude of his feelings that were tied up in the small word that was 'grief'? Alfred took off his glasses and wiped them with a cloth while he thought back to those terrible first few months after Ida died.

'It's a bit like breaking a leg. At first the pain is unbearable, and you can't imagine it ever getting better. You can't function properly and even the simplest tasks seem impossible. Then slowly, as time goes by, you adapt. You learn to live with it. You might be left with a limp and you never quite walk the same, but you do walk again.'

'Sounds rough,' Kian said.

'I'll show you how to make the custard.' Alfred tapped the lid of a tub of Bird's custard powder.

'When we've finished eating, I'm gonna drop Dan back and

then we need to get on. You agreed we'd go to the dealers with all this lot this afternoon, yeah?' Kian prompted.

Alfred couldn't put it off for ever, he knew that. That didn't mean he wouldn't try.

While Kian took Dan home, Alfred prepared his surprise. It was messy and time-consuming taking down all the newspaper from the windows. For days Kian had wanted to rip it all off and Alfred had refused. He carefully lifted the Sellotape from each edge, folded up the sheets and put them inside a folder. They had been part of the fabric of his room for so long, it was unthinkable to throw them away. As the sheets came down, he felt like he was behind a glass case in a museum: *a fine exhibit of vintage man – some wear and tear.*

He stood on a chair and fitted the gingham curtains that had been stored away in the airing cupboard and smelled slightly of mildew. Now it was done, light entered the room in long, undulating panels, creating a hue that he hadn't seen in a very long time.

Kian returned and, just as Alfred had hoped, his enthusiasm for the paperless windows distracted him from going straight to the dealers. Instead he went outside and cut back the hedges with Alfred's ancient shears. Once he'd finished, it was possible to see the coloured front doors opposite, the coming and goings of Alfred's neighbours and even the two cracks on the paving stone right outside his house. It was exactly like when he got his first-ever pair of glasses. He hadn't realized the brightness and level of detail that he had been missing and it was almost too much for him to cope; he'd taken his glasses off again, preferring his blurry view of the world.

Together, they had cleared an alarming amount from his collections. All that remained were two sideboards, a bureau, a small drinks cabinet and a bookcase in the living room, along with his dining table, Chesterfield sofa, velvet armchair, footstool, collection of clocks and ten or so boxes of trinkets. The room was practically bare. Alfred desperately wanted to hold on to everything that was left.

'What do you think?' he asked, pointing at the windows. He plumped a cushion, sat down and placed a blanket over his lap, making it clear that he'd had quite enough for one day.

'That it's time we went to the dealers,' Kian said, dangling the keys for the van in front of him.

Alfred looked across to the hallway, where a row of boxes was lined up like evacuees from his day, waiting to be rehomed. He had one more trick up his sleeve to avoid the inevitable.

'Before that, I've got something for you,' Alfred replied. He stood up and put the blanket to one side.

'No more presents, Al. The watch is more than enough. Let's get going.'

'I had a feeling you needed a little push, and so I sent off for the catering-college application pack for you.'

'You did what?'

'I'll fetch it now and I can help you fill the forms in.'

Kian groaned as Alfred opened up his bureau. 'This is a waste of time. I'm not even going to get in, and we need to get a move on, before the dealers close. Look for it later.'

Alfred started to say something, then hesitated. Something wasn't right. He rummaged through the bureau as a burning heat rose through him.

'Where are my war medals?'

'What?' Kian asked.

'Where are they? They're not here! They've gone!' Alfred tossed out papers, spare spectacles and a carrier bag full of conkers, which spilled out and rolled across the floor.

'You've probably forgotten where you put them. I dunno how you ever find anything in this mess.'

'You think I'd forget something like that?' Alfred spat. 'I always put them in here. Always! I knew you'd taken a shine to them. I didn't think you'd actually steal them, though. Once a thief, always a thief. After everything I've done for you.'

'You've done for *me*?' Kian said, gesturing towards the boxes that surrounded them.

Alfred found the college forms, thrust them at Kian and pushed him towards the front door with trembling hands. Then a detonator went off inside him.

'I trusted you! I let you into my home, cooked for you and helped your brother. To think I cared about your future! Get out of my house and don't come back. I hope you rot in prison.'

'I swear I haven't got them.' Kian stood open-mouthed in the doorway. 'What about me coming over on Christmas Day?'

'Did you hear me? Get out! And take your ridiculous book with you!' Alfred threw the library book onto the path after Kian, as he held back a tidal wave of tears. How could he have been so blind?

29

Temptation

Chris folded his arms on the table in front of him and hunched forward, his eyes meeting Kian's. The window was too high to see out of, but it was open and, outside, a woman was having a massive row with someone. Kian would willingly trade places with her. He hated this room. It was a low-ceilinged box and dingy, like a police interview room. Although there wasn't a spotlight on him or a tape recorder out on the table, it still made him sweat.

'Last two weeks of your programme then. Progress update, yes?' Chris said.

The way he spoke made Kian's lip form into a snarl. If everything had gone to plan at Al's, pretty soon Chris Wilton would no longer be in his life. Now it seemed as if he would never be rid of him.

'We're almost done,' Kian replied. 'I mean the house – it's kinda there really.' He tried not to think about the current state of Alfred's home, and the fact that he was no longer allowed in it.

'Glad to hear it, young man. I look forward to seeing it for myself when I come to inspect your work on the twentieth of December,' Chris said. He was sitting on one of those spinning office chairs and began swivelling it from side to side, like he wanted to remind Kian that his chair was fancier, making sure he knew his place. 'On to your future then,' Chris continued. 'We talked about apprenticeships last time. How've you got on with all of that?'

Kian was grateful he had something to say in reply to this. 'Yeah, good. I'm gonna apply to catering college, to train to be a chef.' Saying it out loud didn't sound so stupid any more. Whether he had a future or not was something else entirely.

Chris leaned right back and coughed, putting his hand in front of his mouth to disguise a laugh. 'A chef, eh?' He scribbled something down in his notes, shaking his head. He didn't think Kian stood a chance. He was probably right. 'All right, well, just in case they don't think you're the next Michelin-star-in-waiting, what have you got as a back-up plan? Applied for any actual jobs?'

Kian slid further down in his seat. His appointment at the Job Centre the previous day had been a disaster. He'd been so wound up, after Al screaming his head off at him, that he'd forgotten his job seeker's booklet for the second time running. Without any evidence of job applications, they put a stop to his benefits. Then, after rejecting a list of at least ten jobs proposed to him, he was forced to apply for one as a pot-washer at the pub he usually drank in with Gav and Ryan. Clearing up after his mates was never gonna happen. He'd have to screw up the interview, which wouldn't be that hard, based on his track record.

'Got a couple of things in the pipeline,' Kian said. 'Just waiting to hear about interviews.'

'You've surprised me, Kian, I'll give you that. With a bit of help from me, you're turning into a half-decent young man. As long as you've got employment or training lined up and have done a good job on the pensioner's house, I'll be happy to see the back of you in a few weeks, knowing you're no longer a menace to society.'

Not as happy as Kian would be. 'Yeah, you've really made me see the error of my ways, Chris. Thanks.'

Kian walked home, smoking his last cigarette. His phone beeped with a voicemail from Ryan.

'Mate, I've sorted New Year – the best party in town. Fire-eaters, jugglers, superclub DJs. It's gonna be awesome. Seriously, you'd better be coming. You owe me sixty pounds for the ticket, and you still need to give me that insurance money, yeah? Laters.'

Sixty quid was nearly two weeks' dole money. It wasn't only the cost of the ticket, either. He'd need a new shirt, the cabs charged double fares at New Year and there'd be a whole night of drinking to fund. And Kian wanted to buy a Christmas present for Dan. But he'd never hear the end of it if he didn't go out to celebrate the biggest New Year's Eve in his lifetime. If he kept turning them down, there'd probably come a point when his mates would stop asking him to do stuff. And where would he be then? All alone, friendless, that's where. They'd realize he was the third wheel they didn't need. He had to get his hands on some money – fast.

As he turned into the side-road that he used as a shortcut home, he spotted a red Fiesta parked half on the pavement. Kian peered inside. A leather handbag was lying on the back seat. It was like it was waiting for him, knew that he needed the money and would come past at this particular time. It would take less than a minute to break the glass. The emergency electricity had run out yesterday and his flat was freezing. His fridge was empty and all he had in the cupboards was half a packet of biscuits and a multipack of crisps.

He hovered in the shadows of the bushes and waited, with adrenaline building inside him. The street lights hadn't come on yet. It was just about light enough to see and almost dark enough to disappear. He looked up and down the street. There was no one around. It would be easy and, right now, money would solve at least some of his problems.

30

All the birds in the air

It may have been Wednesday, or possibly Thursday. With his new curtains firmly closed, Alfred had lost track. He barely knew whether it was night or day – time simply merged into a treacle-like fog. Since deciding to barricade himself in the house, most of his waking hours were spent huddled under a blanket, watching TV. From hours of back-to-back viewing, he had learned the basics of dry-stone walling, discovered that monarch butterflies feed on milkweed to make themselves poisonous to predators, and that goose fat is the secret to perfect roast potatoes. He had watched a programme where a father and daughter were reunited after years apart and cried until his eyes stung.

He knew that if he switched off the television, the house would be as quiet as a churchyard. When you had no one, it was as if you didn't really exist at all. Nothing he did, said or thought had any impact on anyone else. He spent more and more time thinking about Maggie, his head cluttered with fragments of conversations they'd had before becoming estranged. Their small interactions that had enriched him – the interactions that made up a life.

On more than one occasion he had thought of something he could help Kian to cook on his next visit, before remembering that their arrangement was over. He made a shepherd's pie and almost got an extra plate out. Ridiculous, really. He'd lived by himself for years now and had coped well enough. Hadn't he?

Alfred had been caught off-guard, that much was certain. Worse than that, he'd been a complete and utter fool. There were stories about this sort of thing in the paper all the time. He'd been conned. Kian had been very convincing. Alfred had been foolish enough to imagine he enjoyed spending time with him, when all along Kian was just scoping him out to see what he could steal, getting a few free meals thrown in for good measure. There were probably other items missing, too. When he felt up to it, he would go through his inventories and check. If only he'd trusted his instincts and had never let the lad inside his house in the first place.

His medals – his precious medals – were gone. Every time he thought of someone else having them who didn't know their true meaning, a sharp pain rooted itself deep in the soles of his feet and stretched right up to his shoulder blades. They weren't just memories. They were a part of him. He wished he had never shown them to Kian in the first place. He certainly shouldn't have shared his deepest feelings and his private memories.

Alfred needed some air. He pulled on some trousers over his pyjamas and threw on his coat. A little shopping trip was the only way to get through a day like today. He stomped up the street as if a strong, northerly wind was behind him. He ignored the cheerful wave from a man outside, washing his car. He tutted loudly at a woman blocking his way by the bus stop as she counted out her change. And he kicked a neatly swept pile of leaves outside the library.

The first charity shop he reached was the Animal Rescue

one. Once inside, he realized that the woman with the colourful shawl was behind the counter again. He wasn't in the mood for a conversation. He picked up a trilby hat from a shelf and popped it on his head. It was too small and perched uncomfortably above his ears. Then he wrapped a long purple scarf around his neck. Hopefully the disguise would throw her off.

'Hello again. How nice to see you,' she said.

He froze. Clearly he wasn't cut out for a life of subterfuge.

'Is it cold out?' she continued. 'I like your hat. You know, I am sorry I couldn't join you for a walk last time. I'm free today, though. I get off at three, so—'

'I'm sorry?' Alfred said. The smell of freesias overpowered him as she stepped closer. It was the same scent Ida used to wear. He breathed in and closed his eyes and he was sitting at his kitchen table, Ida's hand resting lightly on his shoulder. In front of him was a plate of toast spread with marmalade, and the test cricket murmured from the radio. His heart swelled, but when he put his hand up to touch hers, he felt nothing but his own bones and a scratchy scarf. He opened his eyes. Ida was nowhere to be seen. Instead the woman with the shawl was standing there, twiddling a ball of wool between her fingers as if she'd forgotten something mid-sentence. It was as if Ida had been snatched from him all over again. He unwound the scarf and used it to strangle a nearby coat hanger.

'You said you'd like to go for a walk?' the woman said.

'Why on earth would I want to go for a walk with you?' Alfred replied. 'Although heaven knows, you look like you need the exercise.'

She disappeared into the stockroom with a box of tissues. Alfred picked up the entire basket of bric-a-brac and, without even looking through it, placed five pounds on the counter and left the shop. It was only when he arrived home that he realized he was still wearing the ridiculous hat. He turned out the contents of the basket onto the drop-leaf table. It was mostly rubbish. A letter opener, a bottle of candy-floss-coloured bubble bath, an ashtray engraved with the words *A present from Margate.* He scrambled through each item, certain there would be something in there – something wonderful. He was right. Eventually his fingers found a golden brooch in the shape of a pear tree. It was beautiful. He opened his palm, pinned it to his pyjamas and, at last, his anger dissolved. Things were bad, but he'd get through them. He always did. All he had to do was stay put and not answer the door. He might even use the bubble bath.

31

Looking for answers

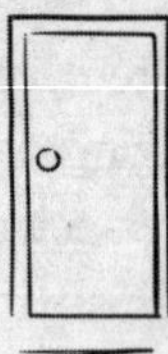

It was so quiet on the street that when Kian picked up a rock, ready to strike through the car window of the Fiesta, he could hear his watch ticking. The sound made him hesitate, long enough to remember how good he'd felt when Alfred had given it to him. He was torn in two. He needed the money – like, really needed it – yet he couldn't risk getting in any more trouble. Also he didn't want to prove Alfred right about him being a thief. Kian was frozen on the spot, unable to think straight, his heart thumping and his mind pulsing. He dropped the rock, stepped out of the gloom right into the middle of the road and carried on his way.

He returned home and ate the remaining packets of crisps while studying the brochure from the catering college. There were pictures of a leafy campus and huge kitchens, of students wearing chef whites and cutting vegetables. He could actually imagine being there. His eyes had been opened. He scrunched up his empty crisp packet. Until meeting Alfred, it had been easy – normal – to pop to the corner shop and load up on cheap crap that it took no effort to cook or eat. Food was fuel, nothing else. But now he wanted to learn it all, to taste it all.

He'd made himself chilli con carne last night, following a

recipe card that he'd picked up in Tesco. Apart from nearly blinding himself by rubbing his eyes after chopping the chillies, letting the rice boil over and spilling half a tin of tomatoes on the carpet, he'd done a pretty decent job. Not only that, but he'd loved every minute of it.

If he had a place at college, the courts might go easy on him when they addressed the fact that his restorative justice had failed, big time. Or maybe Alfred would find his medals and Kian could get on with the job in hand. Either way, he had nothing to lose by giving this a go. It might shut up Chris Wilton, for a start. In the past few days Kian had kept returning to the shortlist he'd written of possible careers: plumber, electrician, telesales. At the very top he had circled the word 'chef'. It shined above the rest.

The next step, filling the forms, was proving a challenge. He had nothing to put in the box headed *RELEVANT EXPERIENCE*, and Kian cringed as he ticked the box declaring convictions and then wrote down his paltry GCSE results. No one in their right mind would want him. He had to at least try, though. He was out of options. The last section was easier: why he wanted to apply for the course. Kian wrote about his short experience of cooking, how it transported him away from the real world and made him happy, how he enjoyed the challenge of creating the perfect flavour combination. He loved the aromas, the rhythm, even the sounds. It was sort of therapeutic, like there was no room for anything else in his head and his worries switched off. He put his thoughts down as best he could and stuffed the form into an envelope.

If he got in, Dan would have a reason to be proud of him. Dan surfaced in Kian's thoughts, no matter what he was doing. He hadn't been able to face looking at the forms to apply to the family court for legal guardianship. It annoyed the hell out of him. He shouldn't have to jump through all these hoops just to have his own brother living with him. No time like the present. He opened up the pack, and reams of legal jargon jumped out at him, making him feel small: *applying for a Section 8 order; existing child arrangements; the Children Act 1989*. He started again, reading from the top: *Three months before you apply to become a special guardian you need to tell your local council in writing that you plan to make an application.* So he'd already lost three months, even before getting to the starting line.

As he reached for his cigarettes, he knocked the library book onto the kitchen floor. He'd have to take it back soon or he'd end up with a fine. He also wanted to see Chloe again. A small piece of paper fell out, a note written in very neat handwriting:

Hi Kian,

I had a quick look on the computer for you and found the name, address and number you were looking for, so here they are, in case you change your mind. Also, my number is at the bottom too, in case you fancy a date sometime.

Chloe x

The fact that a girl he liked was asking Kian out barely registered with him. He was holding his mum's address in his hands. For most of his childhood she might as well have been dead to him, but now she was a real person again. If he wanted to, he could get on a train right now and be there in a little over an hour. He couldn't, though. He wasn't even sure if he wanted to. His hands shook so much he was forced to sit down on the sofa.

His mum might be sitting on her sofa right now, too. Kian

tried to imagine knocking on her door – how it would feel to see her, after all these years. What if he could have a mum again? What if him turning up was a moment she'd dreamed of, something she'd longed for? Or . . . what if, after she'd got rid of Kian, she had another family, better kids than him? What if she slammed the door in his face? There was no way he was going to find out.

He turned the piece of paper over and over and placed it face-down on the table. The thought of being reunited with his mum literally choked him up. He gasped for breath as he imagined her arms around him, telling him the words that he had always longed to hear: that she was sorry, that she'd made a massive mistake walking out on him, that she loved him.

All this time she had lived not that far outside Birmingham. Surely there needed to be mountains, oceans even – some intangible force that had stopped her coming to find him? Not just a county. If he'd had a proper upbringing, he might already be in college and not on some doomed restorative-justice project. Danny would have a proper home, with Kian. This was all his mum's fault – everything was. Why shouldn't he simply go over there and tell her? Demand to know why she had left him like that. He had only been a little kid. He didn't deserve it. His mind was swirling. Before he even realized what he was doing, Kian stood up, put on his coat and made his way to the train station.

The houses were much bigger than he'd imagined – detached new-builds with tarmac driveways that all looked the same. Christmas wreaths hung from shiny front doors. Round his way, the houses and flats were currently decorated with England flags and the occasional inflatable Santa. Either Chloe had given him the wrong address, or his mum was doing considerably better than he was. When Kian reached the right number, his hands began to sweat. He wanted to rip off his coat and turn round. No, he was going to do this. He knocked on the door and waited, flexing his fingers and wishing he hadn't left his cigarettes on the table back home.

'Yes?' A small woman with dyed copper hair, wearing a green shirt-dress, looked at him. It was Cathy. His mum. It was definitely her, although she was older than in the photo and not as skinny. Her face looked softer, sort of blurry round the edges. It was silly, but he'd expected her to still be the mum in the picture that he had.

'It's me – Kian. Remember? Your son,' he said, in a voice that was gritty and cold. Her reaction said it all. He was standing in front of her and she didn't even recognize him. He was a total stranger.

Cathy's face drained of colour and she put her hand to her throat. A silver diamond sparkled from her wedding finger. So she had remarried and there was every chance she had more kids as well. They could be inside, waiting for her to come back in and play Happy Families while he stood outside in the cold. The son she didn't want.

'Kian? I can't believe it. Oh my God, Kian!' She threw her arms around him and rested her head against his shoulder, squeezing him tightly and, just like when he'd imagined this moment, his breath came out in short, sharp bursts. His arms hung at his side as if they didn't belong to him.

'Come in,' Cathy said. 'Come in. I mean, do you want to come in? Look at you, so tall!'

She was acting like an aunty who hadn't seen him for a couple of Christmases, not the mother who hadn't had a clue where her son had been for more than a decade. He hesitated before following her inside, taking in the pale pink-and-cream-striped wallpaper and thick-pile carpet. He listened out for any signs of her new family and was relieved that the place was silent.

Cathy pointed to a plush armchair in the lounge, and he sat down next to a door that led onto a conservatory full of plants and a long wicker sofa. His mum had a conservatory, while he lived in one room. There it was again: the surge of injustice that kicked him from inside. He blinked a few times, wondering if he might wake up and realize this wasn't really happening.

The pair of them stared at each other without saying a word, for what seemed like ages. Kian tried to match this woman, who looked quite normal and sweet and suburban, with the monster who had abandoned her two small children. It didn't seem possible.

He looked around slowly, like a detective trying to put together the pieces of information. There were some photos on a small table in the corner, which were too far away for him to see properly. Would there be one of him and Dan? Did she even think about them? A Christmas tree stood next to the TV, with presents covered in shiny paper underneath. Kian felt sick. The room smelled sweet, like vanilla icing, and he noticed that the bookcase next to him was filled with cookery books.

'You like cooking?' he asked. The questions he really wanted to ask kept getting stuck in his throat.

'I love it. Baking, mostly. I'm doing a cake-decorating course. I've done some lovely birthday cakes for a few of the neighbours' kids. Thought I could set up my own little business. Stupid really. Mark – that's my fiancé – reckons I've got a real talent. Sorry, I don't know why I'm rattling on. Nerves!'

In that moment Kian's heart misfired. He didn't really know this woman, yet he shared something with her. His new-found passion for cooking had, in all likelihood, come from his mum. It had been there all along, just waiting for him to find it – a piece of her in him. And he recognized her insecurity, too.

'It's not stupid. You should,' Kian said.

'Thanks. That's kind. So . . .' Cathy flexed her fingers and Kian flinched, recognizing another trait he'd inherited without knowing. 'How are you keeping? God, I can't believe you're really here. I thought about you the other day, actually. Westlife were on the telly. One of the singers is called Kian, isn't he?'

Kian said nothing.

'I like to think you've done well, like him – got some great job, a lovely girlfriend, a nice house. I always wanted the best for you and Danny, you do know that?'

A switch tripped inside him. 'The best? You wanted the best for me? You abandoned me at the age of eight and thought I'd turn out to have a blinding life? No, Cathy. It doesn't work like that. I hated being in care. Hated you for leaving me. I live in a bedsit that I can't afford to heat. Dan is forced to live miles away from me. I don't have a job, but I do have a criminal record. And I don't have a girlfriend because who, in their right mind, would want to be with someone like me? Someone whose own mum didn't even want them?'

The words were flung from his mouth like knives. He couldn't have her thinking everything had turned out fine, just so she could feel okay about it all. She hid her face in her hands and let out a muffled sob. Did she expect him to feel sorry for her? He should never have come. This was pointless. He stood up to leave, but Cathy put her arm out to stop him.

'No, don't! Stay. Please,' she urged, with tears streaking mascara onto her cheeks.

He stood still for a moment, looking towards the door and then back at his mum. Part of him wanted to run, but something had awakened in him that he couldn't shut down. It was like he was ravenous and full, at the same time. He needed more from her, and he couldn't go yet.

Cathy began biting her nails, another trait they shared. When Kian finally sat down again, she stopped and let out a deep breath.

'I get why you're angry,' she said. 'I didn't want you both to end up in care, I swear I didn't. You were the best things that ever happened to me. I wasn't coping, Kian. I was in a bad place, and you and Danny, you weren't safe with me. I didn't take my medication; I drank too much. I won't go into it all. But I want you to know that I've never stopped thinking about you both, or loving you. Ever.'

'You think you loved us? Then why didn't you sort yourself out and come and get us? You were even allowed contact, but you didn't bother. That's how little we meant to you. We were like dirt that you couldn't wait to scrape from your shoe.' Kian clenched his fists in his lap.

'That's not true . . . I think it just hurt too much. I loved you both fiercely, I swear on my life. I knew I wasn't a good mum. I left because I felt like I had no choice, and I thought staying in touch would screw you up – that you were better off without me. I didn't even think I deserved you, either of you. I'm sorry. I wish I'd handled it differently.'

Kian did too, more than anything, but her actions spoke louder than words. Silence hung between them. He'd wanted to hear her say sorry for such a long time, thinking it would change everything. But its effect barely registered. Her excuses weren't enough. Cathy's eyes had been focused on the floor and now she looked up, staring at him as if noticing Kian properly for the first time.

'You must be, what, nearly eighteen now? I was only fifteen when I had you – just a kid. But look at you. You're so handsome and confident, and I can tell you're kind. I wish I could say I'm proud of you, but I can't take any credit.'

'No,' Kian said. 'You can't.'

She brushed some imaginary crumbs from the arm of her chair and clamped her lips together. Her words replayed in his head. She loved him fiercely. She had only been a kid. Who was he to believe that he wouldn't have done the same in her situation? There was a lot he didn't know about her. In fact, he knew nothing at all. Cathy went to make them both a cup of tea and placed one beside him. He surprised himself by staying long enough to drink it.

'Where've you been all this time?' Kian asked, hoping to hear that she'd been imprisoned somewhere or forced to leave the country.

'Here and there,' Cathy replied. 'I moved to Leicester for a bit. My boyfriend at the time had a place there. Didn't last long. I was homeless for a while. I mean, the past few years have been a bit of a blur, to be honest. I've really tried to turn things around lately. Rehab helped. My social worker's always banging on about how much progress I've made.'

So she'd spent his childhood off her face, chasing after boyfriends and not giving him or Dan a single thought. She was completely irresponsible, and it seemed that he had followed in her footsteps. Another thing to feel let down about.

'When I met Mark, he believed in me, you know? When you

meet someone who genuinely cares . . . I don't know, it makes all the difference.'

Kian thought of Alfred. He was that person in his life – the one who cared, although even that was doubtful now. No matter. It should have been Cathy looking after him.

'Here, I'll show you some pictures of my recent cakes,' Cathy went on, oblivious to the storm surging opposite her. She took down a small album from a shelf and passed it to Kian.

He flicked through the pictures and, he had to admit, the cakes were pretty good. As good as anything he'd seen in a shop.

'Impressive,' he said. He paused on the page that showed a cake with Teenage Mutant Ninja Turtles crafted from green fondant icing. He'd have loved that when he was younger. He thought about all the years that she had never made him a birthday cake, all the years that she had missed. Not *missed* – that sounded accidental. She had wilfully given them up.

'Thanks,' Cathy replied, clutching her hands together across her knees. 'I really am glad you came, you know. I've thought about trying to find you so many times. But I was terrified you wouldn't want to see me. I know I let you down and I don't deserve you, but I'd love to see you again some time. Kian?'

Cathy clearly had a lovely life without him. His life was a wreck. Still, he'd managed this long without her and, now that he'd seen her, what was the point in doing it again? He definitely didn't want to meet her new bloke and find out how great things were without him around.

'You're right, Cathy. You don't deserve me in your life. I've got to go.'

32

The smell of lemons

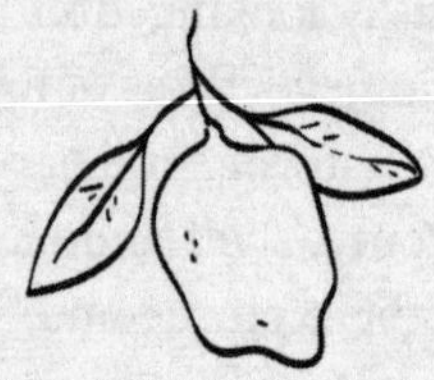

Kian was spiralling. Seeing his mum had screwed with his head. It had complicated everything instead of giving him answers. Cathy's face, her voice, even her bloody perfume were all real now, fresh in his mind. She wasn't a set of faded memories or a ripped photograph. He knew where she lived, what her sofa was like, how good her cakes were and how she'd carved out a life that didn't have a Kian-shaped hole in it. He'd gone straight round to Ryan's after visiting her and downed a few beers while they watched the England match, although he wasn't really concentrating. At half-time he picked up his phone, and that's when his heart dropped to his feet. Five missed calls from Dan.

'Dan? Danny. I'm so sorry. I mean it. I was busy and I forgot. Don't be mad with me, yeah?'

Dan was silent for ages. 'I can hear the match in the background. You're watching it without me.'

Kian signalled at Ryan to mute the volume on the television. He ignored him and started chanting, 'Come on, England!'

'I'm sorry, mate, okay? I messed up. I'll make it up to you.'

'You were going to get me crisps and Coke and we were going to watch it together. You promised.'

How did Kian explain that he was useless – that life had a habit of tripping him up?

'I know, and I meant it. I was looking forward to it, I swear. It's just some other stuff came up. We'll watch the next one.'

'It doesn't matter. I'm going to live with my new family soon, anyway.'

Dan put the phone down, leaving Kian feeling like he'd been slapped in the face. Today of all days, he could have done without the final confirmation that he really was the worst brother in the world.

Heading into town for a big night out had seemed like a good idea at the time. Now that Kian was standing outside Snobs nightclub in front of a bouncer who blocked his way and demanded to see his ID, he wished he'd stayed at home. The guy's face was crooked, as if it had seen a few rounds in a boxing ring, and a scar ran across the bridge of his nose to underneath his left eye. He stared at Kian's fake ID for so long that Kian was sure he was going to turn him away. Behind him, he was aware of impatient women with bare shoulders, shedding perfume-counter fumes, and of men jeering with beery breath.

The bouncer looked Kian up and down again, then let him pass. The place was jam-packed. The carpet was tacky and blotched with stains of indeterminable origin, and there was a faint smell of vomit and disinfectant. Despite the smoke and the mirrored walls that would challenge even someone who was sober, he somehow found his way to Gav and Ryan, who were already eighteen and had been waved straight in. They were standing near the bar, holding bottles of beer with lime squashed into the neck. As Kian was playing catch-up, he ordered two bottles of Hooch and they found some seats in the corner, right by a speaker.

'Lads,' Ryan said, stubbing out one cigarette and lighting up another, 'this club we're heading to later is gonna be awesome. It's got this glass ceiling that opens up.'

'No way,' Kian shouted over the noise of the music. Ryan would believe anything.

'Seriously, you're gonna love it,' Ryan went on.

'Here's to a big night, boys,' Gav said. 'And this is just a warm-up. Christmas round the corner, then it's the millennium!'

'And then Ibiza next summer!' Ryan raised his bottle and clinked it against Gav's. He paused before doing the same to Kian.

Had Ryan said that to make him jealous? Or to make it clear that Kian should change his mind and go with them? With his restorative-justice programme hanging in the balance, he might be banged up anyway. Tonight, though, none of that mattered. He needed to get completely smashed – enough to drown out the feeling that Dan hated him and to forget all about Cathy.

He polished off his first drink and waited for that familiar feeling. The one that signified the start of the weekend, a big one. The buzz of not knowing where the night would take them or who they'd end up with. It didn't happen. Gav and Ryan kept asking him why he was so quiet. More than ever, Kian felt like he was drifting apart from his mates. He kept so much inside when he was with them, whereas when he'd been with Alfred he could really be himself. He hadn't even told them about applying to college, convinced they'd laugh.

As they got up to move to the next club, Ryan tugged his arm and leaned into him. 'Don't worry about that insurance money you owe me, yeah? I know you're broke. Tonight's on me.'

Every now and then, Ryan turned out to be the best sort of friend. 'Seriously? Cheers, mate. You sure? How come you're so flush? You don't start your new job 'til January.'

'Paid a little visit to the old weirdo's house, didn't I? No security in that place. Anyway, found those medals you were on about. Thanks for the tip-off, mate – they made me a hundred quid. Let's have a real bender!'

The repetitive bass pounding through the speakers was replaced by the noise of blood whooshing in Kian's ears. 'You did what?'

Ryan took out his wallet and flicked through a wad of ten-pound notes. 'Enough for us to get wasted tonight, eh, mate?'

'I got the blame for that, you idiot!'

'Yeah, well, maybe you deserved it!'

With huge force, Kian swung his right arm in the direction of Ryan's face. He heard the smack of his fist against the flesh of Ryan's nose before he felt the pain radiate across his hand. Ryan fell backwards onto a table of glass bottles, which smashed on top of him as he stumbled onto the floor. There was blood. A lot of blood.

'You maniac!' Ryan screamed from the floor. 'I'm pressing charges, Kian Matthews. You hear me? I'm sending you down.'

Gav rushed to Ryan's side, and a small crowd of clubbers gathered round. Kian pushed past people who were delirious with drink and dripping with sweat and tried to find his way to the exit through the smog of cigarette smoke and dry ice. He emerged onto the street and the cold air made him gulp. He ran and didn't stop until he reached the edge of the canal.

He stared at the murky depths of water, doubled over, holding his side. Alfred's medals were worth more than a hundred quid. They were priceless. How could Ryan do that? He'd ruined everything.

His heart was beating too fast, a banging cymbal in his chest. He sat on the ground and lit up a cigarette. He breathed the smoke in deeply and was struck by another thought. If Ryan could do that . . . what if it was him who stole the money from Lucy that time? He'd been round often enough after school. Ryan doubtless stood by and let Kian take the blame and lose his home – lose Lucy, who was the best thing ever to happen to him.

The canal suddenly looked like it could drag him under.

Kian stopped off on the way home at the all-night supermarket on the high street. He pulled out his fake ID again and, with his last bit of cash, bought a four-pack of premium-strength cider and a small box of fireworks. With the millennium coming up, every shop had them on special offer. He had one lit in his hand, and it crackled and hissed as he wondered exactly how long he had until it took his arm off. Kian lobbed it towards the sky and laughed as it exploded, sending a trail of orange sparks along the pavement where it landed. He lit another, the fuse burning slowly. When there were only a few millimetres left, he threw it as far as he could. It made a whistling sound as it hurtled to the ground in a haze of shooting white lights. There was one firework left – a rocket, which he was saving for later.

He knocked back another can of cider and kicked over a dustbin at the end of someone's driveway. A cat screeched and

Kian ducked behind a car when the owner of the house came out to investigate the noise. Once he'd gone back inside, he got out his spray can and painted a big smiley face on the side of the car, which was ironic as he was on the verge of having an actual total breakdown. The darkness was back, big time.

He wandered the streets, seething with injustice over what Ryan had done and how he'd messed up Kian's life. What if Alfred never believed him? What if he called the police? He could end up in prison over this.

As if his mind wasn't already spinning out of control, he kept going over the conversation he'd had with his mum. It was like he was walking along the edge of a very tall skyscraper – one that he might fall off at any second. He wanted to head back over to Cathy's and smash her windows in. No, he wasn't so drunk that he didn't remember what happened the last time he picked up a brick. Instead he continued drinking and walked until he reached Lucy's house. She was the closest thing he'd ever had to a real mum, and she might be the one person who could talk him down from doing something he'd regret.

Kian stood in front of the flashing Christmas lights around her front door. The TV was on, so he knew she was still up. He peered through the half-closed blinds and made out a toy kitchen in the corner. Kian had been just one of the kids on the conveyer belt who had been in her care over the years. He didn't really mean anything to her. Fostering was Lucy's job. The fury inside him was a rising steam, surpassing the anxiety shooting through his veins. There was no point ringing the bell. If Lucy had really cared about him, she'd never have let him go in the first place. She would have believed him. Instead she assumed the worst about him, exactly as Alfred did now.

At the side of the house, Kian stood on his tiptoes and looked over the fence into the garden. The football goal was still there. He'd scored countless goals in that very spot while dreaming of becoming a striker for Villa. What he wouldn't do to be the fourteen-year-old him again, when he'd actually thought he might have a decent life to look forward to. There was the swing hanging from a tree at the back, where he sometimes used to sit, even though he was probably too big for it. It was too dark to see if Lucy still had a pond full of fish. All his happiest memories fitted into the space of a small square of garden. Stepping back, he gave the fence three good hard kicks until his foot hurt. Another kick and one of the panels ripped away from the post and crashed to the ground. As he lit the rocket, he heard Lucy's front door open.

He threw the firework upwards and turned to run. Lucy called his name and came outside after him.

'Kian, is that you? Kian, what's wrong? Come inside, love.'

The red blanket on his shoulders was the same one that Lucy used to put round him when he lived with her. If he'd got soaked playing football or had a bit of a cold, she'd wrap him up in it and make him hot honey and lemon. Every time he'd smelled lemons since, it would send a shiver down his spine.

'Sorry,' he said. 'I'm a total state.' He wiped his snotty nose on his sleeve and snorted. 'And it's really late. I'm sorry about your fence. I'll fix it.'

'Hey, love. Don't apologize. Are you ready to tell me what happened?' She handed him a cup of tea and a box of tissues.

He told her everything. All the lies about how well he was doing, the mess he was in with Alfred, what Ryan had done, the situation with Dan. It poured out of him in one long stream, and he was exhausted by the time he'd finished. It was so easy to talk to Lucy; he couldn't begin to think why he'd ignored her all the times she'd reached out to him.

'You've got to tell Alfred,' Lucy said. 'He needs to know it was Ryan and that it had nothing to do with you. And Danny will forgive you – he's your brother. There's nothing that can't be fixed, eh? Even my fence.'

Kian wished that was true. Alfred wouldn't believe him, and Dan had already given up on him. Who could blame them?

The next morning he woke late, with a banging head. He was still on Lucy's sofa, the red blanket tucked around him. When he saw where he was, for a split second he thought he still lived there. Reality soon kicked in, as fragments of last night's events flashed through his head. He wished he could go back to sleep and put off the real world for a bit longer.

'Morning, love,' Lucy said, handing him a cup of tea in a mug that said *SMILE*. 'This is Aisha.' A little girl with her hair tied up peeked from behind Lucy's legs.

'Hiya,' he said, giving her a wave.

'She's a bit shy. Come on, Aisha, let's get some toys out. Sorry, Kian, it's probably a bit early for you. How are you feeling?'

'Pretty crappy. Thanks, you know, for last night. I'm gonna head off now.'

'You know you can stay for as long as you like? I'm worried about you. Have some breakfast at least?'

'You don't need to worry. Seriously, I'll be fine.'

33

Caught red-handed

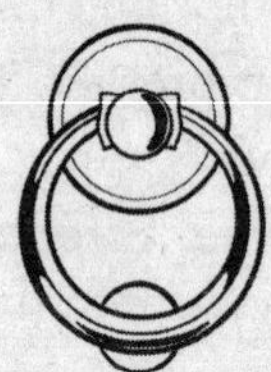

The brass door knocker wasn't an especially good find. Alfred didn't need it. He picked it up and tried to find a reason to leave it behind. Once it was in his hand, though, it was too late; he had to have it. The only way to take his mind off his missing medals, and Kian's betrayal, was to replenish his collections.

'Just this today, Alfred?' Stan, the shop assistant, asked. Alfred pretended it was normal that they were on first-name terms now.

His skin prickled as he looked again at the door knocker. It wasn't enough. Perhaps he should have another look, in case there was something else he had missed. He stopped still. There like an apparition, looking right through the glass shop front from the pavement, was Maggie. Alfred turned round, closed his eyes and began to count. With a bit of luck, she hadn't seen him. Before he'd reached six, Maggie was right behind him, tapping his arm.

'Dad?'

Alfred had been caught red-handed, doing exactly what Maggie disapproved of most, so he ducked into a trench of lies, for protection.

'Oh, Maggie. I'm just selling some items to Stan here. Don't let on that I've made a nice little profit, will you?' He winked, as if he was the sort of person who did that.

His daughter stared at him for a few moments, before getting out her purse. 'Shall we go to that cafe over the road? I could get you a cinnamon bun – you used to love those.'

Used to. Another stinging reminder that their relationship was one that belonged in the past. 'No, thank you very much.' Typical of Maggie to expect him to carry on as if nothing had happened between them.

'Then let me come round,' she persisted. 'We need to talk. How about tomorrow?'

Alfred felt a stab of embarrassment that nothing had changed in his life since the last time Maggie had visited, years ago. He was still miserable, and his house was still in a state.

'No,' Alfred said. 'I'm busy.'

With eyes of steel, Maggie handed him a ten-pound note. 'Here, buy whatever it is you were intending to get before I turned up.'

'I'm selling things, Maggie, not buying!' Alfred replied, although she had already left the shop. The door knocker he'd been planning to purchase had now lost its shine. He bought it anyway and picked up a knitted egg-cosy to keep it company.

In the days since he'd bumped into Maggie, Alfred hadn't left the house. When she'd handed over her money, she'd given him a look of pity. It had made him feel like he was a drug addict, desperate for his next fix. He was now a wisp of a man, ashamed, angry and altogether exhausted. He polished off a whole packet of biscuits on the sofa, without really tasting them, and didn't bother turning over the television to a different channel when a programme came on that he didn't like.

Just when he thought he couldn't feel any worse, a letter from Sandra arrived:

Dear Alfred,

Following on from my recent visit, I'm writing to confirm the date of your forthcoming needs assessment:

Thursday, 20 January 2000 at 2 p.m.

The information enclosed will explain a little more about the process. Really, it's simply a chance for me to find out a little more about your day-to-day needs in more detail, and for us to decide what package of support might be most suitable for you. You can ask a friend or relative to join us, if you would like.

Well, that wasn't likely. He didn't have any friends, and there was no way he was telling Maggie. Alfred stopped reading. A *needs* assessment. What he needed was for everyone to keep their noses out of his business. The date of her visit sounded so futuristic he could almost believe it would never happen. Unfortunately, a quick glance at the calendar showed it was only a matter of weeks away. He oscillated between being convinced that Sandra didn't have a leg to stand on, and picturing the police smashing his door down and carting him off in handcuffs while the neighbours looked on, open-mouthed. Perhaps they'd start a campaign: *Free Alfred*. It wasn't very likely. He'd stopped talking to his neighbours a long time ago and hadn't kept track of who had moved in and out over the years. They probably didn't know he existed, let alone his name.

He held the envelope over the steaming kettle to release the stamp. Somewhere on the street, fireworks were being let off, even though it was only just past lunchtime. Each whizzing rocket and sky-shattering bang made him reel, as though he'd been shot. He turned the radio on and let the Shipping Forecast and glass of whisky that he'd poured pull him into a deeper malaise. There was nothing good about this time of year. It was a trail of inconvenience and misery as soon as summer ended: trick-or-treaters banging on the door, bomb-like explosions going off at all hours, miserable weather, slippery pavements, the pain of Remembrance Day, all building to the garish crescendo of Christmas. It was hard not to be affected by the adverts indiscriminately bombarding him with gift ideas for that special someone, or reminding him that he had to order early to get the sofa he absolutely required in time for the big day, so that he could squeeze everyone in. The whole season was clearly not designed for someone like him. He had no friends, a dead wife and a daughter he'd been virtually disowned by. And what on earth had come over him, inviting Kian to spend Christmas Day with him? He must have momentarily lost his mind. Thank goodness he could now spend the day in his pyjamas and do everything the way he liked.

There had been a Christmas, a long time ago, when the whole family had been snowed in and it was one of the best he could remember. The snow had started to fall on Christmas Eve and they had joked about the odds of having a white Christmas. The next day Ida insisted on playing the Bing Crosby song, as Alfred carved the turkey. Maggie was back from university and had brought a trifle, which they all agreed needed more sherry, so they poured themselves extra glasses to make up the shortfall. The carols from King's were playing as they competed at Monopoly, arguing over who had bought Park Lane. The hours merged into a boozy haze of mince pies and merriment. The snow got heavier and heavier until it reached the windowpane. It was like something from a film.

Alfred wished it was, so that he could rewind it and watch the film over and over again.

34

Room to grow

Sandra's letter had only worsened Alfred's mood, so he treated himself to a few pieces to add to his inventory, which he had found in a trendy vintage shop in Harborne. It mainly sold clothes from the sixties and seventies at extortionate prices, even though you could pick them up from the Rag Market for next to nothing. There was a lot of tat, but a few exquisite pieces were waiting to be found by someone with a fine eye like his, including the new oval tray that now lived on top of his bureau.

That was quickly followed by the arrival of a French dresser, delivered by two men in a van who had grumbled endlessly when he told them it needed to be carried upstairs, where it was slotted next to a wardrobe on the landing. And of course a dresser needs things to go on top of it, or what is the point of it at all? A mirror, a hairbrush with a mother-of-pearl handle and a small selection of photo frames. It was almost the end of December, so he could justify his purchases as little Christmas presents to himself. No one needed to know.

He really should stop there, though, before it all began to get out of hand. He had to remember that he did not want Sandra to put him in care, and he no longer had Kian to help. The boxes waiting to go to the antique dealers kept looking at him accusingly. The best thing to do was to keep himself busy and, without his collections to attend to, that was going to be hard. What did people of his age do with their spare time? He remembered the lies he'd told Sandra about his fondness for badminton. Maybe it didn't have to be a falsehood after all. It was only hitting a shuttlecock over a net. How hard could it be? There was a badminton racket hanging up in the cupboard in the hallway. He'd known it would come in handy one day. And, even better, he found a pair of matching sweatbands squashed into the drawer of the telephone table. They were unworn and still in their packet. He squeezed his hands through them and slung the racket over his shoulder. Surely looking the part was half the battle? This could be the start of a whole new him.

Alfred stood in the way of the automatic doors of the leisure centre, forcing them to open and close repeatedly. He couldn't bring himself to go in. A group of children ran past him wearing armbands, dragging tangled towels behind them. He didn't belong here. It was chaotic and noisy, full of people at the peak of their fitness, their zest for life emblazoned on their Lycra shirts and giant sports bags. He longed to be back in his living room. He couldn't even play badminton, and it was ridiculous taking it up at his age. What had he been thinking?

He slid the sweatbands off. Perhaps he should start with something a little easier. If he couldn't make the badminton lie come true, then he could work on the others: a walking group, and volunteering in a charity shop, if he remembered correctly. In fact, the woman from the charity shop had told him she liked walking. She might be a member of a group that he could join. And if that failed, he might be able to convince her to give him a few shifts in the shop. No, that would be too dangerous. He'd come home with half of the donations.

'Hello again,' he said as he entered the shop, trying to hide his racket behind his back. It took all his effort to walk straight to the counter rather than appraise the contents of the shelves.

'Oh,' the woman replied, closing her eyes for longer than the length of a blink.

It was only then that Alfred remembered their last conversation. Perhaps he had been a little harsh.

'I'm sorry I was a bit . . . offhand last time we spoke. I was having a bad day.'

'I see. Well, apology accepted,' she said, placing a desolate dinner jacket on a hanger.

Alfred picked up a basket of belts on the counter and coughed.

The woman looked at him. 'Can I help you?'

This had been much easier in his head than it was panning out. He put the belts down. 'Ah, yes. Well, I've been thinking of trying a new hobby, only I'm not really sure where to start. I don't suppose you're a member of a walking group by any chance?'

'No. I like to walk by myself. Clears my head.'

'I see. So sorry to have troubled you. I'm sorry, I don't know your name.'

'Meena.'

Alfred nodded, trying to think of a way to ask her what else she did in her spare time that didn't make him sound as if he had an unhealthy interest. He walked to the other side of the shop and pretended to be fascinated by a plain glass jug. He held it up and tilted it from side to side, before placing it back on the shelf. Then he shuffled in Meena's direction again.

'You could come with me one time, if you like?' Meena suggested, as Alfred was about to open his mouth. 'I'm going to walk up to the nature reserve tomorrow actually, for a walk around the lake. It's beautiful in winter.'

Alfred hesitated. In a group he could simply disappear. He wouldn't be open to scrutiny or feel pressured to come up with interesting conversation. A walk with one other person he barely knew was a completely different prospect. But, he supposed, there would be no harm in going just the once. It would be something to tell Maggie about, if she ever called him again. Something truthful.

'That would be nice. I'm Alfred. Very nice to make your acquaintance. Properly, I mean.'

'You too. See you by the entrance tomorrow morning then, ten-thirty. Don't be late.'

It had been nice waking up knowing that he had a purpose for the day. Hopefully the walk would wear him out and Alfred could enjoy a long afternoon nap, before making some preparations for Christmas Day, even though he'd be spending it alone. He had to keep busy. He was still going to roast a turkey, make bread sauce and have a Christmas pudding with a proper silver sixpence hidden inside. His taste-buds were tingling already. If he let the situation with Kian and Sandra and Maggie overwhelm him, he would drown in a well of despair.

The lake had frozen over, and two swans were perched on top of the glittering ice. Their crystal reflections glimmered in front of them as they preened their wings. Crimson berries shone from frost-covered bushes, and the chirruping calls of blue tits and robins surrounded them. Squirrels scurried from tree to tree, fighting over the last acorns. Meena was right – it was beautiful at this time of year, and the fact that there was hardly anyone around simply added to its charm.

Meena was waiting for him a little further along from the entrance to the reserve, wearing a huge scarf and a bobble hat. She had proper walking boots on, a pair of binoculars around her neck and was carrying a flask of coffee and a small bag. Alfred was woefully underdressed, in a trench coat and brown lace-up shoes. At least he'd remembered his gloves.

'You came,' Meena said. 'I wasn't sure if you would. Oh, it might be a bit muddy. Sorry, I should have warned you to wear suitable footwear.'

'It's fine,' Alfred replied, wishing he'd thought this through. Muddy shoes were nothing, compared to his worries about the required etiquette in this situation. Should they walk side-by-side or should he keep a few paces apart? They barely knew each other, after all. He decided to stride ahead, even though he didn't know the way. Meena caught up with him and he increased his speed again. Before long he broke into a sweat and had to stop entirely.

'I love this,' Meena said, pointing to a large owl that had been sculpted from the trunk of a tree.

Alfred looked at it more closely. The craftsmanship was incredible. The wings consisted of intricately carved feathers, and the details in its staring-wide eyes made them look real.

'I can see why,' he agreed. 'It's rather wonderful.'

'Owls are so beautiful, aren't they?'

'A group of owls is called a parliament, you know,' Alfred said.

'Really? How unfair to owls.' Meena laughed.

It wasn't as awkward being alone with Meena as he'd imagined. They continued to walk, and he slowed down a little so that they settled into a matching pace.

'I'll pour you some coffee,' Meena said, once they reached the halfway mark. They sat on a bench overlooking the water, the coffee warming their hands. It was strange to be in company like this, without a care in the world. Being outside in the fresh air was breathing new life into Alfred. He might even suggest another stroll.

He took a deep breath. There was that smell again – the freesias. A shiver danced across his shoulders. 'The perfume you wear,' he commented. 'It reminds me of my wife, Ida. She died. Five years ago now.'

'Oh, I'm sorry,' Meena said. 'I've worn this scent for as long as I can remember. It reminds me of my mother actually. She loved spring flowers. I'm on my own, too. Graham, my second husband, died a couple of years ago. We'd only recently found each other when we discovered he had cancer; and you just hope, don't you, that everything will work out? Only sometimes, it doesn't.'

Alfred bent down and re-laced a shoe that didn't need re-lacing. He had spent so long on his own that he'd forgotten that other people carried grief with them, too. And yet Meena gave no indication of bitterness or resentment. She was out in the world, getting on with things. Maybe he could learn something from her. Maybe he should.

'I'm so sorry. That must have been awful,' he said. 'How did you get through it?'

Meena looked across the lake as though she was lost. 'Sometimes I'm not sure I have. It's been hard, but I decided to keep myself busy – anything to make the days go by and give me a reason to get out of bed. I volunteer in the charity shop, as you know, and I'm a member of a reading group and go to a few coffee mornings. It's friends that get us through, isn't it? How about you?'

A lie made its way to the tip of his tongue. Alfred stopped it. 'I haven't coped well at all. I collect things and, in all honesty, it's taken over, I suppose. I've locked myself away. I . . . I don't really have friends and I don't even see my daughter any more. We've had rather a large falling-out.'

'That's so sad,' she said, lightly touching his arm. 'I'm sure it's not too late, though. I bet she'd love it if you put matters right between you. And you're here, aren't you? Not locked away.'

Alfred was certain it was too late. People were so much more confusing than objects.

'I just seem to make a mess of everything.'

'None of us gets everything right. You're not the final version of yourself, you know. You can still change.'

'Perhaps,' Alfred said, thinking of a similar speech he had given to Kian not that long ago.

'Why don't you come along to my next reading-group meeting? We do a mixture, new books and some of the classics. We're reading an oldie at the moment – *Rebecca*.'

That had been Ida's favourite book. He could picture its exact place on the bookshelf, fourth from the left, three shelves down. Its pages were ragged at the edges from being read so many times. Once, when he'd been very ill with flu, she had read it out loud to him while he flitted between blazes of consciousness, her voice a tincture to ease his aching limbs. He shivered, remembering her warmth beside him. What were the chances of them discussing her favourite book? It was almost as if Ida was speaking to him, telling him that he should go.

'Yes,' he replied. 'Okay, then. Yes, I'd love to come along.'

35

Home is where the heart is

Kian lay on the sofa in the clothes he'd fallen asleep in. Ryan wasn't answering his calls and, in the end, he'd left him a voicemail letting Ryan know exactly what he thought of him and had blocked his number. At least the police hadn't come round. If Alfred or Ryan hadn't rung them yet, there was a good chance they wouldn't. If they did, he had no doubt that Chris Wilton would be begging the prison officer to let him turn the key.

Yesterday Kian had been for an interview with a telesales company and was pretty sure it had gone well. He had managed to get there on time and not mess up the questions he had to answer. The interviewer smiled at him loads and even gave him a tour of the office afterwards, pointing out where he would sit. It sounded like it was in the bag and waiting for the phone call was just a formality. A job would make Kian's case for Dan living with him stronger. The catering-college idea had been delusional, he realized that now. He wished he'd never posted the forms. It was like waiting to hear about an appointment for root-canal surgery. Dreams were exactly that. Much better to know your place, so you couldn't be disappointed.

His feet scrunched on empty beer cans and crisp packets as he made his way to the bread bin. If he didn't tidy up soon, his place was going to end up like Alfred's. He stuffed a slice of white bread into his mouth just as his phone rang. Al? He dived onto the sofa to answer it, nearly choking on his bread.

'Hello, is that Kian Matthews?' a sing-song voice asked.

'Yeah, that's me,' he replied, coughing the last crumbs of bread from this throat.

'It's Arianna from Shalcot Recruitment? Thanks for coming to the interview yesterday. The competition for the vacancy was really tough and I'm afraid you were unsuccessful this time.'

This time and every other time. The hole he was in kept getting bigger. He'd give Alfred a few more days to cool off, then he'd go round and convince him he had nothing to do with the missing medals. Otherwise whatever Alfred told Sandra when she next visited would be fed back to Chris, and Kian might as well kiss goodbye to life as he knew it.

He couldn't just sit here twiddling his thumbs, though. He had to take action. All he had to do was work out what Ryan would have done with Al's medals and see if he could get them back. Ryan was lazy, that was for sure, so he would have offloaded them in the easiest way possible. The local pawnshop had to be a good bet. It was around the corner from Ryan's flat, and he bought and sold games and CDs in there all the time.

Kian surveyed the items in the shop window: a bunch of knackered-looking computer consoles, an unloved Buzz Lightyear toy, a microwave, a portable TV and a selection of rings that signalled broken marriages or unwanted proposals. There, at the back near a selection of *Rocky* videos, he found exactly what he was looking for and punched the air. The medals shone from their silk-lined case. It had been almost too easy.

A young woman walked out of the shop carrying a pink trike with a ribbon on the handlebars. That was going to make some little kid's day. He pushed open the door and a little bell alerted the assistant to his arrival.

'Er, 'scuse me?' Kian said, striding over to the counter. 'How much are those war medals in the window? I mean, I want to buy them.'

'Rightio – two hundred smackeroonies then, please.' He opened up a brown paper bag, ready to drop the medals inside.

'You're having a laugh. I know for a fact you paid one hundred. How much really?'

'As I said: two hundred. Take it or leave it. I'm not forcing you to buy them, am I, pal? Had quite a bit of interest in these already – genuine article,' he said, pushing his glasses up along the bridge of his nose. The guy wasn't going to budge. He haggled for a living and knew the ropes.

Kian left the shop and stood outside, remembering Alfred at the cathedral on Remembrance Day, and what he'd shared about the death of his friend, Jim. He couldn't risk someone else buying them. They belonged with Al and he had to have them back, no matter what the cost.

The guy was still behind the counter, wiping down some CDs with a yellow cloth. He didn't even look up when Kian stood in front of him. He'd known Kian would come back.

'All right, mate, I'll take 'em,' Kian said. 'Can I just pay a deposit, though? 'Til I get the rest of the cash?' He took his dole money out of his wallet and laid the notes in front of him.

'One day only, on deposits. Get the rest to me tomorrow and I'll keep them to one side for ya.'

Everyone knew that Kelly Anderson was not to be messed with. Everyone also knew that she was the fastest way to get your hands on some cash. The address he'd been given in the pub was only a ten-minute walk from Kian's house. As soon as Kian knocked on the door, a huge dog pounded at the glass between them. If its bark was anything to go by, it wanted to tear him to pieces. He took several steps back. A woman shouted at the dog to shut up as she lifted the latch on the door and undid several bolts.

'All right, love, don't mind Jaws,' Kelly said as she answered the door, gripping the collar of the huge Alsatian. It growled, a pool of saliva leaving the corners of its mouth and landing by his feet. Kian could swear it licked its lips as he walked past.

Kelly's hair was tied in a messy bun and she was wearing a tight polo-neck jumper tucked into some designer jeans. Her nails were painted the same shade of pink as her fluffy slippers, and a silver heart-shaped locket hung from her neck.

'Want a cuppa?'

Kian wanted to get out of there as fast as possible. 'No, ta. Let's just get down to business,' he said, as if he was in a boardroom about to pitch a winning proposal.

The sofa in Kelly's front room was covered in plastic and the cream carpet looked brand-new. There were photos everywhere in frames, and little signs that said things like *family* and *Home is where the heart is*. The pictures were of Kelly with her kids or her mates, or some tanned bloke on a beach. Kian didn't know why he was so nervous. She had a family. Surely that meant she wasn't as bad as her reputation made her out to be?

'So,' Kelly said, opening up a black notebook with an elastic band around it. 'How much?' She licked her thumb a couple of times before flicking to a blank page. Jaws had settled by her feet and didn't take his eyes off Kian.

'Two hundred?' Kian suggested. A bit extra would tide him over nicely.

Kelly smirked. 'I don't do less than three hundred, kid. This ain't a charity. You borrow that or nothing.'

It was way too much. Kian wasn't stupid. He'd be paying it back for months. There was no point taking on a huge debt that he didn't need, and the sooner his relationship with Kelly Anderson was over, the better.

'I can't do that. Two hundred quid or I'm out,' Kian replied, trying to disguise the fear in his voice by speaking loudly.

Jaws growled again and Kian shuffled to the edge of his seat, keeping the door in his peripheral vision.

'Shut it, Jaws darlin'. Okay, as it's nearly Christmas and you've caught me in a good mood, I'll let you have two hundred this one time.'

'Cheers,' Kian said. Kelly looked like the sort of person who liked to drive a hard bargain. He'd been lucky. He smiled. 'I mean, thanks. Thanks a lot.'

'Don't thank me, mate. Just make your payments on time or you'll wish you'd never met me.'

Kian stopped smiling. Kelly wrote something down on a piece of paper and explained it was his payment schedule. He had to come round every two weeks with the money he owed or she'd come and find him. And, she said, looking at him with a hard stare, he didn't want that.

Jaws licked his lips again. Kian didn't need to worry about that right now. The repayments were a future problem.

He left Kelly's and stuffed his hands in his pockets. He felt something sharp, pulled it out and held it out in front of him. It was one of Al's wooden soldiers, the one he'd taken when he'd been sure he would never see the old dude again. He tucked it back safely and wrapped his fingers around it. Feeling determined, he headed straight back to the pawnshop.

36

Absolution

Alfred read the letter from Sandra for the fifth time and then consoled himself by counting his tins. With a bit of luck, the millennium scaremongering would come to something. Sandra would no doubt have typed up all her records meticulously, so the possibility that the computer might spontaneously combust on 1 January was the only hope that remained. Then there would be no proof that any of this nightmare had ever happened. The slate would be wiped clean and he could forget about it all.

He poured himself another drink, even though it did nothing to blur his misery. He hated the fact that he missed Kian, and he wondered how Dan was getting on. Just then someone knocked on the door and even though he was still in his pyjamas, Alfred raced to open it. Kian would have to work hard to earn his forgiveness, but wasn't Christmas all about letting bygones be bygones?

An elderly woman in a pale-blue coat that matched her eyes was standing on his doorstep.

'Oh. Can I help you?' Alfred said. She looked too old to be selling anything.

'Alfred? It's Emmeline. I got your letters.'

A soft squawking noise emitted from his throat. How was it possible? He'd completely forgotten that Kian had persuaded him to post the letters he'd written.

'Could I come in?' Emmeline asked.

'Sorry, I'm not dressed. Um, yes. Of course, come in.' Alfred followed her inside. 'Let me switch the stove off,' he called, even though it wasn't on. In the kitchen he leaned against the fridge and closed his eyes. Emmeline was in his living room. His comeuppance had caught up with him, after all. The kettle boiled all too quickly as he carefully assembled a tea tray with shaking hands. Which biscuits would be best to accompany his demise? He decided on chocolate digestives and placed them on the table.

'I won't stay long,' Emmeline said.

Good – quick, painless.

'I'm sorry about the mess,' Alfred replied. 'I'm having a bit of a clear-out.'

'Alfred, I read your letters and I started to write back, then I realized I needed to see you in person.'

'I see.' Alfred dipped his head as if expecting an onslaught of rain. He deserved everything he got. He would let Emmeline do her worst.

'I want you to know that I don't hold you responsible for what happened to Jim.'

'You don't?'

'Far from it. When Jim wrote to me, he talked about you, you know. He said you told him stories at night, when the shellfire was raining down around you.'

Shouldn't she be firing missiles at him? 'Aren't you angry with me? I left him. I didn't mean to, but I did and . . . I'm so, so sorry.'

'I can only imagine what you all went through. I think Jim tried to hide the very worst of it from me. I could tell it was truly awful. I mean, I now know, of course. I know that you did your best. You were a boy, Alfred, and it pains me to think you've carried this with you since then.'

'I've never forgiven myself. You lost so much because of me – my cowardice.'

Emmeline smiled at him. 'It wasn't your fault Jim died. I suppose it probably wasn't even the fault of the soldier who killed him. He was just following instructions, the same as you all were. What could you really have done, if you'd tried to save Jim? He would have bled to death, regardless, and you would probably have ended up being killed yourself.'

'Perhaps,' Alfred muttered. It was very decent of Emmeline to come here and try to patch him back together. He really didn't deserve it.

'I suppose what I came here to say is that Jim's final days were better for having you in them. You made him laugh. You kept him going. You touched both of our lives because knowing he had you, well, that gave strength to me. I can see how hard all this has been for you, but perhaps it's time to let the past go.'

Was it really that simple? Despite what he'd said to Kian about the past being behind you, Alfred didn't really believe it could slip from your fingers that easily.

'I know it must be a shock – me turning up like this. I'd like you to have this. I should have sent it to you long ago. I never reread Jim's letters until recently. I packed them away when his belongings were returned to me. I mean, there wasn't much really: his belt and a watch. A couple of photographs.' It wasn't enough to sum up a man's life.

Emmeline passed him a creased piece of paper. It was a letter in Jim's handwriting. It was addressed to her.

'I don't think I should read this. It's yours. It's personal.'

'Look at the middle paragraph, Alfred. I want you to keep the letter and read that again and again until you see the truth. You didn't let Jim down. You kept him going.'

Emmeline picked up her coat and left. Alfred worked his way through the plate of digestives before reading the letter. He quickly skimmed over the declarations of love for Emmeline until he reached the part that she had wanted him to read:

I'm so lucky to have such a good friend in Alfred. Sometimes I feel like I can't carry on and, in those moments, when it feels like there is nothing but despair, he gives me the courage to keep going. He's so brave, Em, and that makes me stronger. He's like a brother to me. If anything ever happens to me, I want you to make sure he knows that.

The words choked Alfred. He could let himself be defined by guilt or he could see that he had made a difference to someone's life, even if, ultimately, he hadn't been able to save Jim. Alfred stood up, but only got as far as the sideboard before he doubled over and burst into tears. He grabbed a box of tissues, but the sadness was spilling out of him faster than he could mop it up.

37

Christmas spirit

Alfred hardly ever set foot in his bedroom, due to the lack of space. He'd much rather let the room be filled with his prized collections. Today, he squeezed in among the boxes and stared out of the window. The trees swayed in the wind, with bare branches mourning the loss of their leaves, now hidden under a sweep of snow. The garden used to be Ida's pride and joy. Perhaps, when the snow melted, he would plant some bulbs – trumpeting daffodils to herald in the spring.

He remembered when they first set eyes on this house, fifty-five years ago. The smell of paint, the space filled with possibility. They had been so excited as they ran upstairs to look in all the rooms, like children going on a school trip. In this exact spot Ida laid claim to the place. Her dark hair tumbled down past her shoulders and her wool coat was undone. She looked out of the window and said, 'I love it, Alfred, don't you? Plenty of room for Maggie to run around. And just look at the garden. It's beautiful. I'm going to plant apple trees, right over there, and you can have a pie with custard every Sunday.'

She'd known that would persuade him. He did like his food. But it wasn't the promise of weekly desserts that sold it to Alfred. He simply wanted to make Ida happy. The flat they lived in was poky at best and was always damp. The garden was shared, and Ida had dreamed of having one of their own for Maggie to play in. This place was the perfect home for a family. His family. He should never have let Maggie go.

Yes, it was the perfect place for a family and was far too big for him on his own. He'd never leave, though. It was all he had left of Ida. He could feel her in every room, almost hear her laughing over her sewing machine as she made some new cushion covers, or a skirt for Maggie, which she'd subsequently spend the entire summer hitching up to make shorter. The pain created by Ida's absence was still there, a faded bruise that made itself known with only the slightest prod.

Something had shifted in Alfred since Emmeline's visit. Her forgiveness was so unexpected and so generous. It had lit the fading embers of his self-worth and reminded him that change was possible. He wanted to fix matters; he just didn't know how. He walked from room to room, unable to settle until he came across a packet of unopened Christmas cards he'd purchased some years ago. He placed them on the table and took out his Windsor fountain pen. He wrote one for Maggie, even though it was too late to post it. After some hesitation, he wrote one for Kian, thinking of Emmeline's words about letting go of the past. He looked at the remaining eight cards. He could put them away and make them last for the next four years, or he could post them through his neighbours' doors. He had no idea of any of their names. In fact, he was only vaguely aware of their existence when the people next door had their television on too loud. He simply signed all eight *from Alfred at 132* and put on his coat and hat. Despite it being such a small gesture, he felt like Ebenezer Scrooge delivering a turkey to the Cratchits as he waltzed across the snow-covered pavements and popped them through the swinging letter boxes.

When he got back, he unwrapped a slab of Christmas cake, put Tchaikovsky's *Nutcracker* on the record player, closed his eyes and disappeared into a rhapsody of dancing snowflakes and gingerbread soldiers. When Maggie was seven or eight he took her to see *The Nutcracker* at the theatre. It was a night-time performance, and all the Christmas lights were on in town. They'd taken the bus and she kept showing the other passengers her ballet pumps. Once they were seated, Alfred put some coins in the little slot that released binoculars and Maggie was spellbound the entire time. Halfway through, he stopped watching the show and watched her instead.

He put the rest of the cake back in the tin. It was a little dry. Ida used to make the most delicious Christmas cake, covered in a layer of royal-icing snow. The aroma of brandy and marzipan would cling to his clothes for days. They would hang up the stockings and sing carols together on Christmas Eve while Maggie constructed miles of paper chains to decorate the walls. It was magical. However, magic was only an illusion.

He tucked Maggie's Christmas card underneath a magazine. It was probably too late to repair things. She wasn't one of his ornaments or trinkets that could be mended and, anyway, he didn't have the right tools. But he'd realized something. He didn't want to be alone this Christmas and, despite everything, he couldn't think of anyone he wanted to spend it with, other than Kian.

38

The future is now

The letter Kian had been waiting for had finally arrived. He stared at the brown envelope, stamped with the logo of the catering college. There was a chance that it was good news. If it was, maybe Al would let him back in. Then he could give Alfred the medals, and everything could go back to the way it was. The more he thought about it, the more Kian decided he deserved this chance. He was going to train to be a chef. One day maybe he'd have his own little restaurant. Dan could come and have dinner with his mates and say, 'My brother's the chef!' Kian really believed in it now. He would pay Kelly off, get Chris off his back and begin again. He'd get a part-time job, contest Dan's adoption, get a flat big enough so that his brother could have his own room. The year 2000 was going to be his year. About bloody time.

If he got in, he'd ring Chloe, see if she wanted to celebrate with him. Although he'd wanted to, he hadn't yet replied to her note. There had been too much else going on. He pulled on a hoodie, shoved his keys in his pocket and ripped open the envelope as he walked towards the front door:

Dear Kian,

Thank you for your application, which we read with

interest. We regret to inform you that on this occasion you have been unsuccessful in securing a place on our Professional Cookery Diploma course. Although we were impressed with your enthusiasm, we expect candidates to have relevant qualifications or already be working in catering in some capacity. Do apply again when you have gained some experience or qualifications to support your application. Please see an updated list of fees for our 2001 course, which we hope will be useful.

Yours sincerely,

Phil Wise, Admissions Officer

If he was already working in catering, then he wouldn't need to do a bloody course, would he? Kian shouted into his empty flat. And fees? He hadn't even thought about it costing hundreds of pounds. Even if he had got a place, there was no way he'd be able to afford to attend. Why was everything always stacked against him? He paced around the kitchen, unsure what to do. Without reading the letter again, he shredded it into pieces and let his future fall into the bin. Why was he even surprised? He'd been kidding himself by thinking something would go right for him.

To add to his misery, he would have to tell Al, the person who had encouraged him to apply in the first place. Kian had just proved he was useless. And then there was Chris. If he'd laughed before, he'd be hysterical now. Kian hadn't even made it to the interview stage. He rubbed at a coffee-mug stain on the counter until his finger was sore.

His phone rang and he jumped to answer it. It was Dan's foster mum, Simone, who only ever rang him if there was a problem.

'Hello? Is Danny okay?'

'Hi, Kian, Dan's fine. Don't worry. But he's a little upset and he wanted me to tell you something.'

'Tell me what?' Kian said, reaching for his cigarettes to quell the stabbing pain in his chest.

'He met his new parents at the weekend.'

'Already? Did it go okay?' No wonder Dan was upset. Kian should have done more to stop it happening. He was his big brother. He was meant to protect Dan.

'Better than okay. It went really well. He's seeing them again in a couple of days, but he's convinced you'll be cross with him.'

'Cross with him? I'm bloody furious. Not with him – with the whole screwed-up system. Dan should be with me, right?'

'Sometimes it's hard to see the bigger picture,' Simone said. 'The decision's been deemed the best one for Dan. I know it feels hard, but deep down, that's what you want for him, too.'

Simone didn't need to spell it out. It was obvious no one thought Kian had what it took to look after Dan. The adoption was really happening. He hadn't even had time to put a case together and make it all stop. And now it was final. Game over.

He slumped against the door as someone thumped it loudly from the outside. Surely Kelly wouldn't be chasing him yet? Kian froze. If he didn't make a sound, whoever it was might think he was out. Unless they'd been watching his flat. Another bang, more forceful this time. Alfred flashed through his mind. Now Kian knew how it felt to be scared of the unknown threat on the other side of his front door. No wonder the poor guy had a heart attack.

He opened the door a fraction while keeping his weight

pressed against it. Through the gap, he saw two police officers holding up their badges. Al had done it; he'd called the police.

'Kian Matthews? I'm arresting you on suspicion of assault.'

'Assault? What you on about?'

The police officer reeled off Kian's right to remain silent, like he hadn't heard it all before. This didn't make sense. So not Alfred, but Ryan. Ryan, his best mate since they were little kids, had called the cops on him.

'Well,' said Chris. 'Dear, oh dear. What do we have here then? Up for assault, just a few days before I was about to sign you off. Looks like I can cancel my inspection at Mr Ainswick's then. No point now.' He took out his A4 diary and scrawled a line through one of the pages. He followed this up by shaking his head.

Kian imagined the pleasure of swinging for him, but remained sitting on his hands. Having to listen to Chris come over all sanctimonious on him was possibly worse than being arrested. For Chris, it was probably the highlight of his week.

'Yeah, well, it wasn't exactly my fault, was it?' Kian said, not looking up from the floor.

'Never is, eh, lad? Kian, Kian, Kian . . . when will you ever learn? Remember those anger techniques we've been working on? The whole point was to stop you ending up in a situation like this. Looks like you're heading back to the courts. Seems like this is the end of the road. I mean, I've done my best with you – all these file notes back me up on that.' He tapped the folder on the desk in front of him. 'There's a point where it comes down to you, and you alone.'

Kian clenched his jaw. Even though his life hadn't exactly

ever been a picnic, the past few days were the worst he'd ever experienced. His best friend had properly screwed him over, he'd lost Dan, he didn't have a place at college, and Al still thought he was a thief. And now, after all that hard work clearing up Al's place, it looked like he was gonna be banged up anyway.

'Doesn't all that restorative-justice work count for anything? I mean, what was the bloody point of it?'

'I can't stop the police from pursuing justice, now can I, lad? But if we have a positive review meeting with Mr Ainswick and his social worker in the New Year, it might just go in your favour.'

Kian groaned. It was all over. Alfred was the last person to say anything positive about him right now, even if he did get his medals back.

He was going to prison, end of. Al was never going to forgive him. Even so, he had to put things right this time. He had let Lucy believe the worst of him and he wouldn't make the same mistake with Alfred.

39

Reading *Rebecca*

A few days before Christmas, Alfred had stayed up into the early hours reading *Rebecca*, in time for his first reading-group meeting. It wasn't only the gripping plot that kept him awake. Twice he fell asleep, then woke suddenly, thinking about Kian. Chris had called him earlier that day to cancel his inspection. Alfred was delighted to have a reprieve from any authorities snooping around his home, but he couldn't help wondering if Kian was in trouble. Chris had refused to give him any details when he'd asked.

He combed his hair in the mirror and gargled with mouthwash. The last time he'd done anything remotely sociable in a group was when Ida was still alive. What if the others didn't like him? What if he made a fool of himself? It might be for the best if he had a terrible evening, so that he didn't have to put himself through this again.

He read through the notes he'd written on plot and character in his pocketbook, even though Meena had assured him that he wouldn't be put on the spot and only had to chat if he felt comfortable. Then he baked some Florentines to take with him. Rather than being a kind gesture, it was so that he had something to fall back on, if it all became a bit awkward.

Florentines had the sort of chewiness that could account for the longest of silences. After wrapping them up in a sheet of tin foil, Alfred left the house, checking twice that he had locked the front door.

The group met in a room at the back of the Bull's Head pub. The place was heaving with people. Lots of them were wearing Santa hats or bits of tinsel, jeering loudly and singing. Alfred considered leaving, but Meena waved to him from the far corner to show him where they were sitting. He bought himself a large brandy and joined them, clutching his copy of *Rebecca* tightly to his chest as if it were a shield.

'Everybody, this is my friend Alfred,' Meena said. 'Alfred, this is Anne, Ed, Saira and Elaine.'

Alfred's eyes darted across the small assembled group. They smiled and waved. As he sat down, he realized Meena had described him as a friend. If it was true, it was the first time in a long while that anyone had considered him in that way. It gave him a little nudge of encouragement.

'Hello, everybody,' Alfred replied, flicking open his book as though he might be asked a dozen questions about the text right away. He kept his Florentines in his coat pocket, in case of emergencies.

The others asked him how he was, how he knew Meena and what he thought of the book. Without even touching his brandy, he was able to answer everything.

'I'm very well, thank you. We met in the charity shop. And I was struck with the similarities to *Jane Eyre*.'

Anne laughed and put down her orange juice. 'Succinct. That's what I like, Alfred. Not like Meena here. She'll talk us all into an early grave.'

Meena poked her in the arm. 'Ignore Anne. Now, who'd like

to start the ball rolling on *Rebecca*? I must say, Alfred, your copy has a beautiful cover.'

He held out the book for everyone to see. Its dust jacket featured an illustration of Manderley, seen in the distance through a gap in towering green leaves. 'Ah, well, it's a first edition, you see. Pretty rare. I bought this for my late wife, who was a huge fan of du Maurier. It's actually signed by the author.'

There were audible gasps from the group and Alfred let them pass it around, only warning them once to handle it carefully.

'That must be worth a bit?' Ed asked, as he handed it back to Alfred.

'It probably is,' Alfred said. 'But it means more to me than money. Ida, my wife, she loved this book, you see.'

Ed nodded, and Meena patted his shoulder gently. Although Alfred was tempted to expand on the topic of antiquarian books, he wasn't sure that the others would appreciate it. As he'd prepared so well and had written notes on *Rebecca*, he might as well share them.

'I was particularly taken with the theme of escaping the past. Maxim has to face the memory of his actions before he can move forward,' Alfred went on. If only it were that easy for him. His own past was too visceral and binding to extract himself from.

'I noticed that too,' Meena agreed, forcing a hint of colour to spread across Alfred's cheeks.

The conversation was lively and flowed well into the evening. Who knew there could be so much to say about one book? Alfred hadn't even opened the package of Florentines. As the others left, they wished him a merry Christmas as if they were old friends. Alfred stayed behind to share another drink with Meena, surprising himself by not wanting to rush off at the first opportunity.

'How will you be spending Christmas Day?' Alfred asked.

'I'll have tea with some friends in the evening, but during the day I help to make Christmas lunch at the homeless shelter in town.'

Meena was incredibly generous. It put him to shame.

'That's very kind of you. It sounds rather exhausting, though.'

'I ran a cafe for thirty years. It's like water off a duck's back. How will you be spending the day?'

'I was supposed to be cooking Christmas lunch for a friend, only now I'm not so sure. Anyway, thank you for inviting me this evening. I really enjoyed it.'

'Great, we'll see you next month then. I'm planning on going for a walk on New Year's Day. You could join me, if you like? A good start to the New Year, I always find.'

It would be the first thing Alfred would write on his calendar for 2000. Maybe this year it would contain more than the date of his annual dental check-up.

It was late when he arrived home. The previous day he had decided to follow Kian's advice to put up his Christmas decorations and he returned to a glittering grotto, which was a delightful welcome. It was just a shame there was no one else to see it. He found his *Christmas Classics* LP and placed it on the record player. As heavenly voices lilted into the room, Alfred curled up underneath a blanket and treated himself to a celebratory mince pie. It was like a cold-weather front had finally lifted. The flickering lights, the soothing music and the pleasure of connecting with people again had revived him. Perhaps everything would be all right after all.

40

A bad penny

When Kian was a kid, the first thing he'd do on Christmas Day was open the curtains to see if there was snow. Now he knew better than to expect it. They'd had some the previous week, which had melted as quickly as Kian's hopes for Dan living with him. Outside it was grey and dull and, to match, inside his flat looked miserable. The spindly piece of tinsel hanging from one of the kitchen walls and the two Christmas cards above the electric heater hadn't exactly filled the place with festive spirit. He'd also eaten all the chocolate from his advent calendar weeks ago. His microwave Christmas dinner sat in the fridge next to a bag of satsumas that were past their expiry date.

He had no idea what his real family was doing right now. Dan would be at his foster home, probably enjoying the Scalextric he knew he was getting, and maybe playing with the football that Kian had bought him. They'd spoken only once since Kian had forgotten about watching the footie with his brother. Dan hadn't said much, which just made Kian feel even worse, especially now that he knew Dan would be moving to live with his new parents soon. He couldn't wait to see him and properly make it up to him.

He guessed his mum would be cooking something for her

fiancé, not giving a toss about how Kian would be spending the day. Gav and Ryan hadn't spoken to him since the punch-up and he was pretty certain their friendship was over. It was no great loss. Or at least it wouldn't be, if Kian actually had other friends.

He'd thought about this moment ever since he'd left the pawnshop and, as he arrived at Alfred's, Kian felt light-headed as he rang the doorbell.

Alfred opened the front door, wearing an apron over a red sweater. His face fell. 'Like a bad penny,' he said, turning to go back inside.

Kian followed him in, despite the lack of invitation. 'I got you a present,' he said, handing over the badly wrapped parcel. 'Open it.'

'Is this supposed to make up for what you've done?' Alfred put the gift on the table and stared at him. He wasn't going to make this easy.

'Just so you know, I didn't take your medals. I wouldn't do that to you. You're a friend. But I found out who did, and I got them back for you.'

Alfred ripped open the paper. His face lit up as he lifted the lid of the case containing his medals, although moments later his eyes became very watery and he put his head in his hands.

'I'm not sure what to believe, but thank you. Thank you for bringing them back to me.'

Kian could still hear Alfred's words from when they last met: *Once a thief, always a thief*. It didn't matter if the old man didn't believe him. It only mattered that he got his medals back.

Alfred handed him a glass of mulled wine that smelled of

cinnamon and oranges and invited Kian to take a seat at the table, which was covered with a tartan tablecloth and had been decorated with candles, pinecones and holly. There was a Christmas tree, and twinkling lights everywhere.

'You might as well stay for lunch, now you're here. I've made far too much for one.'

Kian hadn't planned on staying. However, the smell of pigs in blankets and roasted potatoes was too good to turn down. Alfred came back holding a huge bronzed turkey and placed it on the table, which Kian now noticed was set for two.

'Expecting someone?' he asked, unsure if he should take off his coat.

Alfred carved the turkey and set the cuts of meat on a huge silver platter.

'To be honest, I was hoping that you'd turn up. I've been worried about you actually, and I've learned some things in the past few days that have made me look at life a bit differently. And you've brought my medals back – that's the main thing. Hungry?'

'Yeah. This all looks amazing,' Kian said, nodding towards the feast laid out before him.

The food was delicious. They ate mostly in silence; there was so much to say that neither of them knew where to begin.

'Now for the *pièce de résistance*,' Alfred said, once they'd cleared the plates away. He passed Kian a fire extinguisher, doused the Christmas pudding in brandy and lit a match.

Kian stepped back as a circle of blue flames formed a halo around the pudding. He tucked into his portion and was about to say how nice it was, when he bit on something hard. He pulled it out of his mouth. 'Argh, what's this?'

'Oh yes, I should have warned you. You found the hidden

silver sixpence! It means you'll have good luck for the coming year.'

'What's lucky about almost breaking a tooth, Al?'

They both laughed and the tension between them eased. They pulled an entire box of Christmas crackers, put on paper crowns and read each other corny jokes. Alfred had won a small box of playing cards and taught Kian how to play Crazy Eights. It was the most fun Christmas since Kian had been a kid.

'I'd like to make a toast,' Alfred said. 'Here's to friendship!'

'Cheers,' Kian replied, tentatively tapping his glass against Al's. He was still half expecting Alfred to start shouting at him again and, even if things were okay between them now, there was little to celebrate. He'd done a pretty good job of pressing the self-destruct button on his life. Once today was over with, he would just go back to an endless list of problems – the worst being that Dan was moving away, breaking Kian's heart into a million pieces in the process.

'So I've got something to tell you,' Kian said as they washed and dried the dishes.

'Go on,' Alfred encouraged him. 'Don't worry about the roasting dish. We can leave that one to soak. I tell you what, why don't we go back into the living room and I'll crack open the sherry.'

Kian hated telling Alfred about being rejected from college, so he made it sound like he wasn't really that bothered. But Alfred evidently knew him better than he thought.

'Well, I shall be writing to that Admissions Officer on your behalf! In the meantime, we'll work something out – a way to get you some experience, so you can apply next year. Leave it with me.'

'Even if I get some experience, there's the small matter of

the fees. There's no way I can afford it. And I didn't mention it before, but I got into a bit of trouble with the police. When we have our review meeting, it's a dead cert that Chris will be telling the courts I failed my programme.'

'But you've worked so hard! Don't give up. We just need to come up with a plan.'

Kian sighed. Alfred hadn't exactly proved that he was capable of problem-solving. He shifted the focus back to where it needed to be. 'Anyway, Sandra's needs assessment is in only a few weeks. It might be too late for me, but it's not for you. We've got our work cut out. You didn't sell any of the stuff we packed up then?'

'No. About that: I was wondering if we could find some temporary storage somewhere. It seems a bit drastic letting these things go. As you've rightly pointed out, they're quite valuable.'

'I thought you didn't care about their value?'

They were back to square one. Kian couldn't blame Alfred. He understood him feeling that it was all a waste of time, like his future was predetermined anyway and whatever he did wasn't going to make a sodding bit of difference. Kian started to clear some bits and pieces away. The mess in the house made his skin itch. If he could get it looking at least a bit tidier, Sandra might go easy on him and then maybe, just maybe, Chris might give him a break.

'Hey, you got a few Christmas cards,' Kian said, noticing the pile of envelopes on the table. Alfred was busy whipping up some home-made mince pies in the kitchen and so Kian opened them for him. The first few were from some of the neighbours in the street. Kian propped them up on the mantelpiece, noting that Alfred, who never spoke to anyone, had more cards than he'd got himself. The last card stopped him still. He let the envelope fall to the floor as he read:

Dear Dad,

I'm sorry to put this in a Christmas card. I wasn't sure you'd open a letter and I've tried telling you this over the phone, and then again when we bumped into each other, but it's been impossible. I thought you should know that I'm sick, Dad. I'm sick and I'm scared. I have cancer and I've recently had surgery. Also, Ethan and I split up, so I'm dealing with this all on my own.

I know this is a lot to take in, out of the blue. I'd like you to come round on Christmas Day. Please. But if you don't, then this is the last time you'll hear from me. I can't keep being the only one of us to try. Life is short, Dad.

Yours, Maggie

'Al? Al, get in here. You need to read this.'

41

Hold on

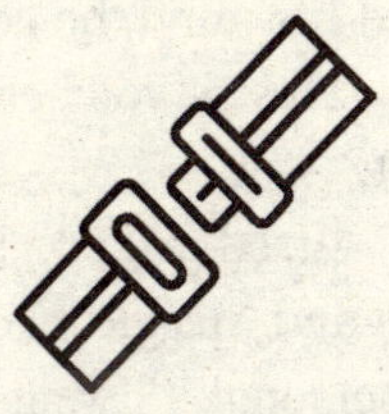

How was it possible to be sweating and freezing cold at the same time? Alfred unbuttoned his coat and did it right back up again.

'You've got your seatbelt on, yeah?' Kian said. 'Just as well Gav hasn't asked for his van back yet. Hold on. I reckon I can get us there in half an hour.'

'I've been holding on all this time, but to the wrong things,' Alfred muttered, his voice disappearing under the noise of the van's de-mister.

Kian pulled off the main road, put his foot down and thrust the van into fifth gear, even though the roads were largely deserted. Alfred tutted, before remembering that he should be grateful Kian was getting him there quickly. It was late afternoon. Maggie would think he wasn't coming. It had crossed his mind that morning that he should phone her to say, 'Happy Christmas', only he hadn't been in the mood for a lecture. Now he'd sit through hours of lectures for the chance to know that she was okay.

'Shortcut,' Kian announced.

Soon the familiarity of high-rise buildings and housing estates gave way to a landscape of smart semis and long lawns.

Although Alfred circled his thumb over his pocket watch, it failed to make him feel grounded. When they arrived in Maggie's driveway, his fingers hovered over the buckle of his seatbelt. He couldn't do this. His legs were leaden.

As if Kian could read his mind, he got out first and opened Alfred's door for him. 'This is your chance to fix things, Al. Come on – out you get.'

'You'll come too?' Alfred asked, his nerves creating a forcefield between him and Maggie's home.

'I dunno. It's a bit personal. I'll wait in the van.'

'It would mean a lot to me,' Alfred said.

Kian followed him up the path. It had been years since Alfred had last visited. The door had been painted a different colour and there were shutters now, instead of curtains. What else had changed? Alfred rang the doorbell and waited. 'I don't think I can do this,' he said, turning to face the street.

'Course you can. We're here now.' Kian ushered him towards the door again.

'I don't know what to say.'

'You'll think of something.'

Alfred was short of breath, like he was being crushed from within.

'Dad?' Maggie had opened the door. Her face was pale, and she squinted as if her eyes were trying to adjust after leaving a dark room. Alfred hadn't even considered the fact that it was Christmas Day and she might have company. Maggie didn't smile as she told them to both come in.

The living room was neat and tidy, a reminder of the huge difference in the way they lived. There was a distinct absence of cooking smells, and Alfred thought guiltily about the huge turkey he had roasted and the invitation he hadn't extended to Maggie.

'Happy Christmas. I've brought some mince pies,' Alfred said, waving a plate wrapped in clingfilm as if it was a white flag. 'You're alone?'

'Yes, Dad, I'm alone. Ethan moved out a few months ago, and I didn't want to impose on my friends. It's a time for families.'

A spear shot through Alfred's heart. He had wasted so much time. He quickly introduced Kian, without revealing too much about their arrangement. The last thing he wanted was Maggie thinking he was only here because he needed her help.

Kian was charming and offered to make everyone tea, so that father and daughter could have a chance to talk. But once he had left the room, Alfred had no idea what to say. It was as if the curtains had been pulled back to reveal him standing onstage in front of a huge audience. His mouth was dry, like it was full of cornflakes, and his legs felt as if they'd give way.

After a few moments of them staring at each other, Alfred realized it really was very simple. There were no adequate words. He would rely on what he understood best: the power of objects. He took Maggie's hand and placed something in it that symbolized everything he could possibly think of to say, and more.

Maggie gripped it tightly. 'Dad, are you sure?'

'Yes.' Alfred had never been more certain.

Maggie uncurled her fingers and stared at the item resting in the palm of her hand: the spare key to Alfred's front door.

42

Rollercoaster

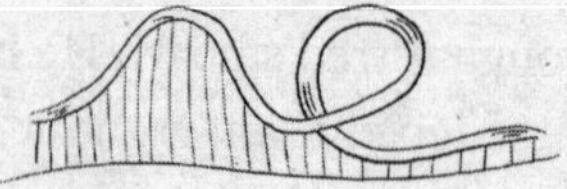

Life was a bit like juggling – a skill Kian hadn't mastered. Sure, he had all the balls; he just didn't have a clue what to do with them. No sooner had one flown into the air than another crashed to the ground. The situation with Alfred was better now. It was everything else that was bleak.

Kian looked inside his wallet as if he was expecting to see something other than the twenty-five pounds that were destined for Kelly Anderson's pocket. Thinking about her made his stomach lurch, like the time he rode the Corkscrew rollercoaster at Alton Towers. Just as it teetered on the brink of a huge loop-the-loop, he'd screamed his head off. Like then, Kian wished he could make it stop. He'd changed his mind and now wanted to get off. Kelly might forgive a little lateness, but not turning up at all would have her starving Jaws of his evening meal, to make tearing him to pieces the next day even more enjoyable. There was no choice but to ask Kelly for a little payment holiday. He'd promised to give Dan a nice send-off before he moved away to live with his new parents, and even though he couldn't bear the thought of saying goodbye, not having the chance to do it properly would be so much worse.

Bracing himself for the assault of barks from Jaws, Kian rang

Kelly's doorbell and stepped back. A tuneless rendition of 'Greensleeves' chimed out and he suddenly really fancied a 99 ice cream.

'Come on in, love,' Kelly said. Jaws was suspiciously quiet, possibly gnawing the bones of a previous visitor. Her black book appeared on her lap before Kian had even sat down. 'So, let's look here a minute . . . That's right. Fifty quid, yeah?'

'Twenty-five,' Kian replied, pulling out his wallet.

'Oh yeah. Right you are, love.' Kelly opened a packet of cigarettes, taking one out and then putting it back again. 'Tryin' to give up.'

Kian exhaled loudly as he took out the money he owed and placed it on the table next to him. At that precise moment Jaws wandered in from the kitchen and snarled. Kian lifted up his feet as the Alsatian passed him and nestled at Kelly's side. He was beginning to wish he'd never borrowed any money in the first place. If he could afford it, he'd pay her back everything right now.

'So your next payment's on . . . the first of January, yeah?'

New Year's Day? Wouldn't Kelly be sleeping off a hangover then, like most normal people?

'Er, yeah – about that. I've got a few things to take care of, so I was wondering, d'you do extensions?' He winked at her and immediately regretted it.

Kelly slammed her notebook shut, a storm brewing in her eyes. 'You havin' a laugh? I told you last time, this ain't a bleedin' charity. You agree to the terms, you stick to them.'

'Yeah, I know. It's just that—'

'Tell you what. I'll add another fifty to the amount you've borrowed. Then you can spread the payments out over a longer period. But your next payment's still the first of Jan – end of. And don't say I haven't gone easy on you, mate.'

'I don't want to borrow any more. I want to pay you back a bit later. I'll give you two payments next time.' Kian's voice had become unsteady.

'And where's my insurance? How do I know you'll pay me back when you say you will? You break this payment, you might break 'em all. Then I might have to break both your bleedin' legs,' Kelly sneered. Jaws, who was now snoring quietly on the floor, suddenly looked friendly in comparison.

Kian needed a bit of extra time, 'til his benefits were paid in again in the New Year. What could he appease her with? The only thing he had of any worth was the watch Alfred had given him.

'I could give you this,' he said, flashing the watch in her direction. 'As insurance. You give it back to me when I come round with the money.'

Kelly stood up and held his wrist as if she was taking his pulse. If she had been, he was pretty sure she'd be ringing for an ambulance.

'Nah. This time I trust you, but don't let me down. Get yourself here first thing, first of January, with my money or else. Fifty quid, *capeesh*?'

'Crystal clear,' Kian said.

43

Should auld acquaintance be forgot

Instead of excitement, the first day of the millennium brought with it a feeling that Kian was standing on quicksand. Another year had passed by, with nothing to show for it. The year that lay ahead of him looked even worse. For some reason, in the game of Snakes and Ladders of life he was at the bottom and some other sod had taken all the ladders.

He hadn't gone out celebrating last night and went to bed before ten, only the constant barrage of fireworks and people shouting and singing in the street made sleep impossible. Gav and Ryan would have been out, having the time of their lives. He realized now why Ryan had said that when they were old, people would ask what they did for the millennium. It was a life-defining moment, and the fact that Kian had spent it alone said it all.

At least he didn't have a hangover, and he'd made it on time to collect Dan. As they stood in the queue at the new multiplex cinema, Kian squeezed his brother's hand and Dan didn't complain that he was too old. After paying for the tickets for *Muppets from Space*, Kian bought two huge Cokes, a tub of popcorn and a tray of nachos. Kelly could wait until tomorrow.

Dan talked excitedly through all the trailers, as if he wasn't moving to Telford to live with his new adoptive parents in a few days, ready to start a new school at the beginning of term. New year, new life. For him, at least. Kian had expected months, if not years, of red tape and panel approvals. Time for him to come up with a compelling reason why the adoption shouldn't go ahead. On the bus on the way over, Dan had shown him a photo of the people he'd soon be calling his family – Sam and Lou. He'd met them a few times, and they'd even had a day at the Science Museum together, which he'd loved. They'd given him a globe as a Christmas present, which Dan seemed more excited about than the football he'd got from Kian. He looked at the photo again. The couple looked nice enough. But it didn't stop him wanting to rip the picture to shreds.

Stepping out into the daylight after the film had finished, Kian pulled his brother in closer. Dan slotted right under his arm, fitted perfectly like the missing piece of a jigsaw.

'It was good, wasn't it?' Dan said, slurping the last of his oversized drink.

Kian had swallowed back tears through most of the film and hadn't really paid any attention to what was on the screen. 'Yeah, it was.'

'Thanks for taking me. I'm going to really miss you.'

'Don't worry about anything, yeah? They're gonna love you over in Telford, right? Everyone loves you.'

'Mum didn't.'

Kian's chest was being wrapped in that familiar choking sensation. He wouldn't let it get the better of him, though. He couldn't let Dan see him like that.

'I didn't know whether to tell you this . . . but I've seen her. Our mum. I tracked her down and went to see her, and do you know what she said?'

Dan shook his head, big eyes looking up at Kian.

'She said you were the best thing that had ever happened to her. It's not your fault she left. She loved you more than anything. She just wasn't cut out to be a mum.'

It pained him to stand up for his mother in that way. She didn't deserve to have history rewritten. He wasn't convinced by Cathy's act, but right now, it was what Dan needed to hear.

'And I love you even more. Don't ever forget that.'

Kian scooped Dan into his arms and wished he never had to let go.

It was starting to get dark after Kian had dropped Dan home. As he crossed the side-road that led to his street, a car pulled up and drove slowly alongside him for a few metres. Then it stopped and two men wearing leather jackets got out. Kian crossed back over towards the railway bridge and walked faster, feeling his heart begin to thump in his chest. The men crossed too, and a feeling of dread unravelled inside him. He unzipped his coat, walking so quickly that he was a couple of paces away from running.

'Kian Matthews?' one of the men shouted.

Kian didn't turn round. Then, out of nowhere, something hard smashed into the back of his legs, and a bright torch was shone into his eyes. He buckled onto the pavement and a series of kicks and blows sent hot flashes of shooting pain through his body. He put his hands up, in a feeble attempt to protect himself, while punches cracked through his ribs and steel-toed boots bruised his back. The frosty ground numbed the side of his face, but his lips were warmed by blood. He could taste dirt as he tried to shout at them to stop, his voice a pathetic groan. He was in agony.

In response someone bent down, right close to his ear, and whispered, 'Kelly sends her love, yeah?'

Kian caught a whiff of the stale cigarette breath and retched. Heavy hands rifled through his pockets, and his watch was snatched from his wrist. Someone turned off the torch and he was left on his own, kicked into the kerb.

44

The beginning of the end

Alfred's needs assessment was hurtling towards him like the InterCity train from London Euston. There was no way of avoiding the impact, not even by hiding under his duvet for the rest of his days. With Sandra's visit imminent, it was rather unfortunate that the house had slipped back to its former state. He wasn't entirely sure how he'd managed to buy so many objects in the short space of time between Boxing Day and New Year's Eve, or even why he had. All he did know was that he couldn't stop. The train had derailed.

Why was he so hopeless? He'd spoken to Maggie on the phone yesterday and promised she could come and visit as soon as she felt well enough, but he was already preparing a list of excuses to put her off. But this wasn't about him any more; Maggie needed him, and he needed her a lot more than he cared to admit. Besides, she now had a key and could surprise him. It should be so simple. He wanted to prove to her that he had changed, only he was like a stuck record, doomed to repeat his mistakes endlessly. Although Kian was going to come round again tomorrow to help him clear up, a weary resignation burrowed inside Alfred. The fight had been lost and he didn't have the energy for another round. He was hanging up his gloves.

At least the first day of the millennium had arrived without any major catastrophe. As far as Alfred could tell, planes had not fallen from the sky overnight and power stations had not gone into meltdown. It was almost a bit disappointing that his preparations had been unnecessary. His wind-up radio, batteries, torch, spare blankets and tins of soup could all be put away again. The public-information leaflet that had been pushed through his door months ago, 'What everyone should know about the Millennium Bug', said on the front, *Keep this booklet for future reference*, so he tucked it back in the kitchen drawer.

That was when he noticed that the brand-new calendar on the fridge had a red circle over today's date. He had completely forgotten that he was supposed to be meeting Meena for a walk today. It was the last thing Alfred wanted to do. He put a packet of biscuits in his dressing-gown pocket and made his way back to the sofa. He paused in front of a picture of Maggie among a group of photos hanging on the wall. He used his sleeve to wipe away some of the dust, revealing her smile. Alfred could remember the exact moment it had been taken. It was the summer she'd turned thirteen. They had been out on a canoe on Coniston Water and had got soaked, but it had been so much fun. He stared at the photo for a few minutes and then got dressed. Going for a walk was one small change he could make that Maggie would approve of. She was always telling him to get some fresh air, and perhaps he had to start somewhere.

The streets were eerily quiet. Spent fireworks littered the pavements and roads, and the air was still heavy with the smell of battlefields. Alfred's breath quickened and he already regretted leaving the house, only he didn't want to be at home, either. To distract himself, he counted to ten slowly as he made his way towards the entrance to the park. One step at a time.

'Happy New Year,' Meena said. Icy puddles crunched beneath her walking boots as she made her way towards him.

'You, too,' said Alfred. 'Though whether it is or not remains to be seen.' It was impossible to stop the bitterness inside him seeping out.

'Good Christmas?' Meena tilted her head to one side, as if waiting for him to share bad news.

'Well, yes, it was actually. I made up with my daughter.'

'Oh, Alfred, that's wonderful news!'

'Thank you. Yes, it is. There's a long way to go, but it's heading in the right direction. I'm so pleased to have her back in my life again. I didn't think it was possible. I just hope I don't mess it up.'

Meena nodded as if she understood, but how could she? It was impossible for Alfred to convey the weight pressing down on him. On their last walk he had felt so hopeful, and now he felt like jumping into the duck pond that Meena had stopped beside. She passed him a slice of bread and Alfred chuckled, remembering his little lie to Maggie about feeding the ducks. He ripped off small bits of crust and threw them, watching the ducks dipping their heads in and out of the water, creating ripples around themselves.

Alfred and Meena stood next to each other until the loaf was all gone.

'Always makes me feel better, feeding the ducks,' Meena said.

She was right. It made Alfred feel better, too. The more they walked, the lighter his shoulders felt. They chatted about the next book-club meeting, reminding Alfred that he had begun to find his way in the world again and had to fight to stay in it. He had to fight to remain in his home.

'We'd better be heading back,' Alfred said, after they'd

stopped to drink coffee on a bench. The sun had gone in and it was suddenly dark. As they left the park, Alfred noticed an ambulance parked on the other side of the road. He recognized the khaki jacket and almost doubled over. The young man being stretchered into the back of it was Kian.

45

The best medicine

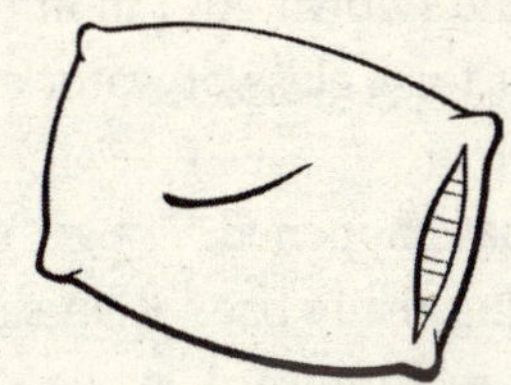

It was impossible to get comfortable in the stiff hospital sheets. The smell of antiseptic, the bright strip lighting and the noise of wheels squeaking along the long corridors had kept Kian awake most of the night. That and the shooting pain in his side, which felt as if a lightning bolt had been captured in him. His face stung and ached all over, thanks to a black eye and stitches to his right cheek. And he suspected he'd got off lightly.

When the police had visited, he'd told them a version of the truth that didn't implicate him in anything. Grassing on a loan shark was like signing your own death certificate. He wasn't lying when he said he had no idea who had done it to him. It wasn't true that he had no idea why. His social worker had visited, too, full of worry and questions. All Kian needed now was Chris to swing by and he'd know he had already died and gone to hell.

'Kian?' The nurse with the Irish accent, who'd been generous with the painkillers, was standing at his bedside.

He squinted up at her, hoping it was time for a top-up.

'You up for a visitor?' she asked.

Had he summoned Chris, just by thinking about him? He rolled into his pillow and yelped as his stitches brushed against the papery pillowcase.

'Kian?' A different voice this time.

He hauled himself up on his elbows, and almost slipped back down when he saw Alfred standing there.

'You look dreadful,' Alfred commented.

'Kick a man while he's down, Al. I'm fine. I mean, I will be.' Kian put his hand out for a glass of water and Alfred passed it to him.

'Who did this? What happened?'

'I've done something really bad,' Kian said.

Alfred sucked his breath inwards while Kian told him about Ryan, and the money he'd borrowed from Kelly to get the medals back.

'And the worst thing,' Kian went on, waiting for the look of disappointment on Alfred's face to deepen, 'is that they took my watch. The one you gave me. I'm really sorry.'

'You don't need to apologize,' Alfred said. 'I want you to know that everything is going to be okay. I'm going to come up with a plan.'

It may have been the haze of medication, but for a moment Kian actually believed him.

46

Worth something

Alfred had barely sat down since returning from visiting Kian in hospital. He tidied away the empty whisky bottles and put them by the sink. It was slightly shocking to see them stacked all together like that. Had he really got through that many? There were no two ways about it: the place was a mess. He picked up the litter of recent purchases from the floor and piled them up against the bin, like a child hiding their unwanted vegetables beneath their fork. It would fool no one. Then he made himself some toast and a cup of tea. He needed a clear head, some space to think.

His anger had been building momentum like a rolling stream. Now the dam had burst. This was something else. Seeing Kian's bruised and battered face had stoked a primeval rage within him. He shouted out loud, 'How dare they?' and realized it was aimed at so many people that it needed to be shouted again and again, until his voice was hoarse. He hovered at the side of his drinks cabinet before deciding against it. Think, man, think.

He could sell his possessions to pay off the loan shark, although that still let the thugs get away with how they'd treated Kian. No, they needed to be taught a lesson. He pushed his half-eaten toast away and slammed his fist on the table. His *What to do in an emergency* notebook yet again failed to be of any use although, in fairness, a loan-shark crisis wasn't something he'd ever anticipated. He threw the book back in the drawer and noticed the folder of newspapers that used to line his windows. A distinct memory popped into his head of an article about a loan shark who'd been prosecuted. He sifted through the pages until he found it. This was exactly why it was a good idea not to throw things away, even if Sandra wouldn't agree.

Alfred sat down in front of his favourite typewriter. It was a thing of beauty and had served him well over the years. They really didn't make them like they used to. It was number forty-seven in his inventory:

Olivetti Lettera 32
Ultra-portable, aqua-blue teal, circa 1965.

Thankfully, it had survived the cull of Kian's clear-outs, mainly due to Alfred's diligence in keeping it hidden in the larder whenever the lad visited. In recent months he had resorted to behaving like a botanist trying to save a rare species from extinction. He ran his fingers over the soft indents on the plastic keys, as words spooled in his mind. After scratching his head a couple of times, he began to type. The clack-clack of the keys was reassuring and filled the room with purpose:

Dear Ms Anderson,

I am acting on behalf of my client, Kian Matthews. In consultation with the Financial Services Authority, I can confirm that you do not have a valid consumer credit licence and, as such, you have lent money to the aforementioned client illegally. If you harass or cause physical harm to my client now or at any point in the future, I will ensure the authorities pursue your immediate arrest.

Yours sincerely,

Alfred Ainswick, Legal Adviser

He waved the paper a couple of times to make sure it was dry and folded it equally into neat thirds. Next he took out his wax seal and carefully dripped melting red wax onto the envelope. He stamped it with the A. A. of his initials and left it on the sideboard to dry. It might just work.

The next step of the plan was difficult, but necessary. Without enough money to pay off the debt, the letter was as useless as a typewriter without a ribbon. Looking around the room at his latest purchases, Alfred assessed what he could quickly make the most money on. He remembered the book on antique-collecting that Kian had borrowed from the library weeks ago, and the boxes they'd packed up together. He'd grown so used to them lined up in the hallway that they'd become invisible. He reached into the depths of his bravery and picked up the phone.

'Maggie, how are you? I hate to ask, but I need your help. Are you up for a little drive?'

'So they just beat him up and put him in hospital?' Maggie said. 'Why haven't you called the police?'

Alfred explained what Kian had told him – that it would only make matters worse. This way was better. He had struggled to get rid of his belongings to save himself, but he would do it to save Kian. He felt a renewed sense of motivation and a fight for life that had been lost in him for so long.

'This is the place,' Alfred said, as Maggie pulled into the gravelled driveway of Eddie's Emporium: a ramshackle barn, with a bicycle hung over the double doors. Outside were tables and chairs, and a little hatch that opened into a booth that sold teas and coffees. On either side of that was a metal suit of armour, a carved wooden dog, a series of huge pots, a sunburst mirror and a red telephone box with a life-sized Charlie Chaplin inside. Alfred would have to pretend he was wearing blinkers. He really was selling, not buying, this time.

Maggie opened the boot of her car and Alfred fetched a trolley from the entrance to load up the boxes. 'I'm really proud of you, Dad,' she admitted.

'That's very kind, but we both know I should have done this years ago. Now why don't you go and get a cup of coffee, and I'll go and charm them into a good price?'

'If you're sure?' Maggie said. 'I'll be right here if you need me.'

Alfred was so grateful that Maggie had come with him. But this next step he had to do alone. He hadn't visited the emporium in years. He was relieved to see that the proprietor hadn't changed. He pushed his trolley up to the counter.

'Eddie! Nice to see you again, after all this time. Listen, you're not going to believe what I've got in here. It's your lucky day.'

After a little bit of necessary small talk, Alfred took out each item one by one and informed Eddie of every minute detail. He knew so much about his prized objects that he could talk about them for hours.

'So this was stolen by one of the servants of Henry VIII, you see. It ended up hidden behind a wall panel during the Reformation and wasn't unearthed for another hundred years. And then . . . Sorry, you must have other things you need to get on with?'

'On the contrary,' Eddie said. 'Do continue, my good friend. This is all absolutely fascinating. You're the most interesting customer I've had in weeks. Don't suppose you fancy a job? I'm selling up in a few months – retiring.'

Alfred almost jumped at the chance before remembering that he had more than enough on his plate right now. 'I'm too long in the tooth for that. Now, as I was saying . . .'

It wasn't nearly as difficult as Alfred had imagined, handing everything over. The fact they were going to someone who was as enthusiastic about them as he was made it *almost* enjoyable to let go.

'How did you get on?' Maggie asked when he rejoined her.

Alfred held out a cheque.

'Six thousand pounds, for all that junk! Sorry, Dad. I mean, wow, that's amazing! What are you going to do with all that?'

'Ah, well, I'm going to give half to you. I want you to book yourself a lovely holiday – somewhere you can really recuperate. And the other half . . . um, if it's okay with you, I'd like to pay off Kian's remaining debt to the loan shark, and give him the rest, so he can afford to go to catering college. I think, more than ever, that he needs someone to take a chance on him and show him that he's worth something. Would that be okay? I know he's not family.'

'Dad, I think that's wonderful. I really do.'

She hugged him, and Alfred felt Maggie's love spin around him like a delicate web that he silently promised never to break.

47

Broken beams

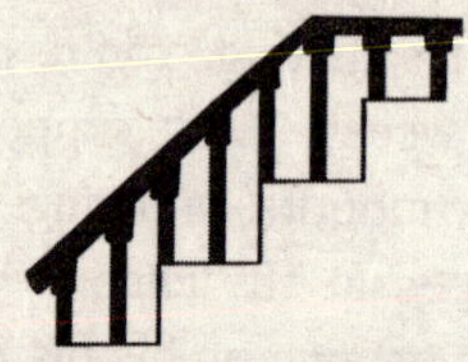

Alfred left the house with three envelopes in his pocket. One he posted through Kian's door, with a cheque and a note explaining its purpose. He included Maggie's phone number, in case anything should happen to him. If he handed it to him in person, Kian would refuse and they would both feel awkward. The other two were for Kelly Anderson. Alfred walked slowly, fully aware of the situation he was getting himself into. It was dangerous. He could end up hurt, or worse. But the spinning gauge of his resolve steadied as he walked. People who took things that didn't belong to them were simply bullies, like the boys who'd taken his belongings in the children's home. He straightened his shoulders and held his head high. Kelly had tied Kian up in an agreement that she knew he had no way of getting out of and it was unfair. He was going to put this right.

All he had to do was look like he meant every word he said and, because he did, it shouldn't be too difficult. When he arrived at Kelly's house, he double-checked the address. He'd been expecting somewhere seedy with blacked-out windows, not a three-bedroom semi with rhododendron bushes burgeoning in the garden and a fibreglass gnome clutching a wheelbarrow. Admittedly the growling of what sounded like a pack of wolves provided a little clue as to what lay behind the white UPVC door. He rang the bell and rubbed his thumb over his pocket watch while he waited. He could do this.

Kelly opened the door with a blank expression. 'Piss off, you old codger,' she said, with a cigarette hanging from her bottom lip.

Charming, certainly. A large dog started barking aggressively at him from behind her legs. Deep breaths. At least it was just the one – so far, anyway. Alfred held steady, both feet on the floor, and summoned up his most commanding voice. 'I've come to retrieve some property that belongs to a young man named Kian Matthews. A watch.'

Kelly looked him up and down, before shamelessly bursting out laughing in his face. 'You, senile? Go on, off you go, like I said, or I'll set Jaws on you.'

Jaws looked only too willing to be given the nod. His top lip rolled back to reveal shark-like teeth. The dog had been suitably named, he'd give her that.

'I'm afraid you don't seem to understand. In this envelope is the full amount owed to you by Kian, and not a penny more. And in this other envelope is a legal letter, explaining what will happen if you go near him again.'

'Police can't touch me. No evidence, so do one.'

'But you admit you have lent money to Kian Matthews – illegally no less?'

'Ooh, listen to you. I don't make a secret of it, do I? I lend money to people who need it. Public service. Only fair that I make something offa that kindness. And if they don't pay back what they owe, they know what's comin'. Plain as. If Kian had watched his payments, like I said, he wouldn't have got a beatin'. How else is he gonna learn?'

Alfred rustled in his pocket and pulled out a small Dictaphone. He had bought it years ago at a flea market in West Bromwich and was pleased that its first outing was one so important. 'I've just recorded our conversation and I think the police will be very happy to take it out of my hands. Unless . . . you'd like to reconsider my offer?'

Kelly's lips pursed together, hollowing her cheeks. There was still time for it all to go very horribly wrong. Alfred stood firm. Don't admit defeat. He stared her right in the eyes. She leaned over to grab the envelope of cash from him, but Alfred swooped his hand away. 'Uh-uh, not until I hear you promise, and until you bring me the watch.'

She swore loudly as her next-door neighbour, an elderly lady carrying a small poodle with coiffed hair, walked up the pathway.

'Morning, Dot, nice day,' Kelly said, with a smile that almost cracked her face.

Alfred uttered a silent thank-you to Dot for her impeccable timing. Kelly huffed loudly and kicked Jaws indoors. She followed him in and returned a minute later.

'Kian won't be hearin' from me again,' Kelly said, taking the envelopes from Alfred and handing over the watch. 'Ugly lookin' watch anyway. Probably a fake.'

'I'll hang on to this, though,' Alfred said, stuffing the Dictaphone into his inside coat pocket and buttoning it up. 'Just in case. Pleasure doing business with you.'

As Kelly's front door slammed, he skipped down the path, letting out a little 'yippee'. He'd done it. He'd actually done it! Who'd have thought he had it in him?

Alfred had planned to go straight to the hospital to let Kian know everything was okay, but as the adrenaline faded, exhaustion caught up with him. He needed a little nap first. He lay down on the divan and looked through his inventory, noting all the listed items that were no longer there. With a pen, he struck them off, feeling each line across the paper as if it were a cut to his skin. No more rococo candlesticks, no more porcelain snuff box. Yes, he had some more space now, but what good was having more room to rattle around in? His eyes closed.

He was nestled inside the bow of a ship. The creaking noise was steady, like a wooden door swinging in the wind. He was warm in his bunk, though. It swayed as the waves smashed the sides of the vessel, threatening to submerge it entirely. The best thing to do was to lie as still as he possibly could until the storm subsided. They always did in the end. The gentle rumbling grew louder, accompanied by a loud groaning as if the sky couldn't take the weight of the clouds any more. Any minute now it would let rip with a sheet of rain that would whip the sails outside. He was safe and dry, and the ship was strong. He had nothing to worry about. He snuggled further into his sleeping bag, when the sky cracked open with a thunderous force that jolted him upright. He wasn't on a ship. He was half-asleep in his hallway and something was very wrong.

Holding his cricket bat out in front of him like a torch, he made his way up the stairs, trying to determine how he would deal with marauding thieves or mutant squirrels that awaited him. Although he was used to clambering over his collections, he cursed as he stubbed his toe on Archimedes, who lived on the seventh stair. The creaking had stopped, but there was a peculiar smell that reminded him of the morning after a bomb blast. Damp plaster and burnt paper.

Before he'd even reached the top, in the semi-darkness it was clear that his bedroom door had vanished. It was definitely there when Alfred had lain down. He would have noticed if it had been missing. When he switched on the landing light, he nearly toppled backwards down the stairs. Whatever he'd prepared himself for, it wasn't this. In truth, his bedroom might have been a little messy before. Now it didn't even resemble a room. In a scene reminiscent of the Blitz there was a mass of rubble, strewn cardboard, broken beams and many years' worth of carefully collected antiques littered across the floor in pieces. His treasures – all ruined. Although it didn't seem possible, the ceiling beneath the loft had collapsed.

The house must have been struck by lightning. His barometer had been warning of a storm for weeks. Alfred ran to the bathroom window, opened it as wide as it would go and stuck out his arm, expecting to feel the force of a gale. The air was cold, but perfectly still – no sign of a storm at all, not even a freckle of rain. He raced back to the bedroom, hoping that he might have dreamed the whole thing. No, it was all too real. He gripped the banister to steady himself and surveyed the unspeakable damage. If he'd been in his bed, he would have been completely flattened. He put his hand to his heart, willing it to remember its job description. He couldn't even shut the door and pretend it hadn't happened, because there wasn't one any more. Not knowing what else he could do, he made his way back downstairs to get a stiff drink.

The kitchen floor was cold on his bare feet, and he realized he'd run upstairs in such a rush that he'd forgotten to put on his slippers. This was an emergency, there was no doubt of that. He took a bottle of whisky and an entire tray of mince pies into the living room and threw a blanket over his legs, in an attempt to persuade them to stop shaking. He switched the TV on – anything to drown out the alarm ringing in his head. His head spun, one thought being quickly replaced by another before it even had a chance to work itself out.

Although he was prepared for all manner of crises, his fire blanket, first-aid kit and extra supply of toilet paper appeared to be of little use in this situation. He got out his emergency notebook and scrambled past the entries for *bee-stings* and *burst pipes* until his eyes landed on the page allocated to the letter C. *Ceiling collapse* was not listed. In fact, the only possible emergency he'd attributed to this part of the alphabet was *choking*. And now that he came to think of it, if he was in need of the Heimlich manoeuvre, there was nobody here to administer it. He would chew the mince pies extra-slowly.

Alfred closed the book and tossed it away. It was hopeless. What would Sandra say? If she thought he'd been fit for a care home before, there was no question about it now. A capable person would not stuff so much in his loft that it collapsed and very nearly killed him.

At least there was one small mercy. His home insurance would cover the cost of the damage. But it wouldn't replace all his items and would undoubtedly make his premium rise. It had only been a couple of months since he'd had to make a claim for his broken windows. He opened the concertina file that contained all his important documents and selected the correct compartment. The insurance policy was missing. Impossible. He emptied out all the papers until they were scattered across the floor like stepping-stones. He examined all of them. Still not there. He ripped off his cardigan and hunted in drawers and ransacked his shelves, to no avail. The pile of papers created an origami city around him. Then he pulled the cushions from his sofa and looked underneath the sideboards, finding a long-lost magazine, a leather bookmark and a tennis shoe, but no insurance documents. They had to be here somewhere!

He was about to give up, when he finally found them wedged inside a photo album. His blood pressure returned to normal as he read down the page, until he saw one alarming detail:

Policy expiry: 24/10/1999.

That was more than two months ago.

48

Old tricks

Kian had been itching to come home for the past few days and now that he was, he wished he was back in hospital. At least he was safe there and free from his problems. Three meals a day were brought to him in bed, it was warm and he wasn't racking up any bills. Best of all, there was no way Kelly Anderson was getting past the matron at the nurses' station. If looks could kill, everyone on the ward would be six feet under the moment she came near.

Now his days consisted of looking repeatedly through the gap in his closed curtains and slamming down painkillers. His body radiated with either sharp stabs or dull kicks, depending on how recently he'd taken his tablets. There was no way he was up to clearing out Al's house in time for his final meeting with Chris. Although he hoped Ryan's case didn't stand up in court, being banged up was increasingly looking like the safest and easiest option.

Kian had cried when he'd seen the cheque that Alfred had posted through his door. For the first time in his life someone was taking a punt on him, believing he was capable of something. As soon as he could, he'd pay it into a brand-new savings account at the bank, one that he couldn't dip into for twelve months. Maybe he'd be out of prison on good behaviour by then. He tried phoning Al to thank him, only he wasn't answering the phone.

He would have to venture out and hope that Kelly's thugs didn't have him under surveillance. He put on his coat and zipped the hood right up over his mouth, even though it was mild outside. Then he put on his shades and a scarf for good measure. He looked like a cartoon spy. Walking as quickly as his injuries would let him, he crossed the road when anyone came remotely near him.

The last time he'd been to Alfred's was on Christmas Day and although there had been no evidence of the collected train timetables, random furniture and drawers overflowing with everything from shoelaces to silverware, there was still loads left to sort out to make the house look anywhere near presentable. It needed a huge clean, for a start. Kian would just have to double up on painkillers and hope Alfred hadn't been up to his old tricks while he'd been in hospital. With only a week until Sandra's visit, he had to make sure Alfred didn't screw it all up.

Alfred did not answer the door. Kian pressed his face up to the glass of his window – the place where their lives had collided what felt like a lifetime ago. Peering through the gap between the gingham curtains, it was clear that all his hard work these last couple of months had been for nothing. The place looked terrible. Kian kicked the badly repaired drainpipe and it collapsed onto the ground.

Ryan had broken in pretty easily, so Kian climbed over the side-gate and gave the door a boot. It gave way with little force. There was no sign of Alfred. Kian called out his name as he ran up the stairs.

'What the actual—' Kian said, before he even reached the top. The only other time in his life that he'd seen devastation like this was when he was eleven years old. One of the tower blocks on the Clevedon estate was being demolished and he and his mates rode all the way to the top of Beacon Hill on their BMXs to watch it. One minute everyone was counting down from ten, and the next a twenty-storey building melted into the ground in a blaze of smoke and noise, leaving behind a wasteland of twisted metal and concrete guts, which they'd picked at afterwards like crows.

It made no sense, but the ceiling below the loft was now on the floor of one of the bedrooms. Alfred was nowhere to be seen. Just when the end was in sight – when it seemed they might actually have a chance of satisfying Chris – Alfred had disappeared, leaving a trail of carnage in his wake. Whatever happened next, it was clear that any chance of a future had been smashed to pieces along with Alfred's house.

49
No return

Among the pile of rubble, plaster and timber that lay in Alfred's bedroom was the occasional distinguishable remnant of something treasured: a glint of broken mirror, half a cigarette card featuring butterflies of the world, the face of a gilded carriage clock cruelly ripped from its body, a copy of *Hard Times* with only a few remaining tattered pages.

It had taken a few of days of ruminating over his options before Alfred admitted that he'd reached the point of no return. He then packed a small case, picked the post off the doormat, shoved it into his coat pocket and left the house. He hadn't been sure where he was going when he arrived at Birmingham New Street station. All he knew was that he had to get away, as far as possible. Before, the mess in his house had been a bit like a fire – one that was small and containable. Now it was like the whole place had gone up in smoke. There was no way to salvage it.

At the station he picked up a newspaper and tried to ignore the date glaring at him. Just seven days until Sandra's needs assessment. Of course if he hadn't given that cheque to Kian, he could have afforded to pay for the necessary building work. He didn't regret his decision, though. Kian's hopes and dreams still lay ahead of him. For Alfred, there were no further adventures to come. He was eroding like an ancient cliff, and the only way was down.

He scanned the destinations board and waited for some sort of sign. Nothing stirred in him as he read the names out loud: Lichfield Trent Valley, Liverpool, Milton Keynes Central, Ely.

Before he'd finished reading the list, an announcement came over the Tannoy: 'We are sorry that the eleven thirty-four service to Barmouth has been further delayed by approximately fifteen minutes. This is due to an incident on the line.'

As Alfred handed over his money at the ticket office, he could almost feel Ida's hand in his.

It had been a long time since he'd last been on the Cambrian Coast Railway, yet he knew the stops off by heart, like a favourite poem. As the train whizzed out of the city, he wrapped his scarf tightly around his neck. He hadn't left the vicinity of his neighbourhood in years and had hoped to feel buoyant and free. Instead he wanted to hide underneath the table until he reached Barmouth. Unfortunately, his problems had come along for the ride. The rhythmic sound of the train's wheels skirting along the tracks seemed to say: *You're running away, you're running away.*

After a while the spires of Shrewsbury Abbey sailed by, and he knew there were still hours to go. Hours of agony until he could leave everything behind. Although Alfred tried to concentrate on the spectacular view awaiting him when the train crossed the viaduct over the estuary of the River Mawddach, he thought of home. There were so many things he would miss. No, he corrected himself, not things – *people*. Maggie, with whom he'd finally been reconciled after all these wasted years; Kian, who had turned his life upside-down and somehow made it better. And Meena, someone he could now call a friend. Just when his life was starting to fill up, the plug had been pulled and it had all drained away. He didn't know what he would do next, or how events would turn out. He did know that he had no intention of being around when Sandra came to call.

Seeing the sea again, after so many years, was like a cleanser for the soul. Seagulls squawked overhead and waves lapped along the shoreline, exactly like Alfred remembered. However, Barmouth had changed a little since his last visit. He stood still, pretending to look for a handkerchief while he orientated himself. The sea front had gathered more cafes, arcades and amusements, most of them now closed for the winter. What had he expected? That when he'd stopped participating in the world, it wouldn't carry on without him?

He wanted to find the pub that he and Ida had sheltered in on the first day of their honeymoon. Only it had been so long ago, he wasn't entirely sure where it was. He might as well pop into the nearest one for a little drink, to help him on his way. No one paid him any attention as he weaved his way to the bar. He might as well have been invisible, which suited him fine. He ordered a double whisky and knocked it back, enjoying the familiar burn as it went down his throat. He ordered another.

Somewhere between the third and fourth pub Alfred's vision blurred, and his stomach got stuck on a spin cycle. It was now dark and the temperature had plummeted. He continued to walk, trying to find a bed-and-breakfast. He was convinced that the hotel he'd stayed in with Ida was just around the corner and so he carried on further, even though he shivered with cold. He knew it! There was the sign for the Starlight Inn swinging in the wind – only the building was boarded up and surrounded by rubble. The fence around it was covered in signs warning of prosecution for trespassing. Alfred rattled it and then croaked out Ida's name. Even though he knew she wasn't inside, he wanted to be with her, right this minute.

He walked around the perimeter of the fence and found a gap that he could squeeze through if he took off his coat. He let it drop to the ground and climbed inside. Immediately he lost his balance and stumbled into a wall, scraping both his hands. It was probably dangerous to be wandering around a building site in the dark. Then again, he had spent much of his life trying to avoid risk and that had got him nowhere.

'Ida,' he said, kneeling down. 'I'm in such a mess. I . . . I'm lost without you. Tell me what to do.'

Of course there was no reply. How was it that he felt so bone-achingly tired? And where had he put his coat? Alfred lay down and allowed his heavy eyes to close. Even though he was as cold as if he was wrapped up in winter itself, it would feel good to rest for a moment.

50

A life-ring

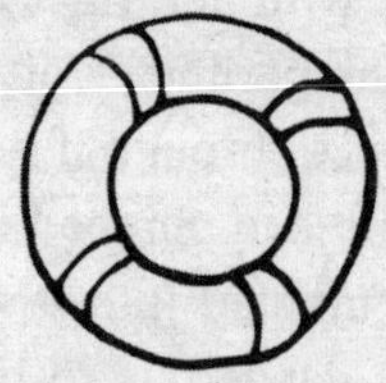

People didn't simply vanish. Kian was torn between ringing Maggie and sending her into a panic, and calling the police and all the hospitals to see if he could work out what had happened to Al. Before that, however, he decided to try one of Alfred's neighbours, in the hope they'd seen him lately. Thankfully the man next door had spotted him walking towards the station with a suitcase the previous day. That was something to hang on to. Alfred had gone away for a few days. Kian was sure he'd be back.

It still left him with a huge problem. Sandra would be coming soon, and Alfred's house was a disaster zone. He rang practically every builder in the Yellow Pages, but none of them could do the work in the necessary timescale. Kian couldn't give up, though. He couldn't hide from Kelly Anderson for ever and maybe now that he'd been beaten up, they were square. Whatever, leaving the house might give him some head-space to think. Without Gav and Ryan to hang out with, Kian had no idea where to go, until he spotted the library book he still hadn't returned.

He checked his hair in the mirror twice, brushed his teeth and proceeded to eat almost an entire packet of Polo mints, just to be safe. Of course he was probably the last person Chloe wanted to see. He'd lost her note with her phone number, and he hadn't even said thanks for finding his mum's address. His mum. She had popped into his head quite a bit over the past few days. Kian knew for sure that he wasn't ready to start a relationship with her. He didn't even know if he wanted to, in the future. For now it was enough to know that she loved him in her own messy, flawed and screwed-up way.

He marched into the library as if he was more confident than he felt. He dumped the book he'd borrowed on the counter and tried to remember if the note Chloe had written to him last year had been signed with a kiss. Even if it had, it was weeks ago. She could have a boyfriend by now. He had probably missed his chance. When the woman behind the counter told him that Chloe didn't work there any more, he knew he had.

When he turned to leave, he thought he saw Chloe walking through the automatic doors. It was hard to be certain, because she was looking down and an old couple were walking in front of her very slowly and blocking his view. He leapt behind the nearest bookshelf to get a better look. He took a large hardback off the shelf and peeked through the gap to give him a good view of the counter. She was nowhere to be seen. It must have been wishful thinking.

'Kian? Hi!'

Kian spun round. Chloe was standing right next to him, smiling, and all at once it was like he'd been thumped in the stomach and had drowned in sunlight.

'You're here!' Kian said, too loudly. What a way to play it cool.

'Yeah, seems that way. Just dropping off some books,' Chloe replied. 'The romance ones are my mum's – honest. Only looks like you're a fan, too?' She gestured towards the book in his hand.

Kian glanced down at the cover of the book and felt his face turn red. The title read *A Secret Lover*, and staring back at him was a dark-haired shirtless man gripping a rose between his teeth. He thrust it back onto the shelf as if it was molten-hot. Then he laughed. 'Yeah. Picked that up by mistake. Um, I'm sorry I never called you. A lot of stuff has gone down lately. And I sort of lost your number.'

'No worries.' Chloe turned to leave.

'Um, wait! You probably think I'm a total loser and everything, but could we – I dunno – go for a coffee sometime?' Kian winced as he waited for her reply.

'Sure, how about now? I mean, once I've returned these.' She held out her pile of books.

'What – seriously? Now? With me?'

'Are you trying to talk me out of it?' Chloe asked. 'Cos, I mean, I can just go straight back home and paint my nails or something.'

Kian grinned. 'No, I'm trying to talk you into it. I'll throw in a cake, too, if you like?'

'Can't say no to that,' Chloe said. 'As long as it's chocolate, you're on.'

Kian was trying to sit as straight as a ruler and drink his coffee without slurping. It was impossible to stop staring at Chloe as she chatted about her Christmas. Her smile made him feel fuzzy inside.

'Did you contact your mum then?' Chloe asked, sticking a fork into the huge slice of chocolate cake that Kian had bought. He'd got himself a piece as well, but felt too nervous to eat it.

'Yeah,' Kian replied. 'It was intense. She'd moved on with her life, like I'd never even been in it.'

'I'm sorry,' Chloe said. 'I mean, my mum drives me crazy, but I can't imagine her not being around. You were really brave, going to see her. Did it give you, you know, closure?'

Kian thought about it. 'Sort of. I'd always wondered why she left. Like, what was so bad about me? Now I've met her, I don't think it was about me at all. I think that was the problem.'

Chloe put her hand out and squeezed his arm. 'She doesn't deserve you.'

Kian's insides melted. He felt so comfortable that he almost told Chloe everything that had happened recently, before deciding it would more than likely put her off. It could wait 'til they got to know each other better. She might not want to see him again anyway. Worse than that, he might be banged up soon, and he was pretty sure she wouldn't want to visit him in prison.

'So, what do you do?' Chloe asked. It was an innocuous question. It was also the worst one she could have asked.

He'd stick to a diluted version of the truth. 'I'm going to catering college next year. I just need to get some experience first. Right now I'm, er . . . helping someone. An old guy – a war veteran. His house is a bit of a mess. Actually a ceiling's caved in.'

'You're joking!' Chloe said.

'Nope. I've tried loads of builders and none of them are free to fix it. I've got the money to pay for it,' Kian said, thinking of the cheque Alfred had given him, which was still sitting on top of the microwave, waiting to be deposited. 'I wanted to surprise him. He's gone away for a bit.' He had no way of knowing if Alfred had any intention of returning. But he clung on to the hope that he would.

'I might be able to help,' Chloe offered. 'My dad's had a load of builders in to do the bathroom and they're about to finish a few days early.' She got out her phone. 'Want me to call him – ask him to see if the builders could squeeze it in before their next job?'

Kian nodded and crossed his fingers in his lap. Maybe his luck was turning. Chloe made the call, but after a few moments of saying nothing, she put it down on the table and gave him an apologetic look. There was obviously no answer.

'Don't worry about it,' Kian said. 'Thanks anyway.' He should have known not to expect things to go right for him.

'Dad's not answering, but the builders will still be there, finishing up. Wanna come back to mine and we can speak to them?'

'Yeah, that'd be great.' Without thinking, he held out his hand across the table. Chloe took it in hers and squeezed it. He had no idea what the builders would say, but after weeks of feeling as if he was drowning, it was like he'd finally come up for air.

51
Reawakening

Ida was wearing a sky-blue nightdress and was laughing so much that she snorted. Her eyes danced and Alfred, who had now opened his, couldn't help laughing, too.

'Shh!' he said. 'I'm trying to sleep!'

'We can sleep when we're dead. Let's get up and go for a walk in Cannon Hill Park. Just like we used to, when we were younger.'

'It's the middle of the night,' Alfred said, ignoring the protests from his knees and getting up anyway. He should stop and get a blanket, a flask of tea and a torch, but when he was with Ida he could cast off his sensible nature like a coat. They ran out into the night empty-handed and full of wonder.

They walked barefoot on the glistening grass, past the cricket pavilion and towards the boating lake where he had asked for Ida's hand in marriage. The rowing boat they had rented was a little rickety and Alfred had sped through his proposal, so that they could get back to dry land as quickly as possible. When Ida had said yes, he beamed with a happiness he'd never known before and no longer wanted to rush to shore. Instead he had been tempted to toss the oars over the side of the boat, so they could stay in that moment for ever.

They reached the shadow of the bandstand and Alfred pulled Ida close, feeling her breath warming his neck. In the moonlight they danced to an imaginary sonata below an audience of stars. This was it; this was real love. Somehow he'd found it, and he would never let it go.

'Don't ever leave me, Ida,' Alfred begged, but her warmth had already disappeared and a glacial chill was settling at his core.

'Alfred?' Ida called, so quietly that he knew she was slipping away from him. 'Alfred?'

Alfred had dozed and woke up to the bitter cold, his head clanging as a taster of how bad he would feel in the morning. Ida had vanished. He was more alone than ever. He stumbled onto the street, finding his discarded coat on the frosted pavement. It was a miracle he hadn't frozen to death, and he shivered as he threw it over his shoulders. He headed back towards the sea front, hopeful that he could find a bed for the night. Is this what his life had become now? He was no better than a convict on the run.

He entered the reception of the Sea Breeze bed-and-breakfast and did his best not to sway while he waited for the receptionist to look up from whatever she was writing. The wall behind the counter was covered with hundreds of mismatched tiles, and next to him was a bookcase filled with walking guides and baskets of tourism leaflets advertising local attractions, reminding him that holidays were meant to be restorative, not a place for an existential crisis. An electric heater glowed in the dim light and Alfred inched as close to it as he could, rubbing his hands together.

'I'd like a room for ten days, please,' Alfred said. By then Sandra would have been and gone, and he might have worked out what to do.

'You're in luck,' the lady behind the desk replied. She had a track of red lipstick on her teeth, which Alfred stopped himself from mentioning. 'I was about to lock up. Fill your details in here, please. Cheque or card?'

'Cheque, please,' Alfred said, clearing his throat and threading his arms fully into his coat sleeves. He was suddenly aware of how dishevelled he must look.

'Perfect. I'll fetch your key and then I can show you to your room. There are extra blankets in the cupboard, if you need them.'

Alfred would pile every single one on top of him and wear both sets of pyjamas that he'd packed. The landlady went into a little office, so Alfred sat down on one of the leather armchairs next to the bookcase. He looked for his chequebook and found the bundle of post that he'd lifted from the doormat that morning. It seemed like a lifetime ago. The first envelope was a gas bill, so he stuffed it back in his pocket. The second was square and stiff, obviously a card of some sort. Who would send Alfred a card? It was long past Christmas, and his birthday was in June. He opened it. It said *Thank You* on the front, in large colourful letters. He read the message inside:

Dear Alfred,

Thank you for helping me with my eleven-plus, and thank you for telling me about the war and letting me come to church with you. I wrote about all the things you told me for my school project and got a head teacher's gold award!!!! I hope I can see you again soon. Here's a picture I drew of you. You can put it on your fridge!

Love, Dan

On an A4 piece of paper folded up inside the card, Dan had drawn a picture of Alfred wearing his uniform. A row of golden medals hung from his top pocket. Next to the picture he had written: *My friend, Alfred. A real hero.*

Without warning, a loud sob escaped from Alfred's mouth, so he clasped his hand over it. The landlady dropped his room key onto the counter and rushed over to him.

'Are you okay? Do you want me to call someone for you?'

'No. No, thank you,' Alfred replied. 'I'll be fine.'

He blew his nose. The thought of ringing Maggie sobered him up like a shot of espresso. The unsalvageable, mangled debris of his bedroom and loft flashed through his mind. He could jump on a train tomorrow and head north to the Lake District. And perhaps, from there, to Scotland. He'd always wanted to visit the Isle of Harris. He imagined himself living as a nomad in the shadow of the mountains, growing a long beard and picking wild berries, perhaps fishing for trout. His whole life had prepared him for such an existence. His bags were already packed. He might as well just keep going.

He finally located his chequebook, filled in a cheque and pushed it across the counter. He looked again at the picture Dan had drawn. An ache materialized below his left shoulder as he thought of Kian and how he'd abandoned the lad at the time he needed him the most. It was no good; no matter how far Alfred went, eventually he would run out of track.

'Actually, sorry, can I write you a new cheque?' he asked. 'I won't need the room for as long as I thought. I've realized I'm needed at home.'

52

Toy soldiers

The yellow rubber gloves pinched Kian's fingers – they were at least one size too small. He had told Maggie what was going on and she'd come round to Al's with a selection of scouring brushes, bin liners and more cleaning products than he'd ever seen in his life. She'd even brought round her own vacuum cleaner, despite Kian telling her that Al had two in the cupboard.

When he'd looked through the front window the previous week and seen the state of the place, it was like he'd gone back in time, as if he'd imagined hauling furniture around and filling skips and rubbish bags for weeks on end. The only difference: there was a new selection of crap to clear out. He'd been an idiot to think that once Al's place had been emptied of clutter, he'd keep it that way. It reminded him of the empty bottles of cider he'd find in the kitchen in the morning when he was a kid. He'd stuff them in the bin, knowing that by the next day there would be another load to replace them.

The builders that Chloe had sorted had done an amazing job. In just a few days the ceiling had been rebuilt, plastered and painted. Kian had hired another skip and cleared tonnes of rubble, broken antiques and rubbish. Maggie wasn't supposed to be doing any actual tidying. Kian wanted her to rest, but she insisted on sorting through some of the boxes of papers upstairs. She came down the stairs slowly and looked fragile.

'You okay?' Kian asked, taking off his gloves.

'I went into the spare room and Dad has kept every card I ever made him, all my schoolbooks and pictures. I can't even . . .' Maggie sat down on the sofa, holding a bright crayon picture of a rainbow. 'It's so ridiculous that all this' – she gestured to the boxes surrounding them – 'became more important than me. I'm the only family he has.'

Kian couldn't blame her for feeling hurt.

'It's not more important. Alfred kept all your stuff because he loves you, right?' He wondered if his own mum had kept anything of his. Probably not.

'You must really care about him,' Maggie said.

Kian nodded. Of course he did, so much so that he'd used the money Alfred had given him for college to pay the builders to fix all the damage as quickly as they could. Alfred needed his home back, and Kian doubted he'd ever get into college anyway.

He got on with the tidying. He came across an old-fashioned camera with a huge lens attached to the front. He took the cover off and clicked one of the levers, wondering if Al had ever used it or if it was simply something he liked the look of. Then he found a violin in a leather case that was frayed at the edges and had broken straps. Could Alfred even play? There was no way of making sense of any of it, and consequently no way of reasoning what to keep.

One of the drawers in the sideboard had a little key in its lock. Kian turned it and discovered a set of writing paper inside.

He decided to sit down for a moment and write to his mum. She'd been on his mind a lot the past few days and he needed to get it off his chest somehow:

Dear Cathy,

There's still a lot of questions I want to ask you, but I don't think I want to see you again.

Kian chewed the top of the pen. What was it that he *did* want? Someone to write to from prison? Someone to blame? Or did he want to get to know the person his mum was now? He could write an entire essay on how much he hated her. Instead he kept things brief. After all, she might not even write back:

A good friend told me that people are capable of change. From what you said when we met, you've changed a lot since I was a kid. I think I've changed a lot recently, too, though I still seem to make a load of mistakes. If you feel like writing back, maybe you can tell me what went through your mind when you left me, and whether you wish I hadn't found you. Then at least I'd know.

Kian

He then got up and threw himself into tidying, in a blur of throwing things out and scrubbing and polishing, until he was sweating and his fingers ached. At lunchtime he made pea-and-mint soup. There were some part-baked baguettes in the freezer, so he cooked them and carved them into chunky slabs, then served them with butter.

'This really is lovely,' Maggie said, helping herself to another bowl. 'Where did you learn to cook?'

'Your dad taught me the basics, and the rest I got from sort of experimenting, I guess.'

'Dad always was a good cook. Well, I'm very impressed.'

'Thanks – tell that to the Admissions Officer at the catering college. They won't give me a place on their course without experience.'

'That's a shame. Don't give up, though, will you? Speaking of which, I think we should stop now. We've been at it for hours and I'm starting to think we're wasting our time. We don't even know if Dad will be back for his meeting with social services, and I'm sure they'll make the right decision. If they think Dad should go into a care home, although it breaks my heart, I think it will be for the best. Right now I just want him back, so we know he's safe.'

Kian looked around the living room. It didn't look much better than when they'd started. Maggie was right. It was like trying to empty a bucket under a waterfall. They would need weeks to do a proper job or hire an army of helpers. He thought of Alfred's toy soldiers, now promoted from their place on the stairs to top ranking on the mantelpiece. He took out the one in his jacket pocket and added him to the front, as if he was the sergeant. He belonged with his troop. An idea came to him. It was a long shot, but it was worth a go.

53

Alchemy

Kian looked at the assembled crowd in Alfred's living room – ten adults, two children and a chihuahua – and began to think he'd made a terrible mistake. He'd expected maybe one or two of Al's neighbours to agree to help out, not half the street. Now that they were here, all squeezed in between the jumble of collections and excess furniture, Kian could almost feel Alfred's burning cheeks. Worse than that, everyone was looking at him to take charge and give them direction. He was used to being told what to do, not the other way around.

Kian rolled up his sleeves and tried several times to get everyone's attention. 'Um, hi . . . er . . . yeah, so thanks to everyone for pitching in. You can see we've got our work cut out, but the fact you're here, helping out, is gonna mean the world to Alfred.' It was more likely Alfred would explode with anger, on returning home and finding out that Kian had let strangers in to remove all his belongings, but that wouldn't make for a very motivating speech. 'Anyway, I dunno if anyone has any ideas where to start or—'

'Hi, guys, I'm Ewan. I live at one-three-four and, just a thought, I've got a huge garage at the back, sitting empty, so how about we store some of the furniture in there?' Ewan's chihuahua, which had been circling at his feet, started to bark as if in agreement. 'Well, Charlie thinks it's a good idea!'

Everyone laughed as Ewan picked up his dog from beside him and nuzzled him.

'Brilliant, thanks, Ewan. And Charlie!' Kian said.

'Hello. I'm Krystyna and this is my daughter, Ania, who is twelve.' Ania smiled shyly and waved. 'We moved in next door to Alfred six months ago, after coming here from Poland, although we've never met him. Actually this is the first time we've met any of our neighbours! We have lots of paint left over from our own decorating, which we could put to good use in here?'

'That would be amazing,' Kian replied. 'I think we might just do this.'

Sophia, from across the road, said she'd go and fetch some plant pots to brighten up the front garden. She remembered Alfred from years before Ida died, and how their front garden always used to look beautiful. Tas, from two doors down, offered to fill his hatchback with rubbish for the tip. Others started cleaning, while another group helped to move furniture into Ewan's garage. Kian couldn't believe all these people were willing to give up their time to help someone most of them had never even met.

Wanting to make himself useful, Kian stepped into Alfred's kitchen and began to bake some biscuits to feed the workers. It wouldn't take long. He used a recipe that Alfred had taught him and, as he weighed out the flour and butter, the idea of becoming a chef resurfaced. His dream hadn't really gone away, despite his attempts to ignore it in the past few days. As he added heaped teaspoons of ginger and baking powder to the bowl, he thought about the alchemy involved. Alfred had told him something previously that Kian had put in his application for college: that, individually, these ingredients didn't offer a whole lot, but putting them together created something amazing. It was a bit like him and Alfred. They had been useless on their own, but together everything was better somehow.

'This is what community is about,' Krystyna said, putting down her paintbrush to eat one of the biscuits. 'It's about people helping one another. These taste wonderful, by the way!'

Kian had never felt a sense of community where he lived. Birmingham was a huge city, with more than a million people in it, and yet he mostly felt completely alone. He knew Alfred felt like this too, and yet all along, he had a ready-made network of people right on his doorstep who were happy to look out for him. If only he'd known.

'You should do this more often,' Kian said. 'I mean, not the painting. But getting everyone on the street together.'

'Yeah, good idea,' Ewan replied. 'My mate in Bristol said their road set up a Street Association.'

'Like Neighbourhood Watch?' Sophia queried. 'Bartholomew Row joined up years ago. The stickers are on the lamp posts, but it doesn't really mean much.'

'No, it's not like that. They get together every few months to have a barbecue or arrange a car-free day, so the kids can play on the street. They put planters out – that sort of thing. Just makes the place friendlier for everyone.'

There were murmurs of approval, as members of the group began suggesting how it might work and who could volunteer for what role. Tas wanted to set up a neighbourhood photo exhibition, and Krystyna wanted to organize a group to paint a mural on the disused garages at the end of the street. Alfred – possibly the most isolated man on the street – had inadvertently become the spark to transform his neighbourhood and bring people together.

After a few more hours the place looked unrecognizable.

'Thank you so, so much,' Kian said as the neighbours trailed back to their homes.

'You don't need to keep thanking us,' Ewan said. 'We're glad we could help. I'm looking forward to meeting Alfred properly, once he's home. I'd love to talk to him about the comic collection I found in the living room.'

Kian smiled. His work here was done.

54

A miracle

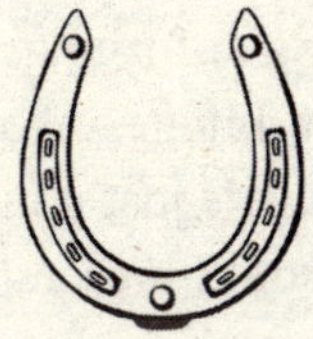

Alfred's brain was as incoherent as a Scrabble board missing half its tiles. The entire train journey home had been spent trying to think of a way to prevent Sandra going inside his house. A gas leak? No, he wouldn't be allowed in, either. An infectious disease? Well, then she'd be shipping him off to hospital. It was no good. Whichever way he looked at it, he was going to be booted out of his home no sooner than he'd got back inside.

As the taxi made its way from the train station, Alfred knew that each corner they turned or traffic light they crawled through was taking him closer to his fate. He thought about the empty whisky and brandy bottles stacked by the sink, the unwashed plates, the smashed-through ceiling upstairs, his new purchases stretching the living room to its seams and the empty well of excuses. He sank his hands into his pockets.

Sandra was due to visit at 2 p.m. and, with only a couple of minutes to go, he arrived home. As soon as he stepped out of the taxi and onto the pavement, her car pulled up next to him. Efficient as ever. She got out of her car with a clipboard and smiled at him.

'Look, there's something I should probably tell you,' Alfred began. 'I'm afraid it might be . . . a bit of a mess. Do you think you could give me a moment, you know, to have a quick tidy-up?' Unless he could persuade Sandra to stay outside for the next few days, this would be a pointless endeavour. Still, if he could at least hide the bottles, throw a few items behind the sofa, it might take the edge off things. Or so he hoped.

Sandra's smile didn't budge. 'Honestly, a little mess is nothing to worry about. Let's just go in and have a cup of tea.'

This was it then. He could pretend he'd lost his front-door key, only he was pretty sure that Sandra was the type of person to have a team of locksmiths at her beck and call. Anyway, it was cold out here and, now that a cup of tea had been mentioned, he was desperate for one, even if it was the last he'd drink from his Hornsea tea set. Maybe he could explain the mess by saying he'd been broken into while he'd been in Barmouth, by someone who left items behind rather than took them away.

As Alfred opened the front door, he ducked as if expecting an avalanche. Instead he was hit by the smell of polish and flowers. The Persian rug in the hallway was at least two shades lighter than he remembered it being. He was either dreaming or he'd come to the wrong house.

He pushed open the living-room door and tried to suppress a gasp. It was exactly like the tale of the Elves and the Shoemaker. It was a miracle! The room was spotless and was nothing like how he had left it. A neatly stacked bookshelf sat next to the television; remote controls were lined up on a little coffee table next to his puzzle book; and on the dining-room table was a vase of violas and winter jasmine. The walls had been painted a calming duck-egg blue. On the mantelpiece some of his favourite items were lined up to greet him, like he was a royal ambassador. Alfred walked over to them and picked each up in turn, silently saying hello to his maritime hourglass, his army of soldiers, his green glass demijohn and his lucky brass horseshoe. It was the tidiest he could ever remember the place looking since Ida had died. And there, in the corner, was something that brought tears to his eyes: one of Maggie's childhood pictures in a frame. A rainbow to lighten the darkest of days.

Alfred coughed, before turning to look at Sandra. She was already making herself at home in the armchair nearest the window. He noticed that this time she did not sit on her coat.

'Doesn't it look lovely in here?' Sandra said. 'I have to say, I wasn't expecting it to be quite so different. Kian did a great job.'

'Yes,' replied Alfred, not quite able to believe his eyes. 'Yes, he really did.'

'Now there's lots to get done, so I'll do my best to rattle through it quickly. I'm concerned, Alfred, that's all. With no family support, we need to ascertain a suitable package of care for you. Now I've got some questions and it really—'

The doorbell rang, cutting Sandra off in her prime. Alfred launched himself from his chair towards the front door. He wasn't expecting someone, but anyone would do.

'Oh,' Alfred said. 'Sandra, this is my daughter, Maggie. Maggie, this is my Sandra, I . . . er . . . mean my social worker.'

'What a lovely surprise to meet your daughter,' Sandra replied. 'I think it's perfect timing, just when we're considering the next steps for you.'

Alfred didn't agree that this was perfect timing. He hadn't even told Maggie about being under the watchful eye of a social worker. She nodded at him, though, as if everything was fine.

'Right, well, let's start again, shall we?' Sandra smoothed out a sheet of paper attached to her clipboard. 'Alfred, tell me a bit about how you think you're managing at home.'

With Maggie by his side, Alfred's artillery had been replenished. He still had some fight left in him.

55

Birthday blues

Kian woke on the day of his eighteenth birthday having slept through much of it. There was a crick in his neck and his limbs ached. After almost twenty-four hours straight of sorting out Al's pad in time for Sandra's visit, Kian was a broken young man. Organizing everyone, shifting furniture, scrubbing skirting boards and painting walls represented the hardest graft he'd done in his life. He'd never have been able to do it without the help of Alfred's neighbours. They'd all gone to so much trouble, and Ania had even picked some flowers from her garden to put in a vase on Alfred's coffee table as a finishing touch. Kian only hoped it was enough.

He rolled over in bed. All he could think about was tomorrow's review meeting, and how bad prison food would be. He'd made no plans to celebrate his birthday and there was no way anyone had organized a surprise party. Adulthood had finally arrived – the day he'd wanted for so long, so that he could take charge of his own life. It had already disappointed him.

He looked at the photo of Dan that sat next to his alarm clock. Telford wasn't that far, but it might as well be on the other side of the world. They'd spoken on the phone a couple of times, and Dan seemed to have settled in well with Sam and

Lou – his new family. Kian was grateful and angry about it, all at the same time. Simone was right, he did want the best for Dan. It was just hard to accept what Kian had known all along: that the best wasn't being with him.

There were a couple of voicemails on his phone, birthday wishes from Lucy and Dan. Another day had gone by and there was nothing from Alfred. Would he ever make it back, from wherever he'd scarpered to? Alfred had once pointed out that the situation he found himself in with Sandra was all Kian's fault. It had taken him a while to see that Alfred was right. Now he desperately hoped he'd been able to turn things around for him.

Kian rang Alfred's number, completely clueless as to what his next move would be if Alfred still didn't answer. Perhaps he'd have to ring the police. The thought made him feel sick. The phone rang out. It looked like all his effort had been wasted, and now he was getting seriously worried. He was about to end the call when he heard Alfred's voice.

'Al? You picked up! Where've you been? What did Sandra say? Are you okay?' He remembered the *No questions* clause in the contract Alfred had presented to him on the first day he went round.

'Steady on, young man: one question at a time. The first thing I want to tell you is the good news. I paid off Kelly Anderson.'

Kian almost dropped the phone. 'Seriously? How the hell did you do that? Have you any idea how stupid that was? She's so dangerous! Are you okay? Is that where you've been – in hiding?'

'I fought in the war, remember. The likes of Kelly Anderson don't scare me. Anyway, you don't need to worry; you won't be hearing from her or her allies again.'

Kian couldn't believe someone would do that for him. Alfred had risked his life!

'And now, with reassurance from Maggie and the house miraculously transformed, Sandra finally seems satisfied that I have the support I need. Not that I require any, but there we go.'

It was a lot to take in. Kian was furious with Alfred for putting himself in danger like that. Only none of that really mattered now. Knowing that Al was okay, and could stay in his home, was the only birthday present he needed.

'Anyway,' Alfred went on, 'I have a rather good memory, and I seem to recall that today is your birthday. Am I right?'

'It's no big deal.' Kian pulled the duvet right up to his chin. 'I'd rather forget about it.'

'Nonsense. I know it was you who sorted everything at the house, achieved what I thought was impossible. Maggie said she wanted to give up, but you carried on and got a team of volunteers to help. I mean, I'm a little embarrassed you did that, but I can't thank you enough. I insist you let me cook you a good old meal to show my appreciation and to celebrate your birthday.'

Kian felt the now-familiar tingling sensation that meant tears could fall. 'I'd like that a lot. Cheers.'

When he got up, there was an envelope waiting for him on the doormat. Inside was a card with a huge silver eighteen embossed on the front:

Dear Kian

Many happy returns. I was so happy to see you again and, even if it was only that one time, it's a memory I'll hold close to me until the day I die. I can't explain things in a way that will make sense, because it doesn't make sense that I left you. I was lost, Kian, and I lost you and Danny in the process. I'm so sorry, and even though I don't expect you to ever forgive me, I hope that one day you'll give me a chance to show you how much you mean to me.

I'm enclosing your hospital tag from when you were born. I've kept it in my purse all these years. Wishing you a very happy 18th birthday.

Love from Mum (Cathy) xxx

The plastic tag was so tiny that Kian couldn't imagine his wrist ever having fitted through it. It had his name and weight written on it. His mum had kept something to remind her of him. A piece of the wall he had built around himself crumbled.

Kian insisted that he help Alfred with the cooking, and so he and Al were huddled in the kitchen making teriyaki chicken.

'You see, I thought I'd try something special, in honour of your birthday,' Alfred said. 'Maggie told me this was one of her favourites. She wrote the recipe down and got me the ingredients. I did try to tell her that she should be resting, but she gave me one of her looks.'

'I think she just wants to care for you. You should let her – you know, a bit.'

'As long as she lets me look after her, too. Anyway, pass me the soy sauce and the ginger.'

Kian opened the cupboard and reached inside. He knew what a good proportion of all these herbs and spices were now, and which dishes they would go well together with. He wiped away yet more tears. He didn't know he was capable of producing so many. 'Onions!' he said by way of explanation, but really it was because he couldn't help wondering if this would be the last time they'd cook together.

'By the way, I also got your watch back,' Alfred told him. 'Remember what I said about every time you look at it?'

'Something about . . . being mine for the taking? That ship's sailed, Al.'

Alfred fetched a cloth and a bottle of Brasso and began to rub at a horseshoe that was on top of the microwave. 'Now this – this could be mistaken for something that deserves to be thrown out. It'll take a while, but if I keep rubbing . . . a little bit of care and attention, and see how it shines? Something wonderful can be found in what appears to be worthless, Kian. It might not happen straight away, but keep putting the effort in and you'll be rewarded, I promise.'

It was a great speech, only Kian knew it was wasted on him. He couldn't believe that Alfred still hadn't realized there was nothing special about him – hidden or otherwise.

56

The end of the road

Kian had been waiting for the day of his review meeting with Alfred, Chris and Sandra for such a long time that he could hardly believe it was finally here. But when he'd started his restorative-justice programme, he'd imagined it would mark the end of something terrible, rather than the beginning of something even worse. He'd wished he'd never allowed himself to think a different future was possible and had simply accepted his fate. It would make today – and what followed – easier.

He had resigned himself to his sentence. Last night, walking home from Al's, all hope had drained out of him as he made a mental list of the things he wouldn't be able to do again for a very long time: cooking his own food, hanging out with Al, and playing footie with Dan when they got to meet up. He hated that his blossoming relationship with Chloe would have to meet a hasty and messy end. Not long ago, drinking in the pub and chilling out with his mates would have been top of that list. Things had changed. He had changed. It was time to take responsibility and learn from his mistakes. Kian now realized that being abandoned by his mum didn't give him a licence to act like the world owed him something for the rest of his life. It was a shame he'd worked it out a little too late.

They were back in the church hall where they'd had their first mediation meeting. A playgroup was finishing up as he walked in, and a toddler held out a bit of soggy toast in his direction. Kian smiled at him, wishing he could go back in time and not have a million problems worrying him. All his life he'd been desperate to grow up and make his own decisions, be in control of his destiny. It turned out that being an adult sucked even more than being a kid.

Kian walked into the small side room and saw Alfred studying a poster on the wall and writing something in a little notebook. He took a seat when he noticed Kian. Last time they met here, Kian couldn't have cared less about the old guy sitting in front of him. Now they were connected so tightly that it felt odd being on the opposite side of the table. He sat down and helped himself to a biscuit. Al winked at him and mouthed the words, 'All right' at him. At least one of them was feeling positive.

'Chris, Kian,' Sandra said. 'Alfred has prepared something he'd like to share, before we begin. Is that okay?'

Kian nodded, and Chris gave her the thumbs-up.

Alfred cleared his throat. 'Well, I wanted to express my thanks to Kian for everything he's done for me over the past few months. This lad has gone above and beyond. In terms of restorative justice, he's paid for his crime, and more. He's turned my life around, given me hope and shown me how narrow-minded I had become. I can't ever thank him enough. He's grown to become someone I am proud of and care for very much. He deserves a chance – a future.'

The words stuck to Kian like glue. Without a doubt it was the nicest thing anyone had said about him, ever.

'Cheers, Al,' Kian responded, as he leaned over to see whether Chris was writing it all down.

'Well then,' Chris said, narrowing his eyes. 'Kian, would you like to tell us all what you've learned from the process?'

Kian took a deep breath. At that moment Chris's mobile rang. He sat back in his chair, mouthed 'Sorry' and took the call. 'Yep. You what? Really, you're sure? Okay, yep, yes. I've got him here with me now. I'll let him know.'

'Let me know what?' Kian asked, crossing his arms.

'It's your lucky day, lad. Ryan has dropped the charges against you. The case won't be going to court.'

'You're messing with me,' Kian said. Ryan obviously had some sort of conscience after all. 'You're serious? I don't bloody believe it!'

Alfred leapt from his chair, slapped him on the back and then hugged him. 'Swearing!' he said, and they both laughed.

'So let's not get carried away,' Chris went on. 'Your court case might have fallen apart, but your probation period isn't over yet. Even though your restorative-justice programme has ended successfully apparently, you still have no employment or training lined up. I'm going to recommend another programme to get you ready for work, under my supervision.'

From a hot-air-balloon high, it was a crash landing. Kian sat down again. He would get a job doing anything, if it meant he would be out of Chris's grasp for good. His track record with interviews didn't give him much hope, though.

'That won't be necessary,' Alfred said.

'I'm sorry, but as I just explained—'

'And as I just said, it won't be necessary. Kian has a job, with me, working in a cafe. With some experience behind him, he can get his place at catering college next year and work part-time, too.'

'You what?' Kian said. 'I mean, yeah, I'm working with Al,

so – you know – cheers for everything, Chris, but I guess this is the end of the road.'

After the review meeting they went back to Alfred's and ate fish and chips in front of the telly, laughing about the look on Chris's face.

'So how exactly are we gonna make this cafe idea happen?' Kian asked, the starter for a hundred questions that followed.

'Well, I have to admit I'm not sure of all the details, but I do know that Eddie's Emporium is up for sale.'

Kian had got his hopes up for nothing. Alfred seemed to have forgotten that neither of them were sitting on mounds of cash. And buying an antiques shop was the last thing he was interested in.

'Anyway,' Alfred continued, 'at the moment it only sells teas and coffees and far too many antiques, but the space has so much potential. It's huge, and in a great location. With a bit of vision, you could really do something with the place. It would be a perfect—'

'Cafe?' Kian asked. 'Maybe we could sell restored furniture and a few antiques too? It sounds perfect! But we can't afford it.'

'Well,' Alfred said, getting out his notebook. 'I saw a poster, you see, on the wall in the church hall. It was advertising a youth enterprise scheme. You can apply for funding for a business idea if you're young and unemployed, and it comes with training and mentoring—'

'And you thought—'

'Exactly!'

In a few short months they had gone from barely speaking

to finishing each other's sentences. Kian had worried at times that somewhere, deep inside him, he was similar to Alfred. Now he recognized many qualities in him that he would be proud to have.

'Anyway,' Alfred went on, 'it could be a great proposal. Something we could work on together, with the right support. If you're on board with the idea of course.'

'Al, I think it's genius!'

It would be a huge amount of work, and Kian was awash with doubt about whether they could pull something like this off. He was also the most excited he'd ever been in his life.

57
Spring sunshine

The syncopated rhythm drifting from his record player made Alfred shuffle a samba, swivelling hips and all, in his slippers across the living-room carpet. Long-quick, short-quick, slow. There was certainly something to be said for having space to move around. He had no idea how long it had been since he'd last danced, and although he wished Ida was in his arms, mirroring his steps and scolding him for treading on her toes, he was still soaring through the sky, gliding on ice and sailing across the ocean, all at once.

Apple chutney simmered gently on the stove, filling the room with the smell of sweet, scented vinegar. Alfred took his pullover off and undid his top shirt button. Then he sat down in his armchair and fanned himself with a newspaper. A sense of peace had descended on him recently. It wasn't that he was grateful everything was back to normal. It was more that he was grateful everything wasn't.

Maggie's visits were something he looked forward to, rather than dreaded. Over the past couple of months they had been on walks or played chess together, while Maggie filled him in on her life. Slowly they were learning to forgive each other. Although his collections were smaller, his life had grown in ways he hadn't known were possible.

The knock at the door didn't faze him these days. It was most likely Kian or Maggie, or even his newly acquainted neighbour, Ewan, who came round every now and again to see how he was and chat about comics. Sometimes Krystyna and Ania from next door would pop round with a cake. He hadn't accepted quite how lonely he'd been all this time.

'Just a minute,' he said as he struggled back into his jumper. He sashayed his way to the door and pulled it open with a flourish. 'Oh, good morning, Meena.'

'Morning, Alfred. I wondered if you fancied joining me on a walk around the nature reserve?'

'Well, I was . . . No, actually I'd love to. Come on in for a moment while I get ready.'

Alfred turned off the stove and fetched his new walking boots. Then he got a pair of binoculars and made a flask of coffee, enough for two.

'Now I can't wait to hear all about the cafe!' Meena said, as they walked.

She was being kind. He had already told her everything there was to know over the phone.

'Kian went for an interview this morning actually. I'm hoping it went well and that we hear soon whether he's got the green light. He's worked so hard on his proposal.'

'It sounds perfect,' Meena replied. 'I'm sure it's all going to work out.'

If there was one thing Alfred knew better than anything, it was not to get your hopes up. Just when you thought everything was going to turn out fine, the rug could be pulled from beneath you. But for some funny reason, this time he did have a positive inkling.

They walked through the blossoming trees that hinted at

longer days and towards the lake, as the sunshine warmed their backs. They sat down to drink their coffee and watched a heron dipping for fish. If you took the time to notice, beauty could be found everywhere.

'So how are things with Maggie now?' Meena asked.

'Really good. Amazing in fact. I didn't think we could ever get back to how it used to be, but we're getting there. She also has me seeing a counsellor, which was like pulling teeth at first, but now I think it's really helping.'

'Wonderful. You didn't miss much at the last reading group, by the way,' Meena continued. 'It was a dreary romance. Everyone asked after you. I think you might like next month's offering, though.'

'Oh yes?' Alfred said, his cheeks warming at the thought of the others noticing his absence.

'We're delving into Dickens, *The Old Curiosity Shop*. Have you read it?'

'Years ago, I think. That's given me an idea. If Kian does get the go ahead, what do you think about the name . . . The Curiosity Coffee Shop? It has a certain ring, doesn't it?'

'I love it! And I've been thinking . . . You can say no if you like, but I thought I could help in the cafe, an extra pair of hands to give some support to Kian while he's training. I wouldn't want paying. What do you say?'

Alfred put his coffee cup down at his feet and stood up as the heron took flight. He followed its path across the lake and noticed the first crocuses of spring emerging from the ground. They had found their way out of the darkness and were reaching towards the light.

'I think that would be wonderful,' he said. 'And I also think I'm a very lucky man.'

58

Full circle

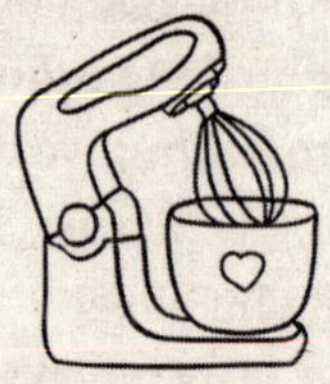

Alfred sat alone in silence. Spring had seamlessly become summer, and the newspaper-covered windows let a soft caramel light into the room, revealing the hazy shapes of cabinets, armchairs and collections of ceramics. His favourite items were displayed on sideboards and dressing tables. In a matter of weeks the collection had expanded in size, spreading from wall to wall like second-season geraniums at the height of spring. It was more beautiful than any dazzling floral display. He opened his inventory and checked through the list. His latest item had just been installed:

French gilt mirror
Original foxed plate and backboard, circa 1850.

It hung on the wall next to a cuckoo clock and a series of seascape paintings.

A bang on the door disturbed the peace and Alfred jumped.

'Al? Al, you in there? Let me in.' Kian again.

Alfred got up from his seat, switched on a light and opened the door. 'Hello, Kian. The day has finally arrived!'

'I know,' Kian said. 'I'm buzzing!'

Alfred smiled. He loved seeing Kian like this – sparkling with enthusiasm. 'I've got something for you, over there on the counter. I meant to give it to you ages ago, but there's been so much going on lately that I quite forgot,' he said.

Kian ripped open the paper. 'A cake mixer!'

'Not just any cake mixer. It's a vintage KitchenAid mixer. It was Ida's, but I want you to have it. To go and make good use of it.'

'I don't know what to say. I mean, thanks, Al – I know what that means to you. I love it. Are you sure?'

Alfred nodded. He had discovered lately that there was more joy to be had in giving items away than in keeping them for himself. He'd given some of his rare comics to Ewan, one of his cameras to Dan, some of Ida's jewellery to Maggie and even a brightly coloured scarf to Meena.

'What's this?' Kian held up a folded piece of paper that had been sitting in the mixing bowl.

'Ah, that's the best bit. It's a scholarship application form for Birmingham care-leavers. You can apply for funding to get you through college, because you will be going to college next year, I'm sure of it. The only thing missing previously was experience, and now you're going to have some.'

'That's amazing. Dan might have a brother he can look up to now.'

'I would bet that he's always looked up to you. You know, when Ida died, I thought all my days would be the same – that there was nothing left to look forward to. And now here we are, almost ready to open the doors of our very own cafe and shop. I definitely never saw this coming.'

'Yeah, tell me about it. I thought I was gonna be banged up, for sure. Anyway, we need to get the paper off the windows, so we're ready for everyone. Only two hours to go! Chloe's coming later to give us a hand.'

Once they'd finished, Alfred made a cup of tea and looked at the invitation list for their official opening. It was funny to think that most of the names on it were ones he didn't know only a few months ago. Now many of them were people he considered friends. And he had a family again. He was no longer shut away from the world. He was a part of its beating heart.

Epilogue

The macarons were all lined up on the counter, shiny like coloured pebbles. They took ages to make, but people seemed to love them. Some of Kian's customers made special journeys to buy them. His brownies did well, too. He'd made an extra batch today, on account of Dan visiting with his parents. It was still strange to call them that, and although it had taken a lot to come to terms with the fact that Dan wouldn't live with him, it now made total sense.

The cafe had its peaks and lulls, and in the quiet moments Kian sat at one of the tables and worked on some new recipes. He'd got to know some of the regulars and looked forward to seeing them – familiar faces in a city where he'd once been so anonymous. There were families who brought their kids to play with the pretend kitchen in the corner while they grabbed a few minutes' peace with a coffee and a bun. There were some who came along to the Friday-afternoon games club that Alfred ran, and others who visited for a good browse among the antiques. Right now Alfred's neighbour Krystyna was sitting at a table creating a poster advertising a new walking group that she was setting up with Meena, while a group of mums with young babies occupied the space in the far corner.

'How's the quiche coming along?' Meena asked, coming into the kitchen with a tea towel draped over her shoulder.

'Yeah, give it five minutes and it'll be out of the oven,' Kian replied.

'You're nervous, aren't you?' Meena said.

'It's Dan, isn't it? He's the most important customer I have!'

Meena laughed. 'That's true. He's very particular about his brownies. Alfred said he's going to pop by with some new items that will be perfect for the shop. He's been busy making bunting this morning for some sort of street party they're planning!'

'Yeah, he said something about finding a use for the sewing machine that I'd tried to make him get rid of,' Kian said, rolling his eyes. 'Told me he knew it would come in useful.'

'Well, he was right.'

As Kian bent down to take the quiche out of the oven, he heard his name from the front of the cafe. It was Dan. He wiped down his apron, put the quiche on the side and ran round to the front of the counter.

'Kian!' Dan shouted, even though he was standing right next to him.

'Hey, little bro!' Kian wrapped him in a huge hug. Dan was eleven now, all gangly limbs and too much hair gel.

Standing a little way back were the people Dan now called Mum and Dad. Lou and Sam were great parents. They were giving Dan a far better life than Kian could have offered. They'd signed him up to a football team and trekked around the region at weekends, taking him to matches in all weathers. Sam was really into hiking and took Dan on adventure weekends where they camped and climbed trees, while Lou loved taking him to the library. Dan was thriving on the love and care they were giving him. He was more confident now, more relaxed.

'Hi,' Kian said, nodding at them to come over and join them. 'Latte for you, Lou, yeah, and a cappuccino for you, Sam?'

'And one for me,' Dan put in.

'No, you can have a hot chocolate. And three brownies coming right up.'

When Kian brought over the refreshments, the four of them sat together, catching up on each other's news. Dan gave a step-by-step account of the amazing goal he'd scored in his last football match and said how well he thought his eleven-plus had gone. Lou, Sam and Kian discussed plans for their holiday next summer in Cornwall. They were all going to stay in a caravan park in St Ives, and Kian and Dan were going to try surfing together.

'Room for one more?' Alfred put a box down on the table and pulled up a chair.

'Hi, Alfred,' Dan said. 'Want to see my football cards?'

'I'd love to,' Alfred replied. 'And I brought mine along, so we can do swaps. Want to open them for me?'

Dan grinned as he took the packet of cards and spread them out on the table.

'Nice to see you again,' Sam said. 'What's in the box?'

'Well, now we're talking,' Alfred responded, opening the cardboard flaps and delving inside.

While he started telling them a story about the model Rolls-Royce he was holding, Kian thought about the toy Tonka truck in his memory box, which sat at the bottom of his wardrobe. It didn't have good memories attached to it. It was a reminder, though, of where he'd come from and how much his life had changed. He looked at the people sitting around the table. Apart from Dan, he wasn't connected to any of them by blood, and yet they were his family: the people he cared about most in the world.

'I've got one more thing in here,' Alfred said, lifting his barometer out of the box and handing it to Kian. 'I think this would look perfect in the window.'

As Kian placed it right at the very front of the display, the dial swung away from STORMY and pointed firmly towards FAIR.

Acknowledgements

So many people have played an important role in my publishing journey – some directly involved, and others cheering me on from the sidelines – and I'm grateful to all of you. First, my wonderful agent, Lucy Balfour: thank you for falling in love with Alfred and Kian, being the best champion for my writing and for making my author dreams come true. I am so glad my novel found its way to you! Thanks also to Florence Dodd at WME for your insight, guidance and all round loveliness.

I'm very grateful for the genuine enthusiasm and care that my novel has received from my editor Maddie Thornham. It has been amazing working with you, and *The Secret Collector* has undoubtedly benefited from your input. Thanks also to the whole Pan Macmillan team who have helped to get this book out into the world, especially my copy-editor, Mandy Greenfield, and desk editor, Rosa Watmough.

I began writing this novel on a three-month Curtis Brown Creative course, so I'd like to thank my tutor, Laura Barnett, for her wise words and for giving me hope that I might be on to something. Also, thank you to Jennifer Kerslake for your warmth and wonderful encouragement. Extra special thanks to two people who went out of their way to offer their time and expertise when I needed it the most: Abby Parsons at CBC and Katie Fulford at Bell Lomax Moreton. Your kindness is very much appreciated.

Thanks to the Airport Writers' Lounge, especially Natalie Lewis, Anna Girling, Lisa Sargeant, Vivian Lord and Steve Brody, who generously read my first draft and gave me useful feedback, and to James Robertson and Colette Bain, for sharing the highs and lows of this journey with me. I really value your friendships and I look forward to seeing your books fly!

I'm lucky to have some amazing friends who have never (publicly) got bored of me talking about my book and whose support has meant the world to me. There are more of you than I can mention here but particular thanks and love to: Johann Chan, Lucy Inman, Fran Phillips, Kerstin Grant, Stacey Kennedy, Jessica Dyson, Nicola Chalmers and Pam Renoata.

Writing a novel isn't easy, and so thanks must go to my family for always being there for me and celebrating my successes. To Rachel, Tim and Eloise, thank you for your love and for being so proud of me – I am lucky to have you all. To my mum, Teresa, I'm hugely grateful to you for so many things, especially for always listening and for giving me a love of reading. Thanks also to my mother-in-law, Judy, for all your encouragement and support over the years.

To my beautiful boys: it has been a joy to watch you grow, and you have taught me so much. Lastly, eternal thanks to my husband, Joel, for your unwavering belief in me, being an expert plot wrangler and for always being by my side. I couldn't have done this without you.